The best way you know how

CHRISTINE POUNTNEY

The best way you know how

a novel

PENGUIN
CANADA

PENGUIN CANADA

Published by the Penguin Group

Penguin Group (Canada), 10 Alcorn Avenue, Toronto, Ontario, Canada M4V 3B2
(a division of Pearson Penguin Canada Inc.)

Penguin Group (USA) Inc., 375 Hudson Street, New York, New York 10014, U.S.A.
Penguin Books Ltd, 80 Strand, London WC2R 0RL, England
Penguin Ireland, 25 St Stephen's Green, Dublin 2, Ireland (a division of Penguin Books Ltd)
Penguin Group (Australia), 250 Camberwell Road, Camberwell, Victoria 3124, Australia
(a division of Pearson Australia Group Pty Ltd)
Penguin Books India Pvt Ltd, 11 Community Centre, Panchsheel Park, New Delhi – 110 017,
India
Penguin Group (NZ), cnr Airborne and Rosedale Roads, Albany, Auckland 1310, New Zealand
(a division of Pearson New Zealand Ltd)
Penguin Books (South Africa) (Pty) Ltd, 24 Sturdee Avenue, Rosebank, Johannesburg 2196,
South Africa

Penguin Books Ltd, Registered Offices: 80 Strand, London WC2R 0RL, England

First published 2005
Simultaneously published in the U.K. by Faber and Faber Limited,
3 Queen Square, London WC1N 3AU

Copyright © Christine Pountney, 2005

*Publisher's note: This book is a work of fiction. Names, characters, places and incidents
either are the product of the author's imagination or are used fictitiously, and any
resemblance to actual persons living or dead, events, or locales is entirely coincidental.*

1 3 5 7 9 10 8 6 4 2

Typeset by Faber and Faber
Printed in England by Mackays of Chatham plc, Chatham, Kent

ISBN 0-14-305203-9

Library and Archives Canada Cataloguing in Publication data available upon request
British Library Cataloguing in Publication data available from the British Library

Visit the Penguin Group (Canada) website at **www.penguin.ca**

To my parents, Michael and Elaine
And to my sister, Michelle

A swift carriage, of a dark night, rattling with four horses over roads that one can't see – that's my idea of happiness.

Henry James – *Portrait of a Lady*

Contents

The wedding girl

Hannah forgets that she's in a hurry. She leans forward on the bureau and holds her face so close to the mirror it clouds over in a fog of breath. She looks around the room. A typical English hotel. Wall-to-wall powder-blue carpet, twin beds, lace doily on a glass-topped mahogany bedside table. Her sister, Connie, sits on one of the beds, trying not to show her impatience. Hannah leans forward again and, holding her breath, stares at her reflection while pumping her mascara brush in and out of its silver vial, like a conductor tapping his music stand.

At twenty-five, she sees her face like a cubist painting, each feature isolated by her intense inspection of it. She can't tell what impression it gives and regularly forgets what she looks like. This is why she must look at herself often. But as soon as she does, her face invariably fractures into its separate parts: eyes, nose, mouth, chin.

This doesn't bother her, though, this sundering of her features, because to see her face as a whole would necessitate having an opinion, and Hannah would prefer to avoid the finality of a conclusion. In fact she welcomes the freedom in forgetting, because you can't be committed to what you've already forgotten.

I think we're late, her sister says, rubbing an empty wrist. Do you have a watch? Hannah glances at her, her face angling away in the reflection, then coming back.

It's when Hannah catches an unexpected glimpse of herself (it could be a mirror in a shopping mall), that she is surprised to find herself beautiful. It makes her wonder how accurately she sees anything at all, and how much her thoughts interfere with her perception. I wish, she thinks, I were capable of a pure, clean perception of the truth, if such a thing exists. A sealed picture carried from the eye to the brain, travelling a straight and uninterrupted path between sight and the knowledge of what is seen.

Because if Hannah had a hard time perceiving herself, she didn't have a clue how others perceived her.

You look gorgeous, Connie says, walking over to the window and pulling the curtain aside.

You see, Hannah had always been doubtful of her beauty. And yet it was this uncertainty that made her all the more attractive. People who noticed it felt as if they were making a new discovery. It made them possessive of it too, as if in discovering her beauty they had created it, and so it belonged to them.

I think the cab is here, Connie says, and Hannah lifts the mascara brush too quickly to her eye and draws a black smudge across her cheek.

Ah, fuck it, Hannah says, and then immediately regrets it as her parents are within earshot. Waiting in the hall outside her room, the door ajar. She hears her father get up from where she left him sitting on the stairs, leaning forward with his elbows on his knees, his fingers steepled as if to reconstruct the absent church, the church they might have been heading to had things been different, and the sound his hands make on the loose change in his pockets as he stands and brushes himself off is sad and isolated, as if, in spite of the conspicuous absence of ceremony, the collection plate had suddenly appeared, like an uninvited guest, a drunk and lascivious uncle seeking reparations.

Hannah feels her heart contract at the deliberate reserve of her father's movements and wonders if today he isn't feeling a little disappointed. She can't shake the feeling that her father would have preferred something more spiritual, more in keeping with the romantic grandeur and religious sanctity of the ritual to come, but dismisses the thought in a flounce of indignance.

It's not like it's his wedding.

Her mother peeks around the door and says (taking it upon herself to dispel the tension, though nobody's asked her to), We'll be downstairs, okay? And Hannah nods without looking at her, eyelids drooping insolently, but even before they're closed she's admonished herself. For chrissake, Hannah, be kind.

But how can I be kind when I'm so fucken nervous?

Connie comes back from the window, sits on the bed and gives Hannah a doleful look with her big brown eyes. It is a look at once sympathetic and slightly reproachful. A look that makes Hannah pause and chew her cheek. She's never been able to conceal her emotions like her sister can, but she doesn't want to feel guilty about it either, not today of all days, though she glances back at her and shrugs apologetically. Connie smiles back and suddenly everything's okay.

Oh, my beautiful big sister. Let's run away together. Just you and me. Find a beach. Go swimming. Dig for oysters.

Looking at Connie sitting on the bed, smoothing a turquoise skirt over her legs, six thousand miles from her home on Vancouver Island, Hannah has this overwhelming and quite melodramatic urge to protect her sister from what feels like the sorrows of the world, but is really her own cloying nostalgia. She can't separate her sister as she is now, wife and mother of two, from the imperious busy-body she was as a child, always arranging things just so. Hannah misses the simplicity of her childhood and has a brief longing to be once again on the receiving end of her older sister's bossy self, because she would find that reassuring. Reassuring to know that no matter how much things changed, no matter how many unexpected turns her life might take, that some things would always stay the same. That there existed inalienable points of reference like permanent character traits to fall back on in times of flux. Because the mere recollection of one of her sister's serious attempts to school her in the necessity of good manners is as grounding to Hannah as the four cardinal points of a compass to an orienteer: North, East, South, West.

Never Eat Shredded Wheat.

Hannah turns back to the mirror and takes a breath, wipes the caterpillar of mascara off her cheek and applies some more. She's already ten minutes late. Ten minutes late for her own wedding and she hasn't even left the hotel.

The family crosses a narrow wet lawn thick with lilac and laburnum. The blue tendrils of wisteria like wet gloves in the bushes. Hannah lets her mother sit in the front seat of the minicab and squeezes into the back beside her father and her sister. Connie leans to pull her skirt free and Hannah shuts the door with an abrupt bang.

It is a Thursday morning in May. People are at work. Finalizing sales. Analysing the stock market. And here I am, Hannah thinks, at this odd hour of the week, a Canadian in England, driving to my wedding in a registry office in Camberwell. Past a building now, where a woman sits behind a desk, biting her fingernails perhaps, and thinking about robbing a bank.

The cabbie seems excited to be ferrying such a precious load at an otherwise uneventful hour and warbles away with Hannah's mother in a south London Jamaican accent. She laughs uproariously and Hannah thinks, I'm not the only one who's nervous. At one point, her mother actually slaps the driver on the knee, taking a shine to him.

Hannah turns to the window and feels her heart beat. A double-decker bus squeaks by so close she can see the bubbles in the red paint. She catches the eye of a young boy sitting on the bus looking down at her. He stares at her silk skirt and lace top. In her lap, she is holding a top hat with linen roses on the brim. The boy tugs at his mother's sleeve and she too leans over to take a look. The woman smiles at Hannah, closing her eyes slightly in a gesture of blessing or pity, wishing her good luck despite the odds, and Hannah smiles back, a polite knee-jerk reaction. Then Hannah looks away, lifts a

4

cool hand to her hot cheek, and decides she is annoyed by the intrusion.

They drive down Denmark Hill and signal at the lights to turn right onto Camberwell Church Street. A Rasta offers to wash the windscreen, but recognizes the driver. He winds the window down and they do that thing with their hands, like white girls in primary school. *Miss Mary Mack, Mack, Mack, all dressed in black, black, black.*

The family sits in silence, staring ahead of itself in faithful anticipation.

Red light. Amber light. Green.

Hurry up. Hurry up.

The cab pulls into the driveway in front of the Camberwell registry office. Here we are, her father says, and the best man comes running over, the flaps of his jacket billowing to reveal the shiny beige lining like the pages of an open book left out to flutter in the breeze on a summer porch by a child who's rushed down to the lake to plunge into the water and drown.

Oh, why does change always precipitate the contemplation of death?

But then Hannah sees the best man's face and it's like Moses coming down the mountain. She emerges from the car and into his arms. Hannah, Peter says. They're both high all of a sudden and he kisses her on the cheek.

You're fabulous, he says.

And you are most certainly the best man.

Hannah looks over at the entrance at all her fiancé's strapping friends, tall and handsome young men in casual suits, and wonders how they see her, whether or not to them she is the ravishing bride. She feels the crushing force of an overflow of feeling. I wish, she says to Peter, I could marry you all.

There's a slight gust of wind and she reaches up to hold on to her hat. She's never worn a hat like this before, but it was either that or the snakeskin trainers with the thick rubber soles. She rests her hand on the reassuring solidity of its top, then plumps the starchy petals of the linen roses bunched around the brim, before taking the best man's arm and letting him lead her to the wedding room.

I just wish I could marry them all.

It's not until she sits down for a debriefing with the registrar and the first thing the registrar says is, You're late, that Hannah realizes it's forty-five minutes past the allotted time.

But it's my wedding, Hannah says, feeling the sting of being chastised. The registrar is noticeably pregnant. Maybe she's the one who's late, maybe that's why she's so impatient. Or maybe she's just slipped prematurely into the slightly intolerant and short-tempered pragmatism of motherhood.

The next couple are waiting in the hall, the registrar says, passing over a form for Hannah to sign. They were supposed to get married fifteen minutes ago.

But it's my hair, Hannah says wistfully, looking down at her feet in their strappy high heels. It takes such a long time to blow dry.

There is a short run in her stockings. Her little toe is sticking out and there is something foreboding about the appearance of this flaw so early on in the proceedings, this chrysalis tearing through the silk, of getting married in somebody else's time slot.

Hannah is ushered into an adjacent room and left to wait there on her own. She can hear the guests but she can't see them. She's in a large canary-yellow room with elaborate cornices and a plaster rose on the ceiling the size of her parents' dining-room table. She is waiting behind a closed set of double doors for the signal to enter. She has her back to the windows. She can feel the warmth of the sun on the back of her legs. She stares at the brass doorknobs and zooms in on the keyhole, like a tiny exclamation mark, letting light in from the other side. It's a green light, and she can't tell whether it's the colour of the other room, bordered as it is on the far side by tall french windows leading out onto a verdant garden of blue-green spruce trees, or the oxidizing effect of air on the copper plate.

There's a snuffling noise like a dog makes when its sleep is disturbed by dreaming, a kind of troubled panting, and she realizes it's coming from her own throat. A door to her left opens and a man in an expensive blue suit rubbed raw on one shoulder says, You can go in now, and closes the door, leaving her alone again in this canary-yellow room, listening to the murmur of voices behind a wall and the Brodsky Quartet doing a cover of a Björk track, reminding her of when she saw four swans fly past her window, and she has never felt so alone. Never so deliciously nor terrifyingly alone, poised on the cusp of a promise that will change her life forever, change it and fix it.

Hannah is standing behind a closed set of double doors, with brass doorknobs and an *Alice in Wonderland* keyhole.

She has a short run in her left stocking.

In the other room, a small gathering of her family and friends.

The man she is about to marry.

If Hannah opens this door and steps over the threshold she is saying yes, a cosmic Yes! the eternal Yes! from which point there is no return or even recovery, from which moment all else (all those potential lives and destinies – all those other men!) will vanish without trace. Hannah puts her hand out and touches the cool brass of the polished handle and turns it under her grip. She feels doubt rising like thunder over distant hills, approaching like rain as over the threshold she goes.

Doubt, she thinks, in my ability to be constant, to feel a love so fierce it cancels out doubt.

Because, as it is, she's still so concerned about appearances, uncomfortable about being the centre of attention, going public with the private contents of her heart. Because I do not trust my heart. It isn't pure. My feelings, Daniel, aren't overwhelming. I'm not transported. My mind isn't full of you.

She is in the packed room now and there's no turning back. She's propped up by rows of smiles and the minty fresh green optimism of the leaves behind the panes of glass. She wobbles in like a cream-coloured peony on a too-tall stem, teetering a bit, giggling and trying to catch all the eyes at once until she feels a hand on her arm (oh, my rock! my salvation!) and turns to look and it's Daniel beaming back at her with a face that may as well be her own, and then she knows that everything's going to be okay.

Everything's going to be just fine.

The registrar stands up behind her desk and says, And how is everybody today?

There is a murmur and a shifting in their seats.

I said, she repeats with evangelical zeal. And how is everybody today?

Fine, the collective responds.

She turns to Daniel and says, Please repeat after me.

Daniel's face in profile. How serious he appears, how his chin is quivering slightly and how red his lips are. They're slightly chapped from drinking with his friends the night before and Hannah envies his ability to please himself, but also wishes he had more vanity. She gave up smoking four weeks ago, even started jogging again so she would look rosy on this day. And he wouldn't so much as buy a new pair of socks.

But what does it matter that she spent the previous night eating a curry with her folks, watching her language and strapping her frantic thoughts to a narrow bed in a London hotel room, when she longed to be with friends, to mark the occasion in some monumental way?

Because I really mustn't be so petty. Mustn't sully the heartfelt moment.

8

Problem with moving around so much is that you leave your friends behind. It's like pulling a travois wherever you go, pine boughs strapped to the back of your heels, erasing your tracks as you make them, obliterating the signs of your existence, as if anybody could exist without proof. One day you realize that you have turned to smoke. And if you leave no trace, how can anyone hold on to you?

I, Daniel Steel . . . the registrar continues.

(This is the moment! It has come at last!)

I, Daniel Steel, her sweet kind gentle fiancé replies.

Do solemnly declare . . .

Do salami declare.

Daniel flashes her a look as if to verify his mistake. He gives her a confident shrug and Hannah laughs. That's what I love about you. This admission of weakness, a crack to let doubt out. She laughs because she cannot cry. Because she also feels despair. She has found a man who loves her though he admits he will never fully know her, a man who won't bend to her will and yet promises to be flexible, a man who will anchor her without pulling her down, will ballast her boat just enough to let her float, and it's like giddy champagne bubbles hitting the roof of her mouth. Her shoulders are bouncing like basketballs and the tears start streaming down her cheeks and she wonders if Daniel will accept these tears as the only tears she can offer him today, and whether or not that will be enough for him.

The registrar fixes her with a serious look and it's Hannah's turn to make her vows. I need to be solemn. But she can't stop giggling. I, Hannah Crowe, do solemnly declare.

The registrar says, Till death do us part.

Hannah wants to say, For a very long time. That's as far as she can see into the future, let alone commit. But she hears herself repeat the line and realizes it's too late. She doesn't have the courage. She lets the tide turn and take her out.

High above their heads, Carl Wilson sings:

9

I may not always love you,
But long as there are stars above you,
You never need to doubt it,
I'll make you so sure about it,
God only knows what I'd be without you.

Now it's done. Just step outside, please, for pictures. Daniel takes her in his arms. Let's move to the patio, he says. He is tender, attentive. Hannah wants to reciprocate but she finds it hard to focus. She is distracted by the people there. The light outside is bright. Her family has flown in from another continent. There are friends of Daniel's she hardly knows. Off to the side, Daniel's grandfather totters into a chair, at a gentle slant in the soft grass.

It doesn't really sink in. The casual procession flows past the gothic church (whose steeple is decapitated for renovations) and down the lane for a round of drinks at Willow's. It doesn't sink in during the ecstatic congratulations that create a tangible froth in the air. Not over her pink slices of roast beef, or when the tiramisu arrives to everyone's delight (there was fear of fruitcake). There is a satiated lull of digestion when Hannah lights up her first cigarette in four weeks and, content to be at one with the world and him, leans into the nook where Daniel's arm meets his chest and exhales. Not even then does she really feel the implications.

Hannah's friend from Montreal, a young lawyer named Louise Samuel, who can best be described as having a safe life but not a safe mind, gets up and tells Daniel he's just married the Marlboro Man. Hannah's mother whoops and winds her arm in the air like someone on the Ricki Lake show, still making up in ebullience what she's lost from years of insecure temerity and critical self-censorship. Hannah's mother has reached that age of aggressive happiness, bullying in her demand for self-respect. She'll be darned if anyone gets in her way, and that's two sugars she takes in her tea, not one. And then Hannah censors herself and wonders why her mother's happiness is so threatening, why at her age she's still afraid of her mother's ability to erase, to dominate her even with an overbearing desire to please.

While Louise goes on to describe her friend as a house of mirrors, Hannah wonders if she will ever silence these critical voices in her head. She's so busy analysing things on the periphery, trying to acquire what lies beyond her grasp, that she often loses sight of what is so obviously right in front of her. Even now, she practically misses the rest of Louise's speech and is surprised to find her at the end in tears because Lou never cries.

Hannah watches Louise Samuel across the restaurant and is filled with a proud love. They have known each other since they were fourteen. A whole history there. Both kicked out of the same high school and attending the next one together. Louise's father had left the poverty of Trinidad when he was a young man. As Montreal's first black school commissioner, Mr Samuel had worked hard to build a reputation and was beside himself with fury. He thought Hannah was a corrupting influence on his daughter, and Hannah had been afraid of him because although she was more reckless than Louise, she didn't have her confidence. Hannah smiles now, remembering the time they both ran away to a motel on St Jacques Street, a strip used by truckers and prostitutes. Just before she walked into the motel office to rent a room, Hannah had looked back at Louise standing under a lamppost in the parking lot. It was a school night and the dark green pleats of Louise's school kilt stuck out like leaves around the hem of her navy blue pea jacket. She had her knapsack on, full of books, and a teddy bear hanging from the end of her arm. Hannah had said, Lose the teddy bear.

Why? Louise had asked.

It doesn't look good.

And now here we are, Hannah thinks. Both of us living in London. Hitched to Englishmen.

11

After Louise's speech, three of Daniel's friends from university get up and sing a song they wrote to the tune of *Sloop John B*. It's a nostalgic song about their student days, a house full of boys, their slovenly hygiene, a saucepan of mushy peas left under an armchair for weeks. They are handsome and funny and everyone appreciates the emotional release of strong laughter.

It is the best man's turn, Peter Straun, and Peter is confident and charismatic in front of a crowd. When I moved to Berlin three years ago, Peter says, I just assumed, in my way, that Daniel and I would fall out of touch. But Daniel persisted. He taught me how a friendship can endure, even in the presence of differing opinions. Daniel, I now understand that if we should ever find ourselves in a pub, with our backs turned in anger, it's only a matter of time before one of us turns round again.

And Hannah knows what Peter is referring to. All those times when Peter expected Daniel to act as an accomplice to his infidelities. Daniel couldn't understand how dispassionate Peter could be about his own deception, and yet he always went along with it in the end, keeping Peter's secrets to himself. Daniel watched as a procession of girlfriends came and went, all equally smitten, and never once exposed Peter or withdrew his love. He may even have derived a certain vicarious excitement to watch, from his vantage as confidant, the dramas spin out like tops.

There are tears in Peter Straun's eyes as he lifts his pint glass to toast the groom. A scraping of chairs on the hardwood floor as people stand to raise their glasses.

Even Daniel cries when it's his turn to speak. He gets up and, looking over at his dad, takes a deep breath and says, I want to thank you, Dad, for being such a clever dad, for managing to hold on to me by the merest of threads when I was growing up. Then Daniel chokes and, holding his champagne flute delicately in both hands, burbles into his glass like he's doing an impression of Benny Goodman.

Hannah is moved by this, but then recovers her self-consciousness. She can't lose herself. Shuck off inhibition. Am I any less genuine for this burden? Emotionally deficient for wont of spontaneity? Hannah would love to get up like Zorba the Greek and do a jig on the scrubbed floorboards of this cosy restaurant to show how healthy is her heart, how robust and bursting from the seams she is with love.

Peter Straun comes over. You're not going to stop loving us now that you're married?

Is it wrong of me, Peter, to want to marry you all?

It is in retrospect that you live anything at all, and Hannah and Daniel sit on the Eurostar headed for Paris, breathless with excitement, drinking another bottle of chilled champagne and picking the red lentils out of their hair. They compare notes, describing different moments of the day, creating a good hilarious story to share with friends, a story to pass down to their kids. The blunders and the high exultant moments.

Wasn't the roast beef good? Hannah says.

And the tiramisu? Daniel says.

I didn't have any.

Why not?

I was too excited.

Babe.

Hannah has taken off her shoes and has her feet in Daniel's lap. He holds them softly in his hands as if they were kittens. From time to time she leans forward, requesting a kiss which he plants on her mouth. A lingering kiss. A kiss that spreads warmth through her body. He keeps giving her these looks, as if he can't quite believe what has happened. Can't believe his good fortune or this sudden shift from what he was, to what he has now become. A man on his own to a man with a wife. It's all taken place so quickly, this act of possession, and his eyes look all soft and buttery with love, and Hannah thinks, how could I ever for a moment contemplate hurting this man? Then just as soon, like a cloud passing over the sun, they enter the Chunnel, blasting their way into that dark passage. Everything goes black and the eye takes a moment to adjust. Then the light rises, artificial and yellow, and Hannah is claimed by that heartfelt promise and ominous responsibility. Speeding down the track into deep water.

2

The preamble

So this is how it happened.

When she was twenty-five, Hannah Crowe went to England:

1. to improve herself,
2. to find herself a husband.

It was new European friends who pointed out (through excessive ribbing) the irrelevance, if not damaging effects, of copious (and to them, supercilious) amounts of North American perfectionism. She didn't know she was a perfectionist. They called her a Puritan. Hannah didn't know she had a Puritan upbringing. She didn't even know that she'd been cured of it, until she was. And she realized all of this through them.

She didn't know, for instance, that she would discover in herself, as she would discover in the English, a fondness for drink. And for eccentricity. And a tolerance for weakness that struck her as merciful. Because there is something compassionate about a culture that casts no aspersions on the businessman in suit and tie puking his guts out on the corner of Old Compton Street at 11:30 on a Wednesday evening because God knows he must have his reasons. And if he hasn't, well, he simply took his pleasure too far and where's the harm in that?

Hannah came to love the sociability, the communal lifestyle, the congregating in pubs, the old world decadence and decay and the fatalistic resignation of a nation that shrugs in the face of disappointment (as if you had it coming) and puts the kettle on for tea. It was this acceptance, this slackening of expectations, that she took to heart and wrapped around her like a soothing compress and started to shiver.

And the husband-hunting part of the equation? The number 2? Well, it started as a joke. A throwaway comment she'd told her friends back home. Hannah was off to England to find herself a husband. She simply didn't know it was going to happen so suddenly. She thought herself immune to the cliché of the natural progression. But this assumed immunity made her all the more vulnerable to it than if she had known herself to be, full-well and intellectually, the marrying type. Finding a husband (it was always finding a husband, never becoming a wife) became something she wanted partly because she'd never given it any serious consideration. It came on like the default option in her internal computer.

And maybe too because she was alone and didn't want to be. The truth is, she later realized, Hannah Crowe went to England:

1. to cure herself of a Puritan upbringing,
2. to not be alone.

Her alone-ness, now that weighed heavily on her. It was relentless and she wanted relief. She wanted someone to come and rescue her out of her oppressive solitude.

You could say that Hannah had spent a lot of her life looking for a place to belong.

The notion of marriage was simply stuck in with all the other lazy-brained, sepia-tinted and romantic notions that cluttered her head like cuckoo clocks in a Swiss cottage. Salinger once said that he was afraid of his capacity for sentimentality because he was afraid he'd turn out to be as soft as a sneakerful of shit.

If only she'd had a fraction of his dog-eared realism.

However, having escaped the jaws of matrimony once before (Hannah's Canadian boyfriend had wanted to marry, but she declined the offer so he broke her heart), and being of a disposition to indulge her appetite for love, Hannah was ready to make the leap of faith. She assumed the role of woman on the lookout and rose to the challenge as a scholar to a particularly rigorous examination.

3

When two solitudes collide

They meet at a contemporary art show at the Royal Academy in London.

Hannah is standing in front of Damien Hirst's fourteen-foot tiger shark preserved in a glass tank of formaldehyde, thinking that it is no longer sufficient to make art for art's sake. Now everything must be polemical and driven by ideas. As if the world has become too complex for the innocent reproduction of life. Mimesis just doesn't cut the mustard any more and art has to be as conceptual as the environments we now inhabit: *The Physical Impossibility of Death in the Mind of Someone Living*. Or given some such slant. Not such a bad thing, really. Progress, she supposes. A concept she happens to believe in. One of the few things she does.

Standing in front of this still-life aquarium, Hannah glances around, then steps forward and puts her hand to the cool glass. She smiles at that shark. Strokes it in tiny movements of her fingers which appear larger if she brings her face close to the tank and squints. Hello there, little shark.

Excuse me, miss.

A security guard from across the room. It causes several people to turn and look.

You're not allowed to touch the glass.

Hannah turns back to the tank with a prickly new awareness of her body. She strikes an intellectual pose by cupping her elbow and bringing a forefinger to her cheek. Now she feels like a voyeur and the work of art full of manly, misdirected hubris. Imagine taking such a fearful beast, an animal of nightmare, and emasculating it like this. To leave it hanging there in blue mid-air to watch its skin grow greyer by the day and start to peel off in lumps like porridge inside a soaking pan? And she thinks how imperious art can be.

Head cocked, Hannah raises an eyebrow. At least the title's good. The title's great, in fact. Best bit really, and so she looks up.

Across the tank is a curiously blue face, a man taking an interest in the shark. Their eyes meet briefly. He is tall and dark-haired, looks Eastern European, of Slavic descent, and has a broad face and almond-shaped eyes that appear smaller through silver-rimmed glasses. Wearing a dark blue denim jacket and a black turtleneck, he is a model of bohemian intellectualism.

Hannah looks at him again and finds that he is looking at her too. His face is kind. They both feel caught and smile at one another.

It's as if that smile, that small act of kindness or flirtation extracts a debt from her and Hannah feels compelled to stay there, not to appear rude or ungrateful, and so she waits, feeling pinned to the spot, somewhat excited and suddenly self-conscious for having made, however small, a human connection. She becomes acutely aware of his presence and of very little else, although she pretends otherwise. She leans forward again and rereads the title in a bid to appear serious in her interests.

The Physical Impossibility of Death in the Mind of Someone Living. Hannah supposes Damien's right, the mental leap from this poor animal, this lump of porridge, to a living shark in the living sea is an impossible one for her to make. In fact, there seems to be no connection at all.

What she's feeling right now, on the other hand, is life that no amount of art could create in her.

If she finds Daniel Steel good-looking, it isn't love at first sight. She just assumes, in her typically promiscuous and sometimes presumptuous way, that here before her is one more potential lover, standing on the other side of a big dead fish, looking at her (because he is looking at her again) and making her feel shy, at once presumptuous and shy.

Hannah moves away from the shark and heads into another room. She feels the man follow her, although he's perfectly entitled. They're both going with the flow, part of the slow traffic at an exhibition.

In another room, there is a model of a naked man made out of rubber and plastic and human hair, laid out on a slab as if in a morgue, every aspect of his body replicated in fine detail although he's no more than three feet long. It's called *Dead Dad* and Hannah imagines her own father lying on his death bed and what she would say to him. If she would be able to break the formality and lay her head on his chest and cry, or whether she would feel the usual restraint. Wonders, at that crucial moment, if she would be soft or hard.

She wanders over to the other side of the room to have a look at a multi-coloured dome tent. Looks like a patchwork quilt. On the inside, the artist has embroidered all the names of all the men and women she has ever slept with. Another kind of death, *les petits morts*. Hannah pokes her head inside and tries counting the names to see if Tracey Emin has slept with more people than she has. If she hasn't, she can at least remember their names.

There's some crowding around the entrance, so she pulls her head out and stands up sooner than she would have liked. Two Japanese girls, comic strip characters with furry pink backpacks and baby-blue platform Kickers, kneel at the entrance. Oh, my God, look at this. I mean, how many people has she slept with?

Imagine seeing your name in here?

Isn't that a famous person?

Then Hannah hears a voice that seems to be addressing her.

I saw this a few years ago, the man from the shark tank says, standing close enough to be looking down at her. When Tracey Emin had a little gallery on Waterloo Road. It was just a tiny place, before she became famous. She was there when I went. Made me a cup of tea and got me to sign her guest book.

19

Really? Hannah says, windblown, scorched from the intensity of his eyes.

Yeah, he says and nods.

Did you see the *Dead Dad* over there? she asks, lifting a hand to her neck and tracing the wingspan of her clavicle.

It's a nice thought to think we grow smaller in death.

It's really good, she says, noticing that he's got laugh lines around his eyes. It's so unbelievably lifelike.

They take in the rest of the exhibition together, loosely together, although it still surprises Hannah how quickly a connection can spring up between strangers. Soon they are waiting, out of a kind of politeness or loyalty for the other person to finish before moving on. At one point, Daniel Steel touches her arm to get her attention to look at the detail in a picture and she can feel the spot where he touched her.

So what did you think? he asks, as they wander out of the building and linger on the steps.

Postmodern taxidermy, Hannah says, holding her hair out of her face and looking up at the sky, at the spongy yellow clouds, the colour of teeth.

Daniel laughs. What did you think of the kebab on the table?

I kinda liked it, she says, feeling a raindrop land on her scalp, right on the exposed, sensitive skin of her part. I mean, I like that somebody's doing that. I don't get it, but I like it.

Well, it's either the democratization of art, Daniel says, flicking a clot of dry grass off the sleeve of his jacket. Or it's the emperor's clothing.

I used to live near this gallery in Montreal, Hannah says, pushing the raindrop into her hair. And someone would always be arranging all the things they found in their backyard and calling it *All the things in my backyard*.

Daniel smiles. I guess the skill lies in the idea now.

I guess so, she says, and they stand perfectly still for a while, silence blooming like magnolia.

You going this way? Daniel asks, pointing his thumb over his shoulder. Hannah nods and together they head towards Piccadilly.

The rain is like grease, smearing itself down buildings. They run across Leicester Square and down a few side streets to the Lamb and Flag. There are small, square, leaded-glass windows on the ground floor and each pane bulges in the centre like the knot in a piece of wood. Hannah follows Daniel into the pub and notices he's got a spring to his step that keeps his heels off the floor. Her grandmother used to say, Never trust a man whose heels don't touch the ground.

They go upstairs where it's less crowded and Daniel says, I'll get the first round.

Hannah shakes the rainwater off her jacket and sits down at a table by the window, misted over with condensation. She watches Daniel go over to the bar and stand there waiting his turn, a full head taller than the men around him, bending slightly to the left to get his wallet out of his pocket, then leaning forward to dry his glasses with a napkin from the bar. His posture exudes patience. He's in no rush. Hannah smiles and shakes her head and leans back with a fatalistic shrug, full of premonition.

After four pints each, it's noisy and it's closing time.

I still can't get over the fact that everything closes down at eleven o'clock, Hannah shouts, waving her hand and knocking a glass over. I mean, finally I'm in this world capital and you can be standing on a corner in Soho and it's only midnight and everything's closed.

I happen to know of a little after-hours den they call the Troy Club, Daniel says.

Hannah pitches forward, the table digging into her ribs, Wanna go?

He likes the fact that she's up for it, this determination on her part to persist, as if pleasure were the most important

21

thing, as if pleasure, now, that was the thing, because he gives her this look that is soft and sneaky and appreciative.

But first I gotta go to the loo, Hannah says.

The toilets are over there, Daniel says, pointing with his eyes.

And that's another thing, she says, standing up and leaning on the table. The British are so fucken polite, but they call the bathroom a fucken toilet.

Hannah's squatting to avoid touching the seat, resting her forearms on her thighs and swaying, head down and breathing heavily, blood pooling to create a pressure across the bridge of her nose, wishing she could pee faster because she's eager to get back to Daniel. A woman in the next cubicle snorts what sounds like a line of coke and says, It's no use. I haven't fancied anyone in ages.

There's a bloke here I quite fancy the look of, another woman says.

Really? she asks. Who?

Again the sound of snorting then a sigh. He's sitting by the windows.

I didn't notice him.

He's with this woman. Some American. One of those loud, obnoxious types.

Hannah's hand on the toilet paper.

He's not, though. Definitely English. Dead sexy, too.

And when she says this, Hannah feels the worth of what somebody else wants and her feelings turn possessive.

I can't help it, the first one says. I still miss Charlie.

What do you mean, you miss Charlie? her friend asks. When you've got him right here. Right where you want him. All cut up in little bits.

That's very funny, the other one says, deadpan.

Look, you've got to forget about him, okay?

There's a bristling like static on acrylic as they leave the stall. The sound of lipstick tubes and the smacking of lips. Another quick pull and hork at the back of the throat.

What I wouldn't do to get him back right now.

But you're not going to, d'you know what I mean? So there's no point in dwelling on it, the other one says, and then she says, almost wistfully, as if she's just fallen in love with herself. Do you like me top? I think it makes me tits look all shimmery.

Daniel leads Hannah through an unmarked door in a tight row of Victorian buildings down a back alley off Oxford Street. There's a whiff of piss in the stairwell and the steps are slippery. Hannah puts a hand to the wall, vibrating with bass, and it's greasy to the touch, as if the building itself is sweating. Downstairs, the heat hits her like a warm wet towel. Hannah stops on the last step and surveys the crowd. There must be a hundred people packed into this tiny room and the whole mass is undulating in the dim orange light, in ecstasy or agony, it's hard to tell. For a moment it's like something out of Hieronymous Bosch and Hannah can hear the crack of a whip, the wails of lamentation. But then there's a man clutching his belly with his head thrown back in pure unfettered laughter, and she's back in a London nightclub, forcing her way into the crowd, using Daniel as a plough.

There's a bar on the opposite wall and behind the rows of bottles, posters of sunny Spain taped to the plaster. To the left is a whitewashed concrete arch, small and crowded, leading to another room. They're playing Spanish flamenco and the music's so loud it's almost tangible, dense as pillow stuffing, you could almost recline on it.

Pressed up against each other, Hannah turns to Daniel and raises her hands above her head and starts moving her hips. They do an impromptu salsa. I'm not, he says, a very good dancer. Let's stop, she says. Normally Hannah would mind about the dancing, but not tonight. She's so high right now that nothing could ruin her mood. She looks around at all the sympathetic, sweaty faces and imagines that it's VE Day. Our men back home safely from the war. Women offering up their bodies to anyone out of sheer gratitude and joy. Oh, to plunge headlong into this seething, hopeful sea of humanity and not drown!

Do you want a drink? Daniel yells, and Hannah nods.

They sip overpriced San Miguel and scream at each other over the noise and the flamenco. They find a space on a bench beside a table of rowdy students who keep getting up and dancing in the narrow spaces between their chairs. In the corner, an old man puts his elbow on a table, but it slips off and he falls forward, jerks upright and opens his eyes. After a second beer, Daniel motions towards the door.

They both let out a sigh when they reach the street. The cool air is a welcome relief. So what now? She is holding her bag between her knees and putting on her coat.

Want to share a cab? Daniel asks.

I'm staying at a bedsit, Hannah says, feeling the chill of sweat on her back.

Right, he says, running his hands over his head, pushing his hair back, no longer feathery but spiky now from sweat.

It's in Clapham, she says.

That's not far from mine, he says.

Your what?

My flat.

They start moving towards Oxford Street. When they get to the corner, Daniel steps into the road, looks around, spots a cab and, putting his fingers in his mouth, rips a whistle out of his lungs.

You know, he says, when they're sitting in the back seat. You're, well. You're welcome to come back to my place if you want. That is, if you feel like it.

Daniel looks so serious and Hannah finds his timidity immensely attractive. It smacks of a sensitive nature. She lets him wait for a second and then she says, in a chirpy voice, Okay.

He relaxes then and lifts his arm and puts it around her shoulder. Hannah leans into the nook his arm makes and notices that it's a good fit.

*

They get out of the cab and giggle and sway with drunkenness as it takes Daniel two whole minutes to coordinate both keys to unlock the front door. Then they're stumbling in like tenpins wobbling on their fat bases, up the stairs and through another door into a large bare room with wooden floorboards, bereft of furniture except for a wide plank on trestles pushed up against the wall to form a desk, two milk crates stacked to make a chair and a lone bookshelf. There's a telephone on the desk and a stereo, a small TV on a stand in the corner, four foam cushions on the floor and that's it.

Have a seat, he says.

Oh, that's very funny, Hannah says, throwing her bag on the floor and walking into the middle of the room. She can see the bedroom, equally bare except for a mattress on the floor and a wooden dresser. The walls are naked. Furniture against your religion?

I just moved in, he says. Don't have a lot of money.

Me neither, she says. I think it's overrated.

Hannah likes the austerity of the place, the monkish quality that suggests this man is serious, focussed, disciplined. Qualities she likes in a man who's just had six pints of beer.

I like it, she says and sits down next to one of the tattered cushions (she can see they're tattered now that she has a closer look). She leans sideways and uses it to prop herself up on an elbow and stretch out her legs, at long last feeling for the first time that evening the sheer dead heavyweight of her drunken limbs.

So what brought you to London? Daniel is hanging up his jacket in the bedroom.

I needed to get out of Montreal, Hannah says. It's a beautiful city, but it's too small. Too easy to get complacent there. Too many ghosts.

And how long have you been here?

About six months.

Are you planning to stay?

If I can make it work.

Do you have a work visa? Daniel asks, walking back into the living room.

My dad's British, she says. I've got a passport.

Even better, he says. So how do you get by?

I've been doing some temping. But what I'd really like is to work for a newspaper or a magazine. You know, do some freelance writing.

Any luck?

Not yet, but then I haven't been trying. You see, she says, I have other aspirations. Hannah lets him nod at that and then says, I'm working on a novel.

Really? What's it about?

It's about a boy growing up in California.

Did you grow up in California?

No. Just spent some time there when I was very impressionable. But what about you? What do you do?

I'm a projectionist, he says. At the Everyman in Hampstead.

London's finest art-house cinema, Hannah says.

So you know it then!

I've heard about it, she says.

I just love this city, Daniel says, shaking his head. I can't imagine living anywhere else in the world.

And Hannah smiles, as if she should feel the same way, but already she's critical of the high cost of living, the bad weather.

Tea? Daniel asks, walking into the kitchen.

That'd be nice. She watches him steady himself to pour water into a kettle and rinse some cups. Never has a man made her a cup of tea as part of the ritual of seduction.

I'm afraid all I've got is Marvel, he calls over the noise of the kettle.

What? she says.

Powdered milk.

Oh, God, no. I hate the stuff. Reminds me of my childhood.

That bad, was it?

The lumps at the bottom.

No milk then.

Actually, I'm okay. I don't need tea.

Glass of water?

That'd be great.

Daniel comes back with two pint glasses of water and sits down on the floor in front of her. They both take sips and Hannah looks away because she knows what's coming next. From this angle it seems sad, almost silly, to make another vain and cursed attempt at intimacy. The booze is making her maudlin but she's as hardheaded as a battering ram ready to knock herself silly for the word, that four-letter trophy L.O.V.E.

Daniel takes off his glasses and puts them on the floor. He blinks and pushes them aside. The silver rims skid across the floorboards and Hannah braces herself against the temptation to laugh.

I guess I should make the first move, he says.

I guess so, Hannah says, trying to corral her drunken thoughts, sincere now in her wish to pacify the saboteur that lives like a crazy woman in her head with a shotgun across her lap ready to shoot the first sign of happiness that comes walking over the hill with the morning sun.

Daniel leans forward and kisses her. Hannah can smell his hot beery breath, a trace of cigarettes as their faces linger, and then his soft lips like paper lanterns, warm and dry, as they brush against hers. They breathe in each other's air. Hannah opens her mouth and he bites her bottom lip and softly sucks it in. The sad feeling passes and is replaced by a voracious, joyful urge to make a human connection. She wants to press and grind her body into his, to paw and dig until she reaches the solace you can find buried in the senses, it feels so much like compassion, so easy to think you're being forgiven when you're being fucked.

Daniel reaches up and holds the back of her neck. Without taking his mouth from hers, he kneels and stretches out beside her until they're both lying on the floor with a big foam cushion under their heads. He pushes his weight into her body and Hannah can feel his cock hard against her pubic bone. She lifts a leg and wraps it around his hip and pulls him forward, taking him onboard.

When they make it over to the bed, hair tousled and rosy cheeked and partially undressed, Hannah looks for the first time at Daniel's body. He is tall and muscular and lean. His chest is hairless and his skin is so pale, has such a frail quality of light to it, that it makes her want to weep.

Entangled on the mattress, they are big and strong and beautiful, paragons of health and vitality. But when they attempt to fuck, he says he can't.

It's been so long, he says. I mean, I want to. It's just that I'm a bit. I can't believe it. I'm really sorry, he says and Hannah is disappointed, though she doesn't show it. You don't mind, do you?

She's not used to the man withholding on account of trepidation and the novelty of it has the unexpected effect of transforming her disappointment into curiosity. It seems almost chivalrous, and Hannah is moved by Daniel's vulnerability and depth of feeling. His ability to be affected. His concern is so heartfelt that it makes her feel safe.

I could fall in love with this man's sensitivity.

No, I don't mind, she says, snuggling up to him with her head on his chest. Honestly.

The alcohol has made them sloppy, they would hardly have been graceful in bed, and soon, before there's even time to turn out the light, sleep overtakes them.

In the morning, Daniel's face on the pillow. Then his body as he bends forward with his hands on his knees and programs the CD player to play his favourite tracks. Hannah lies in bed and watches Daniel focussing all his attention at the stereo on the trestle table in the living room. She loves the look of him.

His body already familiar, fully apprehended. She loves the arc of his back, the veins in his arms and his square knees, the tidy boxes of his joints. If a woman is made of circles, then a man is made of squares.

I could marry this man, she thinks. I could marry this man.

Do you think, Daniel says, wagging a CD cover, that people whose lives are safe can afford to do outlandish things?

My life has always been defined by change, she says from the bed, so I tend to make conservative choices.

You're not bolstered by the accoutrements of an established life.

Hannah laughs. I often feel as if I'm grasping at the straws of some ephemeral identity.

You're like a panicked mistress in a house without furniture.

Daniel gestures around his bare flat, as if it's hardly a metaphor.

It's easier for me to move to a foreign country, Hannah says, than it is to cut my hair.

And if I'm correct, you don't even have a tattoo.

Exactly, I couldn't commit to one.

So you have a strong impulse to preserve.

But I also have a strong impulse to experiment.

To wander, he says, and to belong.

Daniel gets back into bed and they listen to his music.

Hannah was three thousand miles from home. She saw her family once or twice a year. She'd left a clutch of friends in Montreal and sometimes she feared that her life was turning into the sad cliché of a restless hobo. You know the lady tramp, she says to Daniel, in that song by Frank Sinatra?

She likes the free, fresh wind in her hair, Life without care. She's broke, but that's oke'!

Okay, so you know the one.

I do have a range, Daniel says, of musical tastes.

Well, I feel that's me, Hannah says. Happy to stop for a while, make a little love, make a few attachments. If only to suffer the bittersweet pangs of longing when it's time to wrench myself away again and move on.

Hand flung back against your forehead in exaggerated woe? Flinging yourself against the railings of departing ships?

I see it more like I'm straining at the small portholes of planes about to take off.

Either way, Daniel says, you're still feigning.

Yes, Hannah says, rolling onto her back and kicking off the covers. Feigning, it's true. Always feigning.

But here I am, she thinks, and I don't feel like bolting. Where had her Marlboro Man tendencies gone? Didn't she thrive on adventure? Didn't she want to experience as many lives as she could muster, as many lovers as she could juggle? Haven't I always wanted to look back on my life, like Blanche Dubois, and say in all sincerity that I have been *greatly loved*? Wasn't this new impulse to bind herself to a man at odds with her freedom? Or was commitment the surest path to a deeper kind of liberation?

Because it was her freedom that she prized above all else. Her precious independence. What she could achieve on her own, thanks to no one. Hannah was by nature rebellious and right now she couldn't think of anything more daring and spontaneous than to marry this man she'd met in a gallery on the crowded streets of London. It would be intensely romantic and to feel romance this intensely was surely the best antidote to what, in some secret, numb corridor of her heart, she feared the most. That she wasn't capable of feeling much at all.

And so, like a sailor without brains enough or foresight to strap himself to the mast, she wasn't just contemplating slipping into the waves upon hearing the first few bars of the sirens' song but already halfway in the water.

She hears the first few bars of something sweet and it's like honey pouring into her ears, it's feel-good, and Daniel tells her it's *Forever* by the Beach Boys.

Hannah says, The Beach Boys? I always thought the Beach Boys were for sissies. I never liked them. All that do-run-run stuff.

Yeah, but you've just heard their mainstream stuff.

So what's their good stuff?

Pet Sounds, he says. The classic pop record of all time. Or *Sunflower*. Or *Surf's Up*.

And it's true, what she's hearing right now is absolutely beautiful, like nothing she's ever associated with the Beach Boys.

They're very misunderstood, Daniel goes on, stroking her bare breasts. They were better than the Beatles. But when Brian Wilson heard the *Sergeant Pepper* album, he went to bed for ten years. He thought he'd been outdone.

I've always thought of them as saccharine and boring.

People have this misconception about them. That they wrote beautiful music because their lives were easy. But their lives were tragic. Their father was a bully. He made Brian shit on the living room carpet in front of the family once.

Why'd he do that?

Because he could, I guess. Dennis fell off his boat and drowned. Brian can't even swim. He's terrified of the ocean.

Wow, Hannah says. I never would have guessed. What's this song called?

Surf's Up, Daniel says. I want this song played at my funeral, okay?

Hannah laughs. Sure, if I'm at your funeral.

Daniel blushes at his confession.

I love how sure you are of things, Hannah says, rolling on top of him. How unriddled you are by doubt. And she straddles his hips and kisses his mouth and rubs herself against him until she comes.

They are sitting in the Prince of Wales, a crowded pub in Brixton, across from the Ritzy cinema where they've just bought two tickets to see *Breaking the Waves*. They're sipping pints of London Pride and sitting thigh to thigh on a padded velour bench, the backs of their heads reflected in the dimpled mirror on the wall. It's been seven days since they first met.

Earlier that afternoon, in her bedsit in Clapham, Hannah had got a call from Louise Samuel. I can't go out tonight, she said, cause I'm going to a movie with Daniel.

But you've been out with this guy every day since you first met.

Yeah, well, I'm not averse to getting involved.

It was your second priority, Louise said, if I recall correctly. Looks like you might just complete your list.

But when she first saw Daniel coming towards her on the street, Hannah didn't like the way he looked. He didn't look handsome. His hair was limp and feathery like duck down, and the skin around his mouth looked raw. She didn't like what he was wearing (large suede shoes, tapered jeans) and he seemed bereft of style.

Hannah had always thought that style without content was pompous and abhorrent, but content without style was a shame and a waste. She was reluctant to embrace him. But when he smiled, wide open and artless, she chided herself for being so shallow and tried to look beneath the surface at the person she admired. She found him there, sitting on a pile of books, subsisting on a monk's diet of bread and nuts, void of materialistic pleasures, his lifestyle hewn out of granite and philosophical conviction, and she tried to match his ascetic approach. Whereas she'd always taken pleasure in appearances, now she wondered if it didn't make her a little superficial.

I will make, she thought, a conscious decision to eschew my love of style. This will be an effort to improve myself.

Sitting beside Daniel in the Prince of Wales, Hannah renews this prayer to be magnanimous. To withhold judgment. To keep an open mind. God help me not to impose my tastes or assume the worst. To see beyond appearances. To be loving and kind.

Daniel takes another sip of beer and tells Hannah how his mother had a nervous breakdown when he was thirteen. He says, My dad woke us up in the middle of the night. My mum was standing naked on the front lawn. I remember sitting on the couch beside my sister and crying. I couldn't understand it. My mum went away for a few months after that and when she came back, nothing was ever said about it. I did some therapy when I was at college. But after six months of counselling, I reckoned I'd said just about everything I had to say about it.

I did some counselling too, Hannah says, when I was a teenager. My parents forced me to go because apparently I was all fucked up. Well, maybe I was. But what I didn't like was how they were putting the onus of our unhappy family life on me. Like it was my fault. In the end, they weren't satisfied with the results and stopped paying for my sessions after I'd only gone about four times.

What they didn't know, Hannah says, was that this woman was a palm reader and a dream analyst and I quite enjoyed going to see her in the end. She warned me before reading my palms, said she would have to tell me everything she saw in them and that I should think very seriously before accepting her offer. And all of this to a sixteen-year-old. I think she was pretty irresponsible because I've never forgotten what she said.

What did she say?

Well, that I would fall in love with two men when I was twenty-one and that I would marry the one I chose, but that it might not last forever. This never happened, by the way. But she also told me I would have a son at twenty-eight.

Daniel's blue eyes darken. It is the black pupil expanding into the iris. He leans into Hannah. I'll give you, he whispers, a son at twenty-eight.

Hannah touches her chin to her shoulder and then lifts her eyes to meet his. So when's the wedding? she jokes, but her voice sounds breathless, hysterical.

Born into existence at the moment of utterance, now the dream takes shape and form. The future unravels in their minds like bolts of yellow silk thrown down the side of a building. They look away from the sheer intensity of the proposition.

You remember, Daniel says, after a while. When I said the other day that I had something to tell you but wanted to wait for the right moment?

Yeah, it was really annoying. I couldn't get it out of you.

Well, what I wanted to tell you was that on the first day we met, when we went to the Lamb and Flag, remember?

It was only seven days ago.

There was this moment when I realized that. Well. I knew that I was going to marry you.

There is something about being taken. Possessed. The fact that her permission didn't figure now, that Daniel's certainty was such that it disallowed doubt, this excited Hannah. This extraordinary act of confidence won her over. She simply submitted herself, because she never really wanted to be consulted. Tell me what to do because I've never felt anything but confusion all my life, nothing but uncertainty and equivocation and too much power.

And right now, sitting beside her, all six feet three inches of him, is the only man she's ever known who doesn't seem to be afraid of her refusal, who doesn't even anticipate it. Who has what it is she thinks she lacks: an idea of himself that is unshakeable, a confidence that runs deep and isn't showy. It exists independent of the opinions of others. And he is so sure of himself, sturdy as the trunk of an old oak tree, and he is saying, Lean on me. How can I resist? For the first time in her life she is willing to commit. Take me I am yours.

Oh, Danny Boy, Hannah whispers softly in his ear. What are we getting ourselves into?

It seems like a distraction to go to the movie now, Daniel says. But we already have the tickets, Hannah says, and the first

34

scene is of a wedding. The white dress a shock of light reflected on the screen. Afterwards, they walk to Camberwell, down Coldharbour Lane, giddy with excitement now the future has come hurtling towards them. Under a street lamp Daniel holds her still and says, I know we've hinted at it, but I want to be sure.

Hannah looks up at him, his gentle features, the smooth bridge of his nose, and wishes her old boyfriend, Gerald Mansfield, could see her now. Gerald used to poke her in the chest as if to drive the point home, tapping her sternum to the beat of his sentences. If you're gonna be with me, then be with me. Be present. Be here and now and stop holding out for something better to come along because it never will. You're waiting for some flawless handsome stranger to come satisfy all your dreams but that's not real life. It's an illusion for people who would rather nurture a romantic narcissism than love real flawed people like you and me. If only you'd accept it, your ordinariness. Not every compromise is a resignation, you know, and it's not easy, it's the hardest thing in the world, but at some point you're gonna have to give yourself up or you'll spend the rest of your life alone. It's what Forster wrote, Gerald used to say, because all you have to do is connect. Only (sternum tap) connect (sternum tap).

And even though Hannah shrugged it off as best she could, knowing it was Gerald Mansfield's last defence against her reluctance to commit, she has carried his words around like a curse, a crack in the glass, a black cat.

Daniel's eyes are searching her face, roaming wildly across her features, dancing from right to left as if the truth lay somewhere in an eyeball. Will you marry me, Hannah Crowe? And will you be my wife?

Yes, I will marry you, Daniel Steel. And I will be your wife.

The headlights from a passing car slide across the surface of Daniel's glasses. Endorphins spreading through Hannah's body like gossip. Did you hear? Did you hear the news? They're going to get married!

I feel like I'm on drugs, she says.

I know, this is so weird, Daniel says. You wait all your life for something like this to happen and then it does and it's always surprising. I'm not disappointed. In fact, I didn't expect to feel this good. I feel really amazing. I feel so lightheaded. Look at my hands, they're shaking. We mustn't forget this, he says, grabbing her again. When we're old, we must remember what a rush this was.

Back in his flat, Hannah sits on the kitchen floor. Shakes her hands out in front of her like she's trying to get the circulation back into them. I can't believe this, she keeps on saying.

Neither can I.

I feel so high.

Hannah gets up and walks around, then sits down again.

Daniel rolls a cigarette. He takes a drag and Hannah reaches up and he passes it to her.

Daniel and Hannah, he muses out loud. With names like that we should have been Jews.

Wandering Jews, she says.

We should celebrate, he says.

Break a glass?

I'll go out and get a bottle of wine.

But it's too late.

How about some tins from the kebab shop?

Okay, but don't leave me here, she says, standing up. I'll go with you.

Are you okay?

I feel really nervous.

So do I.

So when are we gonna do this?

Soon, he says. Tomorrow, at a registry office, with a witness off the street.

Shouldn't we tell our parents?

I like the purity of doing it alone. Quietly like this, without pomp.

They might feel left out, she says.

But we're doing this for us, Hannah. Just the two of us.

You're right. Of course you are. But what about a ring?

We'll think of something, he says, getting ready to go out.
Don't you want your coat?

No, she says. I'm too hot.

I'll say, he says and comes and puts his hands underneath
her shirt and lifts her up onto the counter.

It's really happening, Daniel, she whispers in his ear. My
husband, she says. The word lingers there on the air like a
sailboat.

Daniel is taking a nap on the foam cushions in the living
room. He is lying on his back with his hands folded on his
stomach, neat as origami. He is guileless in his sleep and
serene and Hannah has a rush of love for him as she would
for a child. She won't disturb him and tiptoes across the room
and into the bathroom. She runs a bath and gets in.

A few minutes later Daniel comes in. Lowering the lid on
the toilet seat, he sits down and watches her. She sinks into
the water and comes up blowing a spout.

You know what I was just thinking? he says. I was just
thinking that I will never fully know you, that you will
always be something of a mystery to me.

And I wonder if you'll ever stop surprising me, says Hannah.
You keep revealing different facets of your personality.

She sticks her big toe into the tap. You're so multi-
faucetted.

Daniel laughs. When he laughs, his face cracks open like a
nut. Hannah is taken aback by the creases around his mouth,
the deep grooves of humour. And she wonders, should it
really be this easy? Have we thought this through enough?

By the end of the week, Daniel has been to the registry office
in Camberwell.

Did you know that it's impossible to get married off the
cuff in this country? he tells Hannah after dinner. First off,

you have to make an appointment in order to give notice of your wedding. Then your notice has to be posted for fifteen days before you can even book the wedding room. And the next available time might not be for a couple of months.

It's just as well, Hannah says, clearing the dishes and filling the sink with hot water. My parents were dropping hints. I think they'd like to be invited.

You told your parents? Daniel asks.

I told them this morning, Hannah says, wringing out the dishcloth.

And what did they say?

They were ecstatic, Hannah answers. My mom started laughing and I couldn't get her to stop.

Daniel drags his mouth down, nodding slowly.

Why don't you tell your parents too? she says, wiping the table. Just tell them and see what their reaction is.

The last thing I want is to be pressured into having a big wedding, Daniel says. I dread being the centre of attention. I'd hate it. I won't do it.

It wouldn't have to be that big.

Is this something you want? he asks. Because this is the first I've heard about it.

I dunno what I want, Hannah says, shaking crumbs into the garbage. I just thought that if we're gonna go public. I mean, our families will be joined. And maybe they have a right to be included.

I don't know about a right, he says.

Hannah wonders what it would be like to stand in front of her parents and declare that she's in love, to say the words, to honour and obey, and mean it without irony. Excuse me, she says to Daniel. He's blocking her way.

Don't worry about those, he says, waving at the dishes. I'll do them.

Hannah walks into the living room and circles like a dog trying to get comfortable before sitting down on the milk crates and picking up the phone. She calls her friend Louise

Samuel and they decide to meet in Hyde Park the following day.

Well, you already know what I think, Louise says in her usual brusque way, flicking her hair back in a familiar gesture. I think you're doing this way too fast. Marriage isn't just for Christmas, you know.

I know, Hannah says, watching her feet climb the gravel.

Louise had always had strong opinions about what to do in a personal crisis, even if she did an about-face and later declared the opposite to be true. It was the force of the declaration that mattered most, to have confidence at any given moment, and it was this certainty that Hannah wanted to take shelter in now. Hannah was so impressionable and Louise so persuasive, it wasn't until Hannah had adopted one of Louise's ideas that she came to realize she had one herself. And this was Lou's gift. By default of espousing Louise's beliefs, Hannah would often discover her own. She came to them in opposition to a strong and benevolent, if sometimes misguided, force.

But if you're sure about it, Louise says, softer now, sensing Hannah's uncertainty. I mean, I know it can happen. I was sure about Martin right from the start. From the very first day I met him, I knew I wanted to marry him. Did that happen to you?

Yes, Hannah says, it was just like that. But like the feeble devotee of some charismatic guru, away from him now, beyond Daniel's sphere of influence, Hannah begins to question her feelings.

Does he pass the crowded room test? Louise asks.

The what?

You know, when you see him across a crowded room, do you get that feeling of, there goes my gorgeous man. What a babe. That feeling of pride and possessiveness?

Hannah isn't sure she does. I don't know if I've ever seen him across a crowded room, she says.

But you're in love with him, right? Louise asks, as if checking off a list.

Yes, Hannah says. I'm in love with him.

And you're sure you want to get married?

Yes, Hannah says. I'm sure I want to get married.

Because it's a lotta work, you know. I mean, I know it's a cliché, but maybe you should let yourself think about it for a while before going through with it. Why don't you postpone the wedding and just try living together for now?

But I've already told my folks. I've told everyone back home.

Who cares about that? That should be the least of your worries. Hannah! Louise pleads, stopping on the path and holding out her left hand, as if something small and delicate lay in her palm, her other hand hooked tightly around the strap of a stiff leather bag, wedged under her arm, the size of a paperback. Do you really want to spend the rest of your life with this guy?

Yes, Hannah says. I think so.

You don't sound very sure about it.

I'm never sure about anything, Hannah says. I lack conviction. You know that about me.

I know you better than anyone else in the world and that's why I'm saying this. You're my best friend and I love you and I'm not convinced this is what you really want.

But I want to get married! Hannah protests, kicking against the scrutiny, the exposure of her weakness. She hates to feel criticized, will do anything to eradicate this feeling. Is already thinking it would be easier to get a divorce later on, than cancel the wedding plans right now. She wouldn't be able to handle the disappointment.

Yes, but to whom? Louise says, adopting her legal voice. It's a minor technical point, but a crucial one.

I just feel like I've started a process, Hannah says. I've agreed to do it and I can't go back on my word now.

You give your word when you make your vows.

It would be like a betrayal.

Then marry him, Louise says, in a huff. Marry him and get it over with.

For two months, Daniel and Hannah talk about getting married. They go out and meet his friends. Hannah is introduced as the woman Daniel is going to marry. There is a wariness on both sides but also a desire to break down the wariness and show a willingness to befriend. Hannah knows it's just a matter of time before she feels at ease, but she finds it hard to relax. She worries about being liked. Feels anguish when she isn't lively enough, isn't funny. Then comforts herself with the reassurance that people like a person who listens. She tries to foster a persona that is quietly self-contained but approachable. Ready with an anecdote but not overbearing. During these two months, Hannah barely leaves Daniel's side for more than a few minutes at a time.

Finally, they decide that Hannah should move into Daniel's flat. She's got £420 in a Barclays account and the rent on her room in Clapham is £65 a week. Daniel has a council flat. He gets paid under the table and his rent is covered by the dole. Move into my flat, Daniel says. You can give up the temping and concentrate on your writing. It's not a difficult decision to make and, in customary style, Hannah comes to it impulsively. Taught to be suspicious of the merits of anything achieved without hard work, Hannah does for a moment, however, experience a dull pang of discomfort in some Puritan corner of her brain at the ease of the move, but dismisses this fear on the grounds that it is self-defeating.

She unpacks her clothes and places them neatly on the right side of the tallboy in Daniel's bedroom. Hannah tries to remember all the different places she's ever lived. She gets to nineteen and loses track. Her father a vicar, she laughs now at the bafflement she used to feel when confronted with the same well-worn excuse that God was calling them to yet another neighbourhood, sometimes a different city altogether.

41

A bearded man picking up a silver telephone and dialling up the Crowes.

Hello, Reverend Crowe. This is God on the line. Just calling to let you know that it's time to move on again. I think you'll like this next parish. Bit of a challenge. So good luck, Reverend. And please don't forget to give my regards to the wife and kids.

She really did believe this as a child.

With equal measures of concern and cowardice, and especially as their daughters got older and their reactions less predictable, Hannah's parents preferred to break the news in a public place, often under cover of a special night out. They would butter up their daughters with freshly baked rolls and frosted glasses of pop at a local family restaurant, and wait until Connie and Hannah had marvelled at the little tinfoil cups that held the coleslaw on their plates and dunked every last french fry into the gravy, before thumping the good news down on the table like a King James Bible.

Mom's already been to the rectory, her father would say. And there are three bedrooms this time, and a laundry chute and a balcony.

Depending on their friends and teachers and extracurricular activities of the moment, one daughter would invariably clap with glee while the other burst into tears. It was at the announcement of their fourteenth move that Hannah refused to finish the food on her plate as a mild protest at having yet another outing ruined. Eating out was such a rare privilege, she felt more indignant about her parents' meretricious attitude towards pleasure than the upheaval of the move itself.

It was then and there that Hannah committed herself to a life of luxury and sensual gratification. She had learned about free will in the Garden of Eden and decided it was time to put it into practice.

She developed an uncanny taste for apples.

It was thus, with all the moving around she did as a child,

that variety stepped in as a surrogate for stability, and a change of scenery became as familiar and welcome as a house pet. There was something miraculous about the sudden reappearance of brown cardboard boxes in the hall and yellow rolls of packing tape. The discovery of a U-Haul trailer in the drive. These objects were the harbingers of change, connected somehow to God's telephone call, and it was as if angels were moving around the house, leaving rectangles of dust on bedroom floors after the beds had been removed, and jangling empty hangers tangled at odd angles on poles in empty closets that once held clothes. Gradually, Hannah welcomed these clues of their divine presence for the new adventures they would often bring, tucked between the feathers of their wings.

It became second nature, counterintuitive for Hannah to stay in any one place for too long and like a gypsy, after a while, she would simply get the itch to move on and would have to go, preferring not to know the outcome. She never made plans. Not knowing was a kind of freedom, and maybe it was reckless, but decisions are like pennies thrown into a well. They sink to the murky bottom without a trace and they're easy to replace. And if she didn't like the features of her new environment, well, that was okay too, because she knew she wouldn't be there for very long.

But when has anything ever satisfied her anyways?

All of a sudden, Hannah finds herself unpacking her clothes and putting them in Daniel's dresser in Daniel's bedroom in Daniel's flat on Daniel's street in Daniel's city. Then she goes and makes herself a cup of tea with Daniel's kettle and Daniel's cup and Daniel's goddamn water. She slams the kettle down on the counter as he's coming into the kitchen.

Making tea? he asks.

Make it yourself, she snaps and walks out of the room. She sits down on the milk crates and fiddles with a soft pack of American cigarettes. She can't get one out. They are taunting her in their inaccessibility, scorning her poor motor skills, giggling in a pack.

What's up? Daniel asks.

Nothing, she says.

You seem pissed off.

Well, to begin with, I can't get a stupid cigarette out of this fucken pack! she yells, shaking it furiously and then flinging it across the room.

This is the first time Daniel has seen her angry.

She looks at him and he's trying to suppress his laughter.

Oh, sure, laugh why don't you. Hilarious, isn't it? she says, rolling her eyes and sliding her jaw to the left. Secretly, she's pleased he's laughing at her. It reveals that handsome imperturbability she likes, makes him appear strong and wilful, a little indifferent.

I'm sorry, he says, kneeling in front of her and putting his hands on her hips. What's the matter, hey?

It's just this place, she says. It's all yours. I mean, I never seem to accumulate anything in life. I left my last relationship with the same amount of shit I arrived with, a box of books and a backpack full of clothes. I'm just afraid it's gonna happen all over again.

But this is different, he says. We're getting married, for starters.

For starters?

Look, it's not my fault this place is mine, he says.

I'm not saying it's your fault, she tells him. All I'm saying is it makes me feel like I have to be polite. Like a guest.

But this is your place too, now. You can do whatever you like with it.

Hannah looks past Daniel's shoulder at the empty fireplace, thinking a plant would sit there nicely. With a mirror behind it. But somehow the thought exhausts her. It feels like defeat, this having to cooperate. These compromises. This sharing.

Can I have another shelf on the bookcase? she asks, needing to make demands.

Well, you already have two, he says.

But you have four!

Yeah, but where am I going to put all my stuff? he asks, and then relents. Look, if you have enough books to fill three shelves then you can have another one, okay?

Better get down to the bookshop then, hadn't I? she says, arching an eyebrow.

Daniel leans on her knees and pushes himself up.

I'm sorry for yelling at you, she says.

It's okay, he says. You're my little feisty one.

You ain't seen nothing yet.

Really?

I love you, sweetheart, Hannah says.

Please don't tell me we're going to start calling each other lovey-dovey names now, are we?

It was a term of affection, that's all.

Yeah, but I don't like it.

Well, I'm sorry.

I just don't like the way it sounds.

No probs, Daniel.

You can call me babe, if you like.

Okay, babe.

Or darlin, without the *ing*. You know? Not darling, but darlin.

How about sir with an f.u.c.k.y.o.u?

Don't be like that.

Don't be like what? she says. All I did was use a term of affection that I kinda thought expressed how I was feeling and it was a nice sentiment and I was feeling happy, but then you had to go and make me feel self-conscious in a bad way.

I didn't mean to make you feel self-conscious, I was just giving you my opinion.

Well, it hurt, okay? And don't be so stupid. You think we're gonna live together for the rest of our lives and never come up with some cute little pet names for each other?

I don't know, he says, walking away from her. I guess I'm not as experienced as you are when it comes to living with people. But look, he says, turning back on his way to the kitchen. If it means that much to you, I apologize, okay? Call me whatever you like.

A thread of anxiety gathers Hannah's brow. She wasn't prepared. She sits on the milk crates, scratching the knees of her jeans, thinking of all the miles she's travelled to arrive at this. A foreign city. Suddenly, Hannah feels very lonely. Her loneliness spreads out into the room like blood underneath a body.

In the afternoon, Hannah arranges her books and they barely take up two shelves. That's all she will claim for now. She puts her Zora Neale Hurston next to her battered copy of *Wuthering Heights* next to *All the Pretty Horses*. Daniel, she notices, has European books. Obscure, thin volumes of film theory and postmodern criticism. There's a bright pink spine and she pulls out a book entitled *Monogamy*, written by Adam Phillips. She flips through the pages and it's a book of short texts. She stops at one and reads:

> Choosing monogamy is not, of course, choosing not to desire anyone other than one's partner; it is choosing not to do anything that violates one's idea of monogamy. Everyone flirts with their (mostly unconscious) standards of fidelity. But one is only ever faithful to fidelity itself, never merely one's partner.

Hannah thinks of what this says about Daniel and again she's full of admiration for his range, the breadth of his understanding and his curiosity for various configurations, various lifestyles and convictions. They have talked about this before. They don't have to follow the standard mould. They can turn this marriage into anything they want it to be.

They will be the marriage inventors, taking old and everyday objects and putting them to novel uses. Our house will be unremarkable from the outside, but inside there will be no ceilings and no walls, the furniture will be floating and all our guests will be asked to undress before entering so as to take nothing for granted.

They go to the pub later that afternoon and sit close together, holding hands and taking in the same view. Hannah and Daniel against the world. Through the window an English plane tree is lit up with evening sunlight. Its bark is like the skin of an elephant and the leaves, bristling softly, are a fluorescent yellow, as if illuminated from inside. The tree is a lamp, bright yellow against the dark backdrop of pewter clouds culminating behind, and the contrast fills Hannah with longing, a visceral ache for something beyond her grasp and maybe it's for a kind of self-obliterating love she only has an inkling of. Even now, at this thrilling point in a new relationship, at the height of passion and discovery, she isn't whole. Or wholly convinced. Looking at herself from the outside in. Impervious to the dark culminating wisdom of her experience. Resistant. A non-believer.

Purity of heart is to will one thing.

Do you think we have the staying power marriage requires? Hannah asks Daniel quietly. Do I?

Who knows? Daniel says. That's what we're going to find out.

But I've been with so many men, Hannah says, fearful of saying something to change his mind, cause him to reject her. She doesn't want to push him away, but she goes on. Sometimes I have a hard time imagining being faithful to just one man for the rest of my life.

Just one man? Daniel asks.

Well, you, she says, smiling and leaning into him. Thing is, I've always thrived on sexual attention. It's a big part of who I am. And to deprive myself of that? Can I do it? To be entirely honest, Daniel, sometimes I have my doubts.

I know you do, sweetheart. I have them too, he says. About all sorts of things. But they don't outweigh the fact that I want to marry you.

Do you realize you just called me sweetheart?

Oh, my God, you're right. Well, fancy that.

47

It doesn't matter, she says, imitating a gruff male voice. Call me whatever you like.

But it was a term of affection, he says, imitating her. You know I never really understood that until now. See what I mean, though? We're good for each other. We'll keep each other on our toes. Improve and expand each other.

You can expand me anytime, Hannah says, then wonders why she's compelled to be so crass. It was precisely this trait she deplored so much in Gerald Mansfield.

I just like the way you challenge me, Daniel says.

But it scares me sometimes, she says. It's the seriousness of it all, the permanence and my own weakness I'm afraid of. I think I'm fairly independent, but when I have the opportunity to be dependent, to rely on someone else, I seem to swing to that extreme. I'm afraid I'm gonna melt into you, lose myself in you. And then end up resenting you for it.

It's not going to be like that, he says. I won't let you. Listen to me, Hannah. I read somewhere that marriage should be the protection of two solitudes. I think it's a quote from Rilke. *The protection of two solitudes*. That's what I want us to aim for. Getting married doesn't have to deprive us of our freedom or independence. It'll just be something that makes us stronger. Going out into the world is so much easier when you've got someone to come back to.

I understand what you're saying, it's just that –

Listen, I don't want to possess you or own you. I just want to share my life with you, that's all. You make me laugh. You really do.

Do I?

Like nobody else.

That's good, Hannah says.

You're the most innocent and cynical person I have ever met.

Well, you'd better get used to the contradictions.

I love your contradictions.

And I love your solidity. You're like a rock and me the

seaweed that slaps your back. The fly that flits around your horseface.

I love you, Hannah, Daniel says.

I love you too, she says, brushing his cheek with the tips of her fingers, then folding her hands in her lap. Sitting humble and expectant as a girl of six. Waiting for a yellow school bus. A bus she's never seen but knows is coming. A bus she hopes she'll recognize when it arrives.

Love isn't something you can reason, but something inchoate, indescribable. Captured in the details that haunt a moment and linger on the body. Evaporate like steam when you try to hold on to them. And Hannah is moved to love Daniel when she watches the thin film of his eyelids as he sleeps, the insect twitching of his eyeballs under the skin, the sleep like salt crystals on his lashes. She loves the way he stands with his two feet neatly together, bent at the waist like a little boy, as he swirls the water around in the tub before getting in. She loves the way he lines his socks up in a tidy row, the way he ties the garbage bag in a cross of knots, or how he laughs so heartily when he's telling an anecdote. Throwing his head back and laughing at the ceiling. His hands clapped together like he's just caught a moth. These are the things she loves about him because they fill her heart with pity.

And what's so wrong with that.

Haven't you ever been in love before?

It is the middle of a quiet Saturday afternoon. Daniel is trying to read the paper but Hannah keeps flicking the pages and poking him in the head. Suddenly he lurches and grabs her wrist and pulls her across his lap. He spanks her hard. Hannah squeals and rolls onto the floor and dodges his next attempt to pin her down. She scurries into the bedroom and he follows her and tackles her onto the bed. They're breathing hard, their faces an inch apart. He kisses her. She kisses him back. He puts a hand between her legs. She sighs. He pushes her shirt up and rubs the hot skin of her belly.

49

You feel lovely, he whispers in a husky voice.

Stop telling me how I feel! she scolds in mock exasperation and they both crack up and Daniel laughs so hard he rolls off the bed and onto the floor.

This is why she wants to marry him.

And because he fucks her standing in the corner. Holding her leg around his waist. Pressed up against the wall.

To confirm that Hannah is making the right decision, the cosmos colludes to show her a sign. She's flipping through a poetry book at a second-hand bookshop on Charing Cross Road when she finds it. It's a translation of a poem by the Greek poet Cavafy. She can't afford to buy the book, so she takes out a pen and copies it onto a page of her Filofax and carries it home like something warm and alive.

When she gets home, Daniel is hanging up the phone. He looks perturbed and it makes her worry.

What's up?

My parents are getting a divorce, he says.

Oh, my God. Really?

No, he says. Just joking. I always wanted to say that to someone, and Hannah's mouth drops open because she never expected this kind of prank from him.

I can't believe you just said that, she says, huffing incredulously and sitting down on his lap. You had me really worried there for a moment. Made me wonder how they were gonna take the news about us, because I've been thinking. We really should include them. In our wedding. Nothing big. Just our immediate families. Maybe even a few friends.

Yeah, he says, obviously distracted. Daniel puts his hands on her waist. We'll talk about it later, okay?

Okay, Hannah says and then, her voice rising more than she intended, Who was on the phone?

Oh, it was just a friend of mine, he says, pushing her off and going into the kitchen. Tea?

Sure, she says and follows him in and lifts herself onto the counter.

Friend of mine I used to work with, Daniel says, filling the kettle and turning it on. He's been going out with this girl Mandi for eight years. Six months ago, they got married. Now they're breaking up. It's really hard to believe because I've only ever known them together. You forget that people had separate lives. That they once existed oblivious of each other. They're practically an institution. And now, just like that, after six months of marriage, it's all over.

Does it worry you?

About us, you mean?

Hannah nods.

Not really, he says. Just makes me feel sad. For the loss of it. The unusual abruptness. I can't get used to it.

It's horrible when people break up.

Is it?

Well, sometimes it's horrible and sometimes it calls for a big fucken party.

Quite.

But I'm glad it doesn't worry you about us, Hannah says after a while. Because I'm not so worried about us any more either.

Daniel comes over and stands between her legs. No?

Hannah shakes her head and touches his face. Daniel bends forward and puts his head on her lap, wrapping his arms around her hips, cradling his elbows in his hands.

In the distance, Hannah can hear choir music coming from the evening service at the Baptist church one street over. In the living room, the red light on the telephone is blinking on, off, on, off.

Hannah looks down at her fingers sifting through Daniel's fine brown hair, the scalp flashing white like young corn. The thought of a lifelong fidelity appeals to her. It is something she wants. It seems like a peaceful thing, though it makes her anxious too. The loss of that praise, the being lusted after. But

51

there's this peace that's looming ahead. It is beckoning and saying, Come, rest yourself. You have been struggling for so long now. Can't you see it? The love that is in your hands? It's all yours. All you have to do is take it. Have faith. Jump. You will be safe.

I mean, there's no point in waiting, right? she says, stroking Daniel's head.

We could wait eight years, he mumbles into her lap, and then get married only to find out it isn't going to work.

But Daniel, Hannah says, we're at a turning point in our lives. One of those metaphysical junctions. I can feel it. Because marriage is gonna change things. It's gonna change us irrevocably. And we won't be able to get back to the people we once were, except by another route. Perhaps even a painful one.

Hannah can't see Daniel's face and it makes her aware of her voice as being separate from herself. It makes her feel disembodied, like she's performing, acting in a play about a wayward woman who redeems herself by marrying the local Baptist minister. Or is it the Baptist minister's fall from grace? She tries a new inflection, like Jessica Lange at her most sincere, her most imploring. And it works. The effect is decisive. Even the early evening sun, slanting in all golden through the window above the sink, has been roped in to provide the spotlighting, to cast a benevolent glow over the proceedings, as if tonight even the gods are well pleased. And it's as if everything on earth has been ordained. Even this. This little scene in a kitchen in Camberwell.

But I'm willing to learn what marriage has to teach us about ourselves, Hannah says. I'm willing to take this trip with you, babe, in order to find out. I wanna give it a shot. I mean, what the hell. What an adventure. And I don't want to be able just to walk away from you. I want to be forced to stay and work through whatever it is that comes up because I've never had to do that with anyone and I want to see how far we can go together, how close two people can be, because it must take a lifetime to get to know someone truly, and even then.

Daniel stands up and looks at her.

And there's nothing to be afraid of, she says. Because, shit, if it doesn't work out. I mean, we can always get a divorce, right?

That's right, he says, almost in a whisper, taking a strand of her hair and tucking it behind her ear. You shouldn't judge the success of a marriage by how long it lasts, but by the quality of the intervening years.

Daniel seems so far away, but then so is she. Hannah is preoccupied. Something like a conversion has occurred. It's as if her feelings, shuffling their feet at the back of the hall, have gradually been incited to action, not out of a conviction of their own but as a result of the hypnotic effect of her words, dragged in tow behind her insistence. It is the potency of language to make things real. She utters phrases like experiments, tries them on like dress-up clothes, but in saying them she makes them come alive. I speak, therefore I believe. Like the sorcerer's apprentice, Hannah is unable to control her own magic. She's in for the long haul now. The whole nine yards. Caught like a fourteen-foot tiger shark in a glass tank of formaldehyde. Hook, line and sinker.

You have such tiny ears, Daniel says, fingering the soft cartilage. They're like elves' ears. They're so soft.

I have something I want to read to you, Hannah says. I think you might like it.

She reaches into her back pocket and pulls out the page she ripped from her Filofax and smoothes it on her thigh. She clears her throat:

Che fece . . . il gran rifuto

To some of us, a day comes when we must say
The great Yes, or the great No.
Whoever has Yes within him
Reveals himself at once; and saying it,
He discovers himself.

The refuser will not repent:
Ask him again, and he will say No again.
But that No, that entirely proper No,
Buries him beyond all hope of recovery.

Okay, Daniel says. So let's have a wedding. We'll embrace this thing. And we'll do it your way, babe.

4

The pre-nuptials

Of course, we could have broccoli quiche if you'd prefer a vegetarian option, or *spanakopita*, the caterer suggests somewhere in the distance behind her.

Hannah turns her head. It's been two weeks since she and Daniel decided to invite a few people and host a small wedding reception at a local restaurant called Willow's, and Hannah has gone to meet the caterer and sample the wine.

No, no, she says, I think the salad and the salmon will be fine, and her stomach folds in on itself like it's full of minnows.

She has given her word. Accepted Daniel's proposal and there is no turning back. She has signed herself away to the promise of a future she won't recognize until it's passed.

Oh, what a foolhardy leap into darkness this marriage business be.

And yet what faith.

Hannah turns her face back to the clouds and the sky and thinks of her earliest memory, of eating parsley in a bright red wagon being pulled by her tall and elegant mother, of children's voices coming from her sister's schoolyard and the heavy-handed heat of a humid afternoon, the soft cotton of her undershirt and the vibrations of the wooden floor of the wagon as the wheels rotated over pavement and pebbles and bits of glass.

They are naked on the bed. Sitting up and making love. For the first time in her life, Hannah feels comfortable calling it love. Not sex. Not fucking. But making love. Yes, indeed, she thinks it could be. Daniel's breath, his hands, his lips, his tongue, his ribs and shoulder blades, his pubic hair and his cock. She has them all inside of her. They are gently nestled in her brain like baby mice. They don't jar with her heart. They can stay there for a while and they don't threaten her. She feels immensely relieved and grateful to him. Hannah pulls herself forward, wrapping her arms around his torso and gripping his shoulders. Sifting down through her pelvis like sand. She doesn't feel self-conscious and Daniel urges her to come. I want you to come, Hannah, he whispers into the tiny conch of her ear and so she obeys him, and as she does, she floats out above Camberwell, beyond London and the world, into thin mid-air and the deadly blue nightshade of outer space, where human souls orbit silent and solitary with only their memories for comfort and nothing else. She passes her parents and they wave. Hello, Hannah, darling, her mother says. Doesn't she look marvellous, honey? So happy and well. Don't forget to give us a call. And she passes her sister and her full round belly full of life, and Hannah's ex-boyfriend, Gerald Mansfield, and his young moon-faced lover, and there's Hannah's best friend from grade seven and the bicycle she fell off when she scarred her chin and the nameless man she lost her virginity to, and there's a professor from university and a little girl she sat next to on a train and entertained for hours and they're all flying past so quickly she doesn't have time to say hello, and as she looks up ahead, the boundless boundary of the galaxy draws nigh, and it's getting darker and inkier and still she's gaining speed, and the satellite faces peter out now and it's just me here, ladies and gentlemen, just me out here, on my own, and it's time. Goodnight, good gentlefolk, sleep tight.

5

Post honey blues

They get back from Paris at midnight and catch a cab from the station to the flat in Camberwell. Hannah gets out and stands on the far side of the taxi while Daniel pays. Just stands there, getting wet in her thin summer dress, looking up at the three arched windows of the living room. The glass is shiny with raindrops and some of the panes lumpy and thicker at the bottom from the slow drip of the last hundred years. The shadows of the branches are like stretch marks on the wall. They bounce up and down as the street lamps shake in the wind. The flat is dark within, everything still. The papers on the desk. The plates in the cupboard. Everything will be as it was left. And the predictability, the deadly stasis of this confined space that now delineates her life with Daniel, begins to fill Hannah with dread.

She can remember standing in front of another house on an evening similar to this. A house in Montreal that had once been the most familiar place she'd ever known and remembers feeling then, too, a dark foreboding. The red brick house she was looking at then belonged to Gerald Mansfield, her boyfriend of four years, and dwarfed by the apartment building across the street, it looked smaller from the outside than it was inside. Being on the corner, it took the brunt of the weather and, though battered by the elements, perhaps because of this, the house had the beckoning look of a refuge, especially in winter, when the windows would be aglow with smug orange light, like a pumpkin nestled in the snow.

Hannah would step into Gerald's house and stamp her boots and the wind would cease as soon as she shut the door and it was cosy inside. Cosy as hell. Cosy as a heroin high. But that block was like a wind tunnel all year round. It would

57

whistle right through her head every time she came home from McGill, sweeping out her thoughts and erasing them almost intentionally, as if at Gerald's behest so that she could enter him, that house, their life, as blank as an empty sheet of paper.

Hannah stands in the London rain and remembers the last time she went to Gerald's house. It was raining then too, and the silver reflective parking lines in the empty parking lot kitty corner to his house shone like toppled white picket fences. Hannah had moved out two months earlier and still thought of Gerald's place as home. Thought somehow it was pure and incorruptible. That she would always be welcome there as if to a place in his heart. But when she walked up to the porch, she was transfixed by what she saw through the square leaded windows of his front door. Past the entrance hall, with its expensive coats and polished leather boots, her eye travelling an uninterrupted path straight on through to the kitchen, there Gerald stood, not alone but with another woman, kissing her, embracing her. Two lovers entwined like tubers in his kitchen. They were so far away and the light soft enough, that it seemed as if Hannah was looking at herself with Gerald. But then the image of their bodies tangled like roots suddenly struck her with all the force of a pure clean perception of the truth. She had been replaced.

And yet her refusal was such that it was like looking at an imposter, witnessing a con. It was her resistance that made the evidence seem fraudulent in her eyes. It was her disbelief that made the truth look forged.

Hannah looked down at her hands and wondered who she was if this girl inside Gerald's house was impersonating her? Until she could figure it out she didn't want to speak to anyone or even be seen. She knew what Gerald would say if she rang the doorbell. He'd already told her (though she hadn't put much store in it). You're getting in the way, he'd say. Please go away. And that is precisely what she did. Hannah slowly turned around and walked down those slippery steps.

She didn't want to know about a pure clean perception of the truth. She just turned around and left.

She was fast becoming a woman of departures.

And the more you leave, the more often you arrive.

So here we are, Daniel says, unlocking the door and holding it open. Home sweet home.

Hannah gives him a tender smile and steps across the threshold. She hasn't lived here long enough for the place to smell familiar and it gets her back up, like an animal catching the whiff of a trespasser. She walks through the living room taking in the details, the cracked tile at the bottom of the fireplace, the lining paper as yet unpainted, coming loose above the radiator.

Before they left, they'd begun to strip the wallpaper above the kitchen counter down to the plaster onto which Daniel's friends from the wedding party, who stayed while they were away, have graffitied their congratulations. *The wedding was great! Hope you had a good one!* Someone's drawn an arrow to a plug in the wall and written, *Socket to her.* Someone else has written, *What's the best way to ruin a good sex life? Get married! Just joking. Love you both!* There's a bottle of wine on the counter with a plastic yellow bow and Hannah notices that her favourite mug is chipped. She goes into the bedroom, sits down on the bed and leans back with her arms spreadeagled. The bed smells old and stale and she realizes they haven't washed the sheets for weeks. It's a smell she's getting used to. It's the smell of a lack of money.

She looks up at the water marks on the ceiling and suddenly feels exhausted, all her muscles drained of energy, crushed by the weight of the future like she's never felt before, stretching out before her like an ominously deep blue and endless swimming lane.

This is where I belong and so shall I stay forever.

Hannah crosses her hands over her chest as if she were dead, in mockery of the melodrama of her own thoughts. Ophelia, I feel ya.

So she's married now and Hannah is living in a mansion of closed doors, like Bluebeard's wife. All those corridors that used to be wide open are now barred to her. And it's her imagination that is constricted. She doesn't know what to do with this surplus of romanticism. It's as if the part of her mental life that was devoted to dreaming about getting married, the part of her psyche that was reserved for imagining what her perfect partner would be like, has suddenly been amputated. The wide-open green space of the unknown is gone and in its place, the stringent limits of a certain future. All she's left with are the ghost feelings of a discarded habit, unsanctioned desire without referent or object or practical outlet, and she begins to feel the ache and poignancy of a longing which is prohibited, for something inaccessible, forbidden and out of bounds. Such thoughts of illicitness arouse her and Hannah has the urge to fuck someone and then she realizes that from now on that someone will always and only ever be Daniel, and she can't help but somehow resent him for it.

She hears him laugh out loud, rummaging around in the kitchen, and this makes her feel contrite. Put your slippers on, Hannah, shuffle into the kitchen and let Daniel absolve you with a hug. He touches her face and she is forgiven. He claps his hands and rubs them together.

It's good to be home, innit? he says, his wolfish eyes bright with contentment. Cuppa tea? Toast and Marmite? Mmm, mmm, he purrs, rifling through the cupboards.

Hannah nods. Yes, she says, and it is true. It's good to be at home with you.

But how could she possibly tell him that she's only been married for seven days and already she feels trapped and busting at the seams? How could she have known that this was going to happen?

She's already analysing her feelings, balancing the pros and cons, and it doesn't make her feel close to him. It makes her feel her heart's not in it. Can you still want a person when you catch yourself asking that very question?

I need some air, Hannah says.

I'll open the windows, Daniel says. Bit stuffy in here.

I think I'll go outside.

What, right now? he says. But it's the middle of the night.

Solvitur ambulando, she says. I'll go once around the block and then I'll be back.

Are you okay? Daniel asks. Because I always worry when you start talking in Latin.

I'm fine, she says, dragging her mouth into a smile. Her face feels so heavy it's like hoisting a sail.

Well, seeing as you're going out, Daniel says, could you get us a pint of milk?

Hannah walks when she's upset. She walked for miles that evening when she saw Gerald in the kitchen with that girl. It was a year and a half ago and she can remember walking around Montreal until the skin on her thighs began to tingle and she no longer felt the motion of her walking. She walked past the house her friend Louise Samuel used to live in before she moved to London. People move, Hannah thought. They change. They do new things with other people.

Eventually, Hannah stopped at a diner and ordered a cup of tea. She didn't realize she'd been crying until the waiter gave her a sympathetic look. She remembers leaving her tea on the table and walking to the back of the restaurant and dialling Gerald's number. The phone rang twice before he answered it.

Is she still there? Hannah asked.

Who? Gerald answered.

Don't give me that shit.

You mean Harriet?

Of course I mean Harriet. Harriet. Hannah. What's the difference, eh? It's all the same to you. We're interchangeable.

That's not true, he said.

Well, you didn't leave yourself much time to get over me.

Look, he interrupted, I don't know why you keep calling. You were the one who left me.

I know I did, Hannah said. I just wasn't too keen on your ultimatums.

You're the one who couldn't be with me, Gerald said. In fact, I don't think you're capable of being with anybody.

Oh, yeah?

Listen, Hannah. You gotta sort this one out on your own, okay? Sort this one out and you'll be in good stead for the rest of your life.

You're like Pontius Pilate, you know that? A real fucken coward.

I don't want to be alone, he said. What's wrong with that?

You treat women like batteries. When they run out you just get another one. But let me tell you something, Hannah went on, her voice rising. Don't kid yourself because you haven't got anything special going on here. If I'm so easy to replace, then so is she. There will always be another Harriet, you know.

Not even Harriet is a Harriet, he said, and then hung up, leaving Hannah alone again, standing at the back of a cheap diner, with a sympathetic waiter leaning against the counter and a cup of tea breathing into the empty air.

What did he mean by that? Not even Harriet is a Harriet. Hannah thought about it for twenty minutes. Nothing made sense to her any more. She wasn't capable of plucking the tiniest assurance from the rubble of her past.

A few days later Hannah called Gerald again and pleaded to see him one more time. Come out to dinner, she said, and he accepted. It ended in a fight. A couple of weeks later she begged to see him again. This time it'll be our farewell dinner, she promised. But it was just one more in a long series of farewell dinners because she could never get enough of apologizing to him. She kept trying to attain some level of indifference, of decorum. But she failed to convince Gerald of her happiness without him. She accused him of being emotionally dead and then felt the need to make it up to him somehow, to prove to herself that she was over him. But of course it never worked. She just lost her temper whenever she was confronted by his stoicism, so that in the end, all she could do was walk away from this cycle of humiliation empty-handed.

The last time she saw Gerald Mansfield was in a cheery Mexican restaurant that served sizzling fajitas with refried beans and guacamole. The walls were painted in large geometric shapes of red and orange and terracotta. Vibrant colours to dispel the gloom. They drank margaritas and Hannah told Gerald about her new job and he filled her in on the news about friends she hadn't seen since they broke up. Whether from the booze or her intractable need for an explanation, by the end of the meal Hannah was feeling maudlin.

Would you like anything else? she asked, typically lavish on a tight budget. Tea? Coffee? Me?

Gerald glanced at her nervously and Hannah rolled her eyes. Just joking, she said, and thought, what cowards men. He looked so tired, so old, so scared of her then. Beads of sweat had appeared on his upper lip. Don't worry, she said. I'm not gonna eat you for dessert.

I should be getting back, he said. Harriet's waiting up for me.

Gerald said this without thinking and her name was like a splinter jabbed under a fingernail. There was a pause and then Hannah said, Look, I'm sorry I can't be more gracious about this, but it's hard taking second place, you know? Hard to lose out in a competition.

Hannah hadn't wanted to say this but she had. And there it was. Out on the table like a cold dead fish.

But there's no competition, he said. You took yourself out of the running.

I took myself out of the house, she said.

It was the same thing.

Maybe for you it was.

Please don't start this all over again, Gerald said. I really don't think we should see each other any more.

What, like forever?

For a long time, he said.

Whatever you say, she said. Just tell me one thing, okay? Just for the record. Indulge me. If you had to choose, right now, you know? Between Harriet and me, who would it be?

Harriet is my first choice, Gerald said, sighing like a sarcophagus, dragging his scarf around his neck and then pulling on his jacket without standing up, slowly, as if it was full of lead. And you are my second choice, he said. If Harriet was hit by a bus tomorrow, then you would be my first choice.

Gerald got up and thanked her for dinner and left the restaurant. Hannah was stunned, not so much by her own emotional masochism, or even by her inability to sever the bonds of affection and move on, but by the sheer perversity of his final comment.

She sat for a while longer, immobile. Under the table, out of sight, she clenched her fists and promised herself over and over again that this would be the last time, the last time she would reach out to him, to blame Gerald or to vindicate herself.

She put her hands on the table and opened them up. Eight tiny pink grins where her nails had dug into her palms. A reading for her future.

You will experience much laughter.

And then she knew that she had to get out of Montreal.

Nighttime and Hannah tries to quell her restlessness by binding herself physically to Daniel. He is on top of her and she wants him to crush her, to crush all feeling right out of her body. She wants the scouring force of sex to scrape her body clean. To be as numb as a bag of frozen peas. She pulls him down and clenches her fists behind his back. She tightens her stomach, lifts her head off the pillow. She can see down the length of his back, see his ass pumping in and out. He is banging hard into her now. She tightens her cunt around his cock and tries to squeeze all the bitterness out like the juice of a lemon. But all she produces is a cramp in her hip and Ow! Ow! Ow!

What's wrong?

I've got a cramp, she says, straightening her leg and stretching it out. Hannah laughs, but she's annoyed.

You okay? Daniel asks, stroking her face, slowly moving in and out of her, making her body move on the bed. Does this feel any better?

He is so oblivious to her frustration and he is being so gentle with her that she is ashamed of her selfishness. She wants to protect his innocence and unexpectedly her mood changes. Daniel's breath comes in short vulnerable bursts close to her ear. Hannah holds his head and looks into his face and finds it to be open. Like the inside of a shell, surprising and delicate and beautiful. She thinks of archers running back onto the field, arrows at the ready. Daniel's body stiffens, his whole body undulating, rising and falling with every dragging breath, and as he comes, Hannah's hands fly up to his shoulders. She strains and pulls and tries to come, but she doesn't succeed. She can't do it. And then just as suddenly, her mood swings again and bearing Daniel's full weight as he pants into the pillow, her eyes fix angrily on a spot in the ceiling. I can't knock it out of me, she thinks. And starts to cry. She is crying out of sheer frustration.

Daniel strokes her wet face. Everything's going to be okay, darlin. I'm right here.

Oh, shut the fuck up. Give me a break. I'm fine, okay? Just fine. I don't need your pity. But Hannah doesn't say any of this out loud. And she doesn't bury her face in his chest. Or admit that, like a baby, what she really wants is a mother's lavish love to come and console her. Instead, she pushes Daniel off, then curls herself around his back and wraps her arm around his chest and tucks her hand into the soft, hot downy patch of his armpit. And wonders, altogether dispassionately, what it is about sex that brings to the fore so many forgotten wayside

65

thoughts: the tea towel left to simmer a little too close to the stove, and did I turn off the gas? And will there be enough electricity on the meter to heat the flat? And should I cut my hair? Or wear my Levi's rolled?

She cradles him because she fears that her contradictions may be damaging and she wants to protect him from what she cannot alter, which is herself.

6

Getting to know you

September rolls around, uncommonly cold. Hannah and Daniel push their way into a crowded pub in Covent Garden. There's a fusty smell of wet wool and old carpet. There they are, Daniel says and Hannah looks in the direction of his wave. Ursula Bishop and her boyfriend George Tuff are sitting in the corner with their backs to the wall. They are friends of Daniel's from Sussex University. Ursula Bishop is blonde as a Viking princess, in a beige angora turtleneck and toffee-coloured corduroy skirt. A woman at ease in the loose, lighthearted banter of men (a fact that both vexes and delights George in equal measure). She smokes and drinks and looks at home in the city, while George Tuff appears ill at ease. He has the torpid scruffiness of a public school boy and a clipped manner that suggests he might be happier if he didn't have to be sociable at all. They appear to have been sitting in an atmosphere of rancorous silence, the kind so familiar to couples who have traded in boredom for something less tolerant. They seem grateful for the company.

It's about time, Ursula says letting Daniel kiss her on the cheek.

George Tuff stands to shake Hannah's hand and says, Nice to see you again.

You too, Hannah says and hangs her jacket on the back of a chair. She looks at Ursula Bishop and nods hello. Ursula flashes her a smile and the weather station at Crystal Palace registers a dip in the temperature.

Where's Eddie? Daniel asks.

He's on his way, Ursula says, and grabs Daniel by the sleeve. Ursula pulls Daniel down beside her and Hannah looks on with a mixture of admiration and envy. Ursula is the perfect English rose, skin like alabaster and a face as sculpted as a Roman soldier's little sister. Shorter than Hannah but with breasts to die for, breasts with attitude, breasts that lean their elbows on the table and blow smoke rings while other people are eating.

Hannah has heard people talk about Ursula's beauty. She's heard about the men who've fallen in love with her, and wonders if George will be enough to make her happy. Hannah can't help making a comparison and often feels diminished by the powerful attributes of others, as if Ursula's beauty by force eclipsed her own. Hannah knows this to be envious logic, but even Daniel these days seems to praise Ursula more often than he praises her. I feel undesirable, Hannah thinks, and this insecurity isn't going away. Another weakness to overcome, I suppose, but it's hard when you have no money for clothes and you're not getting any male attention, like you don't need to hear that you're beautiful any more, now that you're married.

The thing she couldn't get used to was this: Hannah wasn't accustomed to being sexually unavailable. The general lack of come-ons was making her feel depressed. Oh, how she longed to impress a man in a bar. Knew so well how the lust in a stranger's eye could sustain her for days. Hannah looks at Daniel and nods towards the bar.

No, no, it's my round, George insists, standing up again. What's your poison?

I'd love a beer, Hannah says, watching him walk away, taking an exaggerated interest in her surroundings to mask her shyness. She watches a young man in an orange puffer jacket seduce a woman in red high heels and low-slung jeans and realizes that even if her curiosity is disingenuous, a foil for her discomfort, it makes her all the more observant. As if being a more observant person were the consolation prize for a lack of confidence.

But what Hannah wants right now, more than anything else, is to be taken outside herself. Lifted out of her precious subjectivity, so easily offended, so quick to think the worst, and learn to love these people.

I must remember to look at things from the other person's point of view. If I concentrate on reassuring them, then my fears will go away. Because my fears only exist by virtue of my thinking them. And if I thought them into existence, then I can think them into oblivion.

There he is! shouts Ursula, and Eddie Webb walks over to the table. He's in his usual state of disarray, hair like a pile of leaves and holes at the elbows of his russet coloured jumper. He is flustered by the crowds and his own impatience to get a drink down his gullet. Daniel stands up to make room for him.

Hello, four-eyes, Eddie says, leaning in and patting Daniel on the back, like a sparrow in a bird bath, fluttering his hands at Daniel's shoulders, at once availing himself and making short shrift of the physical intimacy of the gesture. Eddie Webb turns to Hannah and gives her a pope's handshake, knuckles pointed at the ceiling, Evening, Mrs Steel.

Hi there, Eddie, Hannah says, and I resent the erasure of my identity by that nomenclature.

I'm astonished, Eddie says, you never agreed to take the name Steel. I so want to take a man's name. And Steel, my God, that's so hard, so binding.

You'd be surprised how often Hannah Steel has taken my place since I got married.

Are people that old-fashioned? Ursula says.

Who would have guessed, Hannah says, that Daniel and I would become the marriage inventors?

What I'm dying to know, Ursula says, turning to Eddie, is how you feel about the recent return of our friend Ingmar?

Ingmar being, Daniel tells Hannah, the secret object of Eddie's affections.

And Ursula, George says, putting down a tray with four full pints of beer, being the object of Ingmar's.

I couldn't possibly talk about that, Eddie says, running his hands over his head. It's far too early in the evening and I haven't even had a gin yet.

Let me get that for you, George says.

No no no, Eddie says, I intend to drink one at the bar while I'm waiting for my second. You can talk about the latest in footwear fashion while I'm gone. I'm sure Ursula can come up with a few compelling reasons to support Indonesian child labour.

It's India, Ursula says, feigning great tedium. And all our factories are locally run with a mandatory minimum age requirement of sixteen.

When Eddie's gone, Ursula leans forward and says in a conspiratorial voice, So! Ingmar got back from Norway yesterday and apparently Eddie went round to his flat and they stayed up all night, drinking and commiserating. Seems things aren't going so well with Ingmar's girlfriend. She finally decided to pack it in. Or at least Ingmar thinks so. He hasn't heard from her in weeks. Which of course pleases Eddie no end, because with Sara out of the way, well, it means he'll have Ingmar all to himself again.

Apparently, George says, they were out on Ingmar's balcony at six o'clock this morning trying to wash the pigeon shite off the patio furniture.

Can you imagine the two of them? Ursula says, grinning and shaking her head. Standing on Ingmar's balcony in their woolly jumpers, with their soapy tea towels, shooing the pigeons away?

Laurel and bloody Hardy, George says.

Come to think of it, Ursula says, he'd make an excellent scarecrow, don't you think? Can't you just see him standing in the middle of a field, all dishevelled and waving his *Guardian* at the birds?

Somehow I don't think he'd be assertive enough, Daniel says.

Too sensitive for his own good, George says.

Mustn't forget, Daniel says. We are talking about the man

who once apologized to a flower. And he laughs at this, head thrown back, clapping his hands together.

I'm just afraid he's setting himself up for a fall, Ursula says, pleading all of a sudden, touching Daniel on the arm. You know how he gets. He dotes on Ingmar's every word.

And Ingmar's having none of it, I suppose, Daniel says, sympathetically.

None of what? Eddie asks, returning from the bar with two double gin and tonics.

Oh, we were just talking about Ingmar, Ursula says.

Did you hear the news? Eddie asks Daniel, arching his eyebrows. Ingmar's bird finally flew the coop. He can't find her. Doesn't even know where she is.

Maybe you could get your brother to track her down, Daniel says, a little cruelly.

Is he a detective? Hannah asks.

No, Daniel says. An ornithologist.

A what?

Birdwatcher, Eddie says to Hannah. My brother's idea of entertainment is to sit in a swamp all day keeping an eye out for tits. In fact, I think he's spotted a couple on you, Ursula.

Honestly, Ursula says, giving George a peripheral glance, but George is too busy sending a text message on his mobile phone.

Shame about the legs, though, Eddie says. You'd be perfect if it wasn't for your legs.

Well, at least I'm not a fat fuck like you, she says.

Touché, Eddie says. Those ankles may never launch a thousand ships, but your face, darling, now your face –

Well, never mind about my face, Ursula says. It's not my face your brother finds so distracting.

Does your brother's wife know about his interest in Ursula's tits? Daniel asks.

God, no, Eddie says. She wouldn't tolerate it. She's the very jealous type.

Bit henpecked, is he?

Not that he minds, Eddie says. After all these years, she's still HFC.

What's HFC? Daniel asks.

Hot for cock, Eddie says.

Daniel jerks towards the table, stifling a laugh with his mouth full of beer.

Now there's something you know a thing or two about, Ursula says.

I'll admit it, Eddie says. It's the only thing I have in common with my sister-in-law. Only not with respect to my brother, of course. Yuck. I can hardly bear to think about it. They still have more sex than anybody I know. It's absolutely disgusting. All that soft, sticky anchovy flesh. Honestly, I don't know what you men see in it. If only we could ship all the women in Britain to some remote island in the North Atlantic where they could get their nails done and go shopping all day long and have their needs met by short, hairy-chested Vikings.

I think the place is called Reykjavik, Daniel says.

Wreck your dick, George mutters.

You still wouldn't have any luck getting laid, Ursula says. There'd still be all those straight men for you to fall in love with. And stop being such a misogynist.

I'm not a misogynist, Eddie says. I abhor discrimination of any kind. Except when it comes to the Tories and that hideous cow Widdicombe. She should be banned for life. Exiled for having such enormous baps. I mean, they're even bigger than yours.

What is it with you and breasts? Ursula asks. You know, sometimes I think you're a closet heterosexual, Eddie.

What a horrible thought, he says. But honestly, I think it's time we asked Hannah what it's like to have such small tits.

It's a load off, Hannah says, and Eddie laughs.

But you're married now, he says. So I suppose your shagging days are over. Now you'll just have to content yourself with Mr Hand. Just like the rest of us.

Eddie, George admonishes, putting his mobile away and rejoining the conversation. You're fucking outrageous.

It's my fucking prerogative, Eddie says and pulls a mobile out of his breast pocket, as if taking his cue from George. For not having got laid in a month of Sundays.

Speaking of which, Eddie says, punching in a message with his thumb, Ingmar's on his way over and he may need a little cheering up. In other words, he says, tucking his mobile back in his pocket and bending his face to meet the lip of his glass arrested at some fixed point just below his chin and taking another slurp of gin, take no prisoners.

Well, I don't blame Sara at all, Ursula says. You can only wait so long for someone to commit. If it doesn't happen after six months, well –

Then it's a case *sera*, Sara, Daniel says, and they all groan. George flicks a coaster at him.

The problem with Ingmar is that he can't get past that stage of wanting to keep all his options open, Ursula says, once the joke has settled.

Too bloody right, Eddie says, and then in a wistful tone, I mean, how tempting could he possibly think a shagfest *à la Norvège* actually is?

Well, you tell me, Ursula says.

He certainly has a way with the ladies, Daniel says.

For a troll, Eddie says.

Oh, you're just jealous, Ursula says. And then, leaning forward with her hands on the table and pushing herself up, she says, Right. Who wants another drink?

Sit down, pig legs, Eddie says. I'll get the next one. But first, I have to go shake hands with the unemployed.

That night in bed, Hannah turns to Daniel in the dark. She wants to want him. Wants to dispel this uncomfortable feeling of having fallen into the cliché of a sexless marriage when all she's ever wanted was to live a life intensely. She moves her head onto his pillow and touches his hair, then runs her hand

73

over his flat belly. She gets up on an elbow, leans over his face and kisses his mouth. He kisses her back, but it's a perfunctory kiss.

Hannah lies down again.

Sorry, Daniel says. But I'm not really in the mood tonight.

I see.

You don't mind, do you?

I mind a bit, she says.

I just think we should respect it when the other person doesn't want to have sex.

Of course we should respect it, Hannah says.

I mean, Daniel says, I don't think we should force each other to have sex if we're not in the mood.

Wouldn't want to force you.

Because there will be times when we don't feel like it.

I know, she says, trying to sort her intellectual accord from the sting of rejection.

Hannah thinks of times in her life when she's had sex and not really wanted to. The way it made her clench up inside. How it made her so disdainful, and remembers how, when she was sixteen years old, she would visit a certain apartment in the city to buy a dime bag of pot. How the dealer had taken her into the back room one day and sat her down on a bed and pulled out his cock, and how he had a wad of toilet paper wrapped around the end of his penis and how this had distracted her, but before she knew it, his cock was in her mouth and she was letting him move it in and out and not resisting him, and how quickly he had come and how objective she felt, and only slightly dismayed, and not a little curious about the way some people could behave, herself included. And what it all meant to feel so indifferent, so detached from her own experience. And feeling sometimes afraid of her own capacity for cynicism, although she had an adventurous spirit open to new experiences and a curiosity without judgment, she still wondered whether that kind of behaviour made a man feel superior. Or a woman loved, for that matter. I mean, why else would anybody do it? And apparently unscathed, always seemingly unscathed, remembers how she had looked around to see if there was anywhere she could spit his come and, there being no such place, swallowing it.

I guess it does more harm to have sex when you don't want to, Hannah says, feeling the reluctance of her pride, begrudging her this acquiescence, than it does to abstain on the other person's behalf.

Exactly, Daniel says. He gives her a big kiss on the mouth and strokes her hip then turns away from her.

Daniel isn't moved by her and this hurts her. Hannah wants to set him up, make him feel inconsequential too, but she holds back. I will understand the merits, she thinks, of restraint. But isn't that another word for indifference?

I just don't want us to get into the habit, Daniel says, of confusing sex with sleep. He pulls up the covers.

And that about settles it.

Hannah turns away from him as well and pulls her knees up to her chest. She stares at the shapes the lights from a neighbour's window make on the wall of their bedroom, overlapping parallelograms of pale yellow and green. She agrees with Daniel's logic (she's so susceptible to argument) but doesn't like this feeling of having been denied. Of having been cautioned against asking Daniel to go against his nature. As if she had the potential to corrupt him.

She feels her mouth tense and her face set hard against the world. She reaches down and slides a finger between her legs, slippery as aloe vera.

7

Dinner with Louise

Holding her knife and fork like goal posts, Louise Samuel is inspecting three plump scallops in garlic and white wine, clustered at the centre of a large white plate. She is wearing a beautifully tailored, chocolate-brown pinstriped suit and a crisp white shirt. Her clothes echo the colour of her skin and the bright whites of her eyes. The stiff white collar makes Hannah think of envelopes. Of all the correspondence Lou must produce at work. Hannah looks down at the Thai spring rolls on her own plate, crossed on a bed of watercress and framed by three red dots of chilli sauce. She can see the shadow of her head on the white tablecloth, cast by the dramatic spotlighting overhead. It is so clear she could trace the stray hairs with a pencil. Her knife flashes platinum and she looks at her hands. She is wearing three big silver rings, one on the same finger as her wedding band. They overlap. A man shouts on the other side of the busy restaurant and Hannah looks up. The air is blue. She looks at Louise and they laugh.

Thank God the nineties are coming to a close. It's been a decade of small portions, Louise says, taking a scallop in her mouth and rolling her eyes with pleasure. Oh, but they're delicious.

A toast, Hannah says, raising her champagne glass. To wealthy friends.

To wealthy friends, Louise says, taking a sip. But I haven't got any, she says, putting her glass down.

Shut it, Hannah says in a menacing voice.

Don't you find, Louise says, that food always falls into one of two categories? Food that tastes like food, and food that tastes like the human body. All the delicacies, truffles, caviar, they all have tastes reminiscent of the human body.

Sexual tastes, Hannah says.

Exactly, Louise says. Like lobster.

Or sushi.

Or garlic.

Fried onions, Hannah says.

You know, there's nothing I like better than the smell of a man's armpit, Louise says. Not stale, but freshly sweaty.

Or the neck, Hannah says. A man's neck and shoulders can smell amazing.

They say, Louise says, dabbing her lips with a napkin, that if you want to know what a person's essence smells like, you should smell their temple. That the oil the skin produces there is very pure and individual.

Really, Hannah says. Where do you get all this crap from, eh?

Magazines, Louise says, as if the answer is obvious. You know, for someone who claims to be pursuing a career as a freelance writer, I don't think I've ever even seen you read a magazine.

Please don't remind me. I've been a complete failure when it comes to work.

What's the matter? Louise asks.

I don't know if I'm bored or lazy or scared, Hannah says, but I just can't figure out what to do with my life. I seem to have lost my confidence.

London can be overwhelming, you know? Louise says, putting the last scallop in her mouth and chewing it slowly.

Hannah pauses, and then she says, So how are things with you and Martin?

Great, why?

What do you do when the thrill of excitement wears off? I mean, I know you're supposed to go to a deeper level, but what if you miss the thrill of meeting someone new?

The fantasy phase?

The passion.

Louise shrugs, You have to work at it.

77

Work at passion, Hannah says. Yeah, that's never made a lot of sense to me. How do you work at something that's supposed to take possession of you?

Booze and lingerie, Louise says. That's always been my motto.

Hannah laughs, So your sex life is good then, is it?

It's fine, Louise says, taking a sip. I can't complain. It's really good. Why?

Daniel and I aren't having much sex these days, Hannah says, letting out a sigh, the heaviness of which surprises them both.

And you're missing it?

He just doesn't seem to notice me. I don't turn him on. It's like, now that we're married, something's changed. There's no urgency or need to keep things alive. What do you think the average is?

Once a week, I think, for most people. At least, that's what the magazines say.

I wouldn't know, Hannah says, adopting a superior air. I never read them.

You're just going through one of those inevitable sexual troughs, Louise says. Things'll pick up again.

I hope so.

Sure they will, Louise says. Now cheer up. Can't be that bad. I'm paying, remember?

Well then, for God's sake, let's have another bottle of champers, Hannah says, getting the waiter's attention with a little wave.

You know, the more you drink, Louise says, the more camp you get.

Must be from hanging out with Daniel's friend Eddie. I'm sure he encourages me.

Well, let's just have a good time tonight, Louise says, leaning forward and holding Hannah's wrist. While we still have the chance.

What do you mean while we still have the chance?

Louise looks down at her plate.

What? Hannah says.

I thought I'd leave it till later, Louise says. But it's in the air now.

What is?

Martin has finally agreed, Louise says, unable to suppress a smile. To move back to Montreal with me.

Really? Hannah says. When?

Soon, she says. In a month or so. I'm in negotiations with a law firm there.

Well, you kept that pretty quiet.

It's been quite a struggle to convince him, Louise says. Martin's lived here all his life. He's never lived anywhere else but London.

Hannah shakes her head. And these London boys sure love their city.

Tell me about it.

Oh, Lou, Hannah says, a dull ache in her stomach she can only guess is a fear of loneliness. But I just got here.

I know.

And you're part of the reason I came to London.

Am I?

I thought of you, in Montreal. I'd left Gerald and I remember thinking how good you and Martin seemed together. And he's English. And maybe –

Maybe you needed an Englishman?

It worked for you.

But Hannah, I'm really ready to go back home.

I know, Hannah says. But I'm gonna miss you so much.

Me too, Louise says, and they sigh into their champagne flutes, before knocking back the rest of it and holding their empty glasses out for more.

8

Vulnerable

The next afternoon, Daniel and Hannah are at Safeway buying groceries. Hannah loves to food shop, it's the only real spending she does these days, and she deliberates over every choice with a lavish, almost melodramatic attention to detail. Now this, Daniel, is what I call a good bulb of garlic.

What, it should be hard, tight, a touch of purple?

Like the arsehole of a Catholic priest. Lately, Safeway has upgraded. And I find, Hannah says, this spiritually uplifting.

Yeah, there are more speciality items, Daniel says.

More whole foods, less junk.

They pass the security guard. Hannah has a block of Parmesan in her pocket. She won't tell Daniel until they're outside because it makes him nervous, though not on moral grounds. (He would be mortified if she got caught.) Two months ago, Safeway hired a security guard and Hannah has seen him chase and tackle two men so far. He grabbed one by the sleeve but he slipped away, leaving the security guard, a tall black man, wheezing on a street corner, holding a grey jacket in his hands. And Hannah didn't know who to feel more sorry for.

She follows Daniel down the meat and dairy aisle. They need cheese and milk and eggs. I'll get the eggs, Hannah says, and lifts the lid on a dozen to check for cracks. They look like a busload of frightened lab technicians, something out of Orwell. Someone hisses and Hannah glances at a scruffy couple down the aisle. They're dressed in tracksuits and the man is wearing an old bomber jacket. The leather is so dry it's cracked. They must be drunk because they're swaying, standing so close they look as if they're holding each other up. The man is stuffing a pound of ground beef into the shallow pocket of his jacket and they're arguing in loud whispers.

Hannah wishes they'd be more discreet. She wants to tell them how to do it. Look around. Check the ceiling for mirrors, for cameras. She doesn't want to witness another violent arrest. She wants to scream, The security guard is coming!

But instead she just closes the lid on the eggs and catches up to Daniel. She puts them in the basket and follows him to the checkout.

Daniel empties the entire contents of his wallet to cover the cost of the groceries and pushes past Hannah to get out of the line. Can't stand these narrow lanes, he says, standing behind the cashier and shaking air into a plastic bag. They make me feel corralled.

Hannah takes the change and reads the receipt and as they're leaving, asks Daniel to name the most expensive item.

It's the cheese, he says.

Then what?

The coffee. Then butter and the fish.

You forgot the red meat.

Okay, coffee, then the meat.

I love this game.

Me too.

Hannah says, The cashier must have made a mistake because the olive oil only cost us two ninety-nine. Normally it's closer to four pounds, isn't it?

Maybe it was on sale.

No, Hannah says. I think it was a mistake. I remember her typing in a barcode. She must have made a mistake.

It feels like a karmic gift of undeserved good luck and Hannah wants to return it to the world. Put it back in circulation. They are approaching the man who sits at the edge of the parking lot begging for money. He is always crouched there with his back to the wall, hands resting on his knees, reading a paperback. The well-read beggar. Rain or shine. Once she saw a woman give him an umbrella. For a while he had a chair.

If he stayed there long enough, would a shelter rise up around him in increments? Built from the scraps of generosity?

Hannah turns to Daniel and says, I'm gonna give this guy the extra pound.

Don't do that, he says.

Why not?

What's he done to deserve it?

Well, what have we? she says, and hesitates, and now they've passed the beggar and Hannah's missed her chance. She could go back, but she's upset, feels chided in a moment when her heart was open. She stuffs the receipt and the change into her coat pocket, and scraping her knuckles on a sharp corner of her pilfered block of Parmesan, thinks about what it means to deserve.

And the quashing of spontaneous acts of generosity.

There was this one sunny afternoon, Hannah says, when I was seventeen years old. I was hanging out in the park with my friends, and I saw my parents walk by. I hadn't seen them in a really long time. I'd left home the year before. And my first reaction was one of joy and excitement. Hey, there are my parents! I ran down the hill in my bare feet, skirt flowing, hair like a wild mane, imagining some affectionate reunion. What I'd forgotten, though, was how I was wearing a chain of liver-coloured hickeys around my neck. I bounded into them and reached out, for the first time in months, Daniel, it was like breaking the deadly silence of the kitchen table.

What did they do?

My father said, What the hell have you done to your neck? Haven't you got any self-respect? How could you let a boy do that? What's the matter with you? I felt like a horse with a bit in my mouth, reined up hard.

Was that all he could say?

It was too much to bear, you know? His disappointment.

He was stamping down your enthusiasm.

And it was days again before we spoke. Or maybe it was years.

I guess one shouldn't thwart good intention.

It kills the will that's left, she says.

Yeah, he says, it leaves an empty distance you can't cross over.

9

A phone call from Louise

It is the middle of the night. The phone is ringing. Hannah wakes startled, full of fear. Am I dreaming?

It's for you, Daniel says, shuffling back into the bedroom, bleary-eyed and scratching himself. He can hardly see without his glasses on. His face looks unprotected, his eyes have a bewildered look. It is his bedroom face, a private face that Hannah cherishes because she's the only one who gets to see it.

It is cold in the flat and her hips are stiff. Hello? Hannah says hesitantly, pushing the curtain aside to look down at the dark and empty street.

He's not coming! a voice wails down the line.

Lou? Hannah asks. Is that you? What's the matter?

Martin says he won't come with me. He doesn't want to go. I can't believe it. He's such a bastard.

Oh, Lou, Hannah says.

We have the plane tickets and everything. We did all the paperwork for immigration. I've got a job lined up. He knows I have to go now.

Do you want me to come over? Hannah asks. I can jump in a cab right now.

I'm in a hotel room.

A hotel room?

Well, where the fuck was I supposed to go?

Just tell me where you are, Hannah says, grabbing a pen and folding back the cover of a paperback on the desk. Just give me the address.

Louise wipes her nose with a ball of Kleenex. Martin can't change his mind, she says. This move. He's so afraid. I mean, neither of us foresaw. It's taken us both by surprise.

Hannah watches her cry and feels helpless.

I ripped up his clothes today. I smashed a soapstone chess set he bought on our last holiday together. I put all these things in a pile and set fire to them.

You burned his clothes?

Well, they smouldered and went out, Louise says, pulling a fresh Kleenex out of the box on her lap.

You have every reason to be angry, Hannah says, and yet it's great that your anger hasn't turned in on itself.

I have to go meet Martin in Russell Square, Louise says out of the blue.

Okay, Hannah says.

He wants his grandmother's wedding ring back.

Really? Hannah says, and Louise snaps back, No, I'm joking, and Hannah sighs and sits down on the bed beside her. She puts her hand on Lou's back.

Would you come with me? Louise asks.

Right now?

In the morning, Louise says. Look, sleep here and I'll get you a breakfast and you can come help me with Martin in the morning, okay?

They walk towards Russell Square tired from a sleepless night. They pass a Tesco's on the way and Louise heads inside. Hannah figures she wants to do some food shopping. She can understand how this might be comforting, is encouraged by the return of appetite, but all Lou buys is a whole raw chicken.

While they're standing in line at the checkout, Louise turns to Hannah and says quietly, candidly, unusually self-deprecating, All those times I told you how great everything was between Martin and me? Well, it wasn't strictly true. We haven't had a good sex life for years. But I couldn't bear to admit it.

Hannah puts a hand on Louise's shoulder and wishes she could transfer love through the palm of her hand. Oh, God, Hannah prays, love my friend Lou. Please make her happy. May she have a happy life.

85

When they get to the park, Hannah can see Martin Mercer waiting on the other side. He's standing in the middle of a gravel path with his hands in his pockets, unaware of the people walking around him. Louise says, Wait here, and takes the chicken out of the Tesco bag. She gives the bag to Hannah, and as she's walking towards Martin, Lou peels the chicken out of its plastic wrapping. Hannah notices where the plastic lands in a little shrub along the path and then, feeling the need to give them some privacy, takes a few steps back behind a tree. It is thus, partially concealed, that Hannah watches Lou and Martin exchange their final words. He doesn't seem to notice the chicken in Lou's hand. Lou takes something out of her pocket and gives Martin what must be his grandmother's wedding ring. He says something and they stare at each other. And then, before turning and walking away, Lou hands Martin the chicken.

Hannah will never forget the stunned paralysis of the husband. The heavy yellow chicken hanging sideways by a leg. Lou's nervous jog as she returned. Or how bad she felt. Martin's humiliation had been so public. He hadn't put up a fight. And while Lou had always been a literal person – brave, daring, funny – Hannah wasn't sure she'd ever seen anything quite so poetic, or Greek.

How was that, then? Louise says. And they both giggle, though neither of them is laughing.

That, Hannah says, was a thrilling *coup de grâce*. But after seeing Louise off to work (she gets on a red double-decker bus at a corner of the park), Hannah sits down on a bench and feels giddy with guilt. The wind picks up and suddenly there is manic desperation everywhere, in all the leaves of all the trees as they tremble in the park. Because who do you feel sorry for when everybody suffers?

10

Broke

Hannah didn't know what a Cash Converter was until she went to one.

A pawnshop? she asks.

That's right, Daniel says, pulling the door open and walking in.

They had been sitting at the kitchen table, each with a baked potato on a plate for lunch. The hot white stuffing so neat in its crinkled jacket, dignified as a butler, but lacking in personality. Salt and pepper was all they had. No money, not even enough for a small block of butter.

This is so fucking depressing, Daniel said, and Hannah started to laugh.

What? he asked.

Reminds me of the time my sister and I came down for dinner one evening and my parents had put a box of condoms on our plates. I was about fourteen, Connie fifteen. And my father, who never talked about sex, said, If you're gonna muck about, muck about safely. And that was the end of the discussion.

There must be something we can do, Daniel said. Something I can pawn.

Pawn? Hannah said. It had never occurred to her to pawn anything in her life.

I pawned my stereo a few years ago, Daniel said. When I was doing my degree in film studies, when I was really broke.

That's very inner city of you, Hannah said, impressed.

Yeah, well, needs must when the devil drives.

And so they had looked around and found Hannah's old Walkman stashed in a drawer.

You don't mind, do you?

No, Hannah says, but it's not very reliable.

Inside, the Cash Converter smells like mildew and mothballs. There's a counter as soon as you walk in, and behind that, a wall with a small window in it. Stacked around the window, from floor to ceiling, are speakers and stereos of all varieties. Through the window Hannah can see a messy office. Daniel is fiddling with her Walkman, so Hannah just stands quietly by his side, romanticizing the grimness of her own life. There's a woman in front of them. She's got a blender in a baby blanket, which she's hugging to her breast. When it's her turn, she unwraps it on the counter with such demented care, Hannah wonders about her sanity. The door opens and in comes a skinny man with hollow cheeks and pock-marked skin. He walks as if he's shaking spiders off his legs. He can't stand still and fidgets with a camera. The flash goes off in his face and he jumps back. Like he doesn't know how to use that camera. It might not be his. He might have just nicked it.

It's like Christmas, innit? he says, smiling when he notices that Hannah's watching. She smiles back and turns around.

When it's their turn, the man behind the counter takes a cassette from a cardboard box and finds a pair of earphones and plugs them into the Walkman. He's a tall, young black man with a retro Afro and an underground t-shirt.

Got any batteries?

Daniel shakes his head.

The man takes out another cardboard box, this one full of batteries, loads the Walkman and presses the play button. Nothing happens. He looks at Daniel, who takes the Walkman and taps it against his palm. It whirs into life and the man starts bobbing his head to the music. He takes the earphones off and hands them to Daniel. Daniel listens for a while, also bobbing his head, then passes them to Hannah. She puts them on and feels like she's at communion.

Isley Brothers, the man says, when she hands them back.

Hannah nods sagely and the pawnbroker says to Daniel, I can give you four quid.

Whoah, Hannah says, appalled by such a paltry sum but then, considering the volatile nature of the place, thinks better than to make a fuss.

There's no market for Walkmans these days, the man tells Daniel. Chances are I'm not going to sell this. I'm doing you a favour, mate.

Daniel accepts the money. They go outside and he gives two pounds to Hannah. They linger on the sidewalk, then decide to go to the pub. After one pint each, they've drunk Hannah's Walkman.

When they get back to the flat, two men in dark blue overalls and long-sleeved yellow t-shirts are standing at the door. They are delivery men from IKEA. A big yellow truck is idling in the road behind them. One of the men is trying to recover a notice he just slipped through the mail slot.

Just in time, the other one says, handing Daniel a clipboard to sign.

It is the twenty-third of September and in the truck a dusky blue, three-seater sofa-bed, courtesy of Daniel's father. A wedding present.

11

Lyle

Ingmar is throwing a party in his spacious top-floor flat in Highbury. So Daniel and Hannah walk to Denmark Hill and stand on the platform and wait for a train. It is a cold wet dark grey day. The trees rising up from the banks on either side creak like wooden ships. The sky looks like curdled milk. Like it's giving off a bad smell.

Sitting on a bench across the platform is a middle-aged woman in brown tights and black leather shoes. She is wearing a calf-length floral skirt and a nylon burgundy jacket. The lenses of her glasses keep catching the light and there is a splotch of white cream at the corner of her mouth. She is holding an armful of arum lilies and their green stems hang down over her lap like the closed tail of a peacock. The contrast between the woman's homely appearance and the ardent beauty of the lilies creates a tightness in Hannah's chest.

Aren't we, she thinks, all of us, all the time, striving towards beauty, despite how uneven our chances of achieving it?

Hannah looks down at her faded army pants, her scruffy trainers and her coat, loosening at the hem and thinning at the elbows. Her coat is too thin for the weather and she's shivering, wishing she had enough money to buy a new one, a whole new wardrobe for that matter. She thinks, I hate the way I'm dressed and I don't know anything any more. I haven't read enough. I'm stupid and I'm selfish. Bored by everything and I have nothing to say.

And immediately she knows what this will mean. Within minutes of her arrival at the party, Hannah will have drunk enough booze to numb her insecurity. She'll get overexcited and metamorphose into somebody loud and funny and flirtatious. For a while it will be showtime! But in the morning, she'll awake, her usual guilt-ridden self, punished with a hangover and riddled with remorse, the brand-new owner of a family sedan of resolutions, still living the same old life, with the same old habits, beside the same old man. The repetitious nature of her life making her feel invisible, the way a pattern obliterates uniqueness. When all she wants is to be the exception to the rule.

Daniel comes back from checking the timetable and tells her when the next train is coming and where they'll have to change. He does this automatically, this taking charge. It comes naturally to him. Whenever they go to buy a ticket or ask for directions, he's always the first one to jump in. This makes Hannah feel undermined, but short of cutting him off or having an argument, she doesn't know how to stop it. It makes her feel weak.

Nobody warned me, she thinks, how love can weaken a person. How it can make timid even the boldest of people. Hannah feels cramped by her fear of losing it, now that she has this love. The burden of maintaining it. She feels meek and angry at the same time. In need of Daniel's approval, while wanting to defy that need too. Gone, she thinks, is the resilience of my solitary existence. As if love were a force that exposed the tender pulp of her insides. I don't like it, but there is something passive in my nature. I am letting myself become subordinate to Daniel, indistinct, as if I'm not even here.

They arrive at Ingmar's and Hannah follows Daniel up the stairs with all the anticipation of an intoxicated motorist about to take a breathalyzer.

Daniel turns and gives her a look before knocking on the door.

What you looking at?

You okay? he asks her.

Yeah, she says, suddenly remorseful for being so petulant, so paranoid and selfish, touching his waist for reassurance.

He stops and stares at her for longer this time. Sometimes it's only his awareness of her that draws her out of herself. You sure you're okay?

Yeah, I'm sure, Hannah says, and then because she can't help herself, Do you love me, Daniel?

Very much, he says, and smiles without opening his mouth. It is a practiced response. This is how he always answers her. Then he turns and knocks on the door.

Eddie Webb opens the door and the noise of the party explodes towards them. Hannah takes a deep breath, steadies herself and thrusts into the room with a: Hey there, Eddie! Ya big poof! How the hell are ya?

And there are kisses all around.

Come on in, come on in, Eddie Webb says, with his usual impeccable politesse, as if he were the host. And he may as well be, Hannah thinks, he spends most of his time here. He's standing with a man Hannah's never met before. He's tall and thin with straight brown hair that falls down across his eyes, and this half-concealed look creates a feeling of suspense, of something withheld, something to discover. He has a narrow, wry mouth and his whole attitude suggests a superior indifference to what the rest of the world cares about. He flicks his hair to the side and their eyes meet briefly and Hannah gets that internal ping of a chemical attraction.

Oh, God, no. Please. No no no no no.

Then Hannah notices that his expression is not so much aloof as it is tired, and there's a certain resignation and a sadness to the eyes. Hannah imagines that by extension he is also sympathetic, in possession of the kind of compassion that only comes from suffering, and she wants to be a recipient. Longs for sympathy. To be understood.

I'd like you to meet a very good friend of mine, Eddie says. This is Lyle. More commonly referred to as the rock god.

Eddie likes to flatter me, Lyle says, putting an arm around Eddie's shoulder. But really, the epithet has no bearing on reality whatsoever.

Not yet, at any rate, Eddie says. And this here is Mr Steel and his better half. Arty-farty types, who the hell knows what you people do, but individuals of enormous promise, I'm assured, recently betrothed and in the same penurious boat as you've been ever since I've known you.

Congratulations, Lyle says, shaking Daniel's hand.

I'm sure we're deluded, Daniel says.

On getting married, Lyle says.

Oh, right, Daniel says.

And you are?

Hannah, she says, imprinting herself for life at the first warm touch of Lyle's hand.

Lyle withdraws his hand without, Hannah realizes, the slightest trace of interest. And why should he be interested? I'm a married woman. First and foremost, a married woman. And Hannah has never wanted to be something less in all her life.

Rock god, Ingmar salutes Lyle, coming out of the bathroom and passing him on the way to the kitchen.

I've been in the business for ten years now, Lyle says, and only in the last couple of months has there been any talk of a record deal.

One day you'll look back on these humble years and be grateful, Eddie says.

Yeah, I'm really grateful for being skint, Lyle says. Frankly, I wouldn't mind a return to the days of the patrons. We could start with you. Fancy donating?

I'd love to help, Eddie says, but I've spent all my money on gin. Talking of which, I must refill this glass before I get to the bottom.

I thought the whole point was to get to the bottom, Lyle says, and Eddie gives him a withering look.

They follow Lyle and Eddie into the kitchen. Daniel puts a reassuring hand on Hannah's shoulder and now it is unwelcome. He is oblivious to the constant shifting of her allegiances, satisfied with his lot and God she wishes she could be too, but she can't be. She is not. There is too much to choose from. Too much she wants.

Let's ask the rock god! someone shouts and it's Ursula, leaning on the edge of the kitchen counter in a sweater and skirt Hannah's never seen before, a new pair of knee-high boots, and she looks fantastic. Who sang *Don't push me cause I'm close to the edge*?

I'm try-ing not to lose my head. It is Daniel who takes over, bending his knees and swaying from side to side. *It's like a jungle sometimes, it makes me wonder how I keep from going under*.

Who was it? Ursula asks, shaking her hands out in front of her.

Grand Master Flash and the Furious Five, Daniel says.

Grand Master Flash! they all yell.

And you thought it was Run DMC, Ursula tells George, who is apparently more interested in rolling a joint than taking part in the conversation.

I said it might be, he mumbles.

Don't push me cause I'm close to the fridge, Ingmar jokes. *I'm try-ing not to drop these drink*s. He kicks the fridge door shut while holding two bottles of beer in each hand and a bottle of aquavit under his arm. There you go, ladies, he says to two young women who have come into the kitchen in search of libation. Pass them round, he says with a generous sweep. When they've taken the beers, Ingmar flips the bottle of aquavit over his back and catches it. They smile and thank him and Ingmar winks, and as they're leaving the kitchen, he actually gives one of them a pat on the bum. When they're gone, Ingmar turns to his friends who have been watching his performance, and still holding the aquavit, points to his chest and says, Am I good? Or am I good?

There's a collective sigh and rolling of eyes.

What? Ingmar says.

94

You have about as much discretion as a slapper in a brothel, Ursula says.

I'd slap her in a brothel any day, Ingmar says, making his eyebrows leap up and down.

You know, Ursula says. I've been looking at your eyes all night, and there are only two reasons your pupils could be that large. So is it drugs or love?

He's in a constant state of sexual arousal, Eddie says.

No, you are, Lyle says, and Eddie blushes.

Didn't Ingmar just come out of the toilet? Daniel says. There's a mirror above the sink, you know.

Of course, Ursula says. Ingmar's just fallen in love with himself. Haven't you, Ingmar?

And Ingmar says, You guys. He says it bashfully, charmingly, with genuine affection. Loving the attention.

Hannah pulls out a chair at the kitchen table. Her face is aching from smiling so much. She wants to partake in the banter, but, man, you had to be fast. Instead, she resorts to drinking three quick beers. The alcohol kicks in. It emboldens her.

Ah, booze, she thinks. Getting drunk is like walking through a beaded curtain onto the hot white sand of a tropical beach, only to look down and find that you've lost all your clothing, but it doesn't matter anyways, because suddenly you've got the body of a fucken supermodel.

By three in the morning, George has left. The music's on softly and the party has dwindled to the diehard core. It's just Ingmar dancing with Hannah, and Ursula dancing with Lyle. And Eddie and Daniel sitting on the sofa. Daniel has a leg over the arm, smoking a rollie, his head on Eddie's shoulder. Eddie is slumped like a duffel bag in the middle, chin resting on his chest, and he's burping little bubbles of gin vapour into the room like he's finally become, at this early hour of the morning, his very own distillery. Daniel says something and they both turn their heads in unison to gaze at the others.

Ursula and Lyle dance at arm's length. They are staring at their feet.

Is that salsa? Daniel asks.

Rudimentary salsa, Eddie says.

And what about Fred Astaire over there?

Ingmar is spinning and dipping Hannah around the room.

That, Eddie says, is called spinning and dipping.

Ingmar dips Hannah and she throws her head back. She can see Lyle and Ursula upside down. Hannah's body is torpid and padded from the booze. Her mind alcohol-logged. But there's an intimacy she feels with these people. A fondness like love.

It's one of those moments in the quiet aftermath of a party, when the exuberance of an eight-hour buzz wanes, and the fuzzy murmur of tired voices can wrap a group of friends in an air of complete and restful benevolence, and they are cosy in their little bubble of contentment (never mind the drugs), basking in the soft lush chords of Spanish music, burgeoning like begonias, savouring the warmth of human companionship, the idle chit-chat, the bloody nonsense and the jokes.

By five o'clock the sky is growing light. Lyle is lying face down on the carpet, his nose in a dark stain of beer. He's wearing an army green parka with the hood up and his head is hidden. He had almost managed to leave. His arms are straight by his sides and the soles of his Converse All Stars meet pigeon-toed at the tip. The group is posed around him like a tableau vivant. The Verve is crooning *Urban Hymns* into the whale-grey morning and they are whispering, out of courtesy towards Lyle, and sheer post-party exhaustion.

Maybe we should move him, Ursula says eventually, tapping Lyle on the shoulder, this new guy who has appeared on the scene and whom they have all taken a fancy to for his good looks and his charm. She tries to coax him awake, but he doesn't stir.

Do you think he could suffocate like that? she asks again.

Well, I don't think he'll die, Ingmar says, stretching out on the floor, giving in to gravity. He rolls onto his back and crosses his ankles and puts his hands under his head.

But the carpet under his face is wet, Ursula says.

So move him, Eddie says.

I don't know him well enough, Ursula says, shy all of a sudden.

Fine, Eddie says. I'll do it. He pulls the hood back on Lyle's parka, lifts his head and turns it to the side. Lyle grunts and settles back into sleep.

Poor Lyle, Eddie says, dropping his hood again like a lid. Just split up with his girlfriend of seven years.

There are tuts of sympathy. Ursula gets up, goes into the kitchen and comes back with the last dregs of aquavit.

Oh, no, not the aquavit, Daniel says.

Ursula takes a swig and shudders. I've got some news too, she says. George and I aren't living together any more. I moved out of his place six weeks ago.

Really? they all say, sitting up and moving their bodies to accommodate the shock.

Oh, Ursula, Ingmar says, putting a hand on her thigh. Why didn't you tell us before? At which point Ursula crumples into tears.

It is the following afternoon. Daniel and Hannah are at home, lounging in the bathtub, both facing the same direction. She's got her head on his chest and the warm water is like a rug. The sound of cars going by on the street is the only reminder that the rest of the world is at work.

God, it's hot in here, Hannah says, lifting her leg and hanging it over the side of the tub, feeling the cool air peel the heat from her skin, like a clean white sheet softly falling.

This is the life, Daniel says, dragging a warm, wet facecloth over his head and leaving it there.

Daniel, Hannah asks, her voice suddenly plaintive, hitting a higher register. Are you happy with me?

Of course I'm happy with you, darlin, he says, pulling the facecloth off his head.

I just feel so boring, you know? Now that we're married.

Well, thanks a lot.

Oh, I don't mean you. I mean. I saw a billboard the other day that said the average woman is twenty-five when she gets married. It depressed me because that's how old I was. I thought we were being so daring.

We were being daring, he says. For us.

But maybe all we have is a perfectly ordinary marriage. With all the ordinary flaws. Destined for a perfectly ordinary divorce.

What's the matter with you today? Daniel asks.

Sometimes I feel like I'm gonna end up alone in life.

Is that what you think, or is that what you want?

I fear my own capacity for sabotage.

Well, why don't you try and resist it for a change?

What, and miss out on all the excitement of breaking up?

You think breaking up is exciting?

Not exciting –

You do, he says, sitting up in the water and pushing Hannah forward. It's all part of your romantic fantasy life. One more dramatic chapter in the Crowe biography. Well, I don't think splitting up is very exciting. I think it's sad. I want you to know that I would consider it a significant failure in my life if this marriage doesn't work out. And I don't particularly relish the thought. I'm sure Ursula is going through hell right now. Didn't you see how upset she was? And Lyle, too, for that matter.

I wouldn't know, Hannah says.

That's because you're too wrapped up in yourself.

No, it's because I couldn't get a word in edgewise. You kept going on about the fucken Beach Boys.

Hannah is sitting sideways in the tub. She looks down at her hands, wrinkly from being in the water so long. Topographic maps. Tiny mountain ranges. Quietly she says,

Don't you ever look down on your life as if from a great height?

No, Daniel says abruptly, I don't.

Well, I do, Hannah says. And I'm sorry if it offends you, but I can't help it. When I was a teenager, they used to call me the Ref because I never got involved. I was kind of aloof, impartial. They used to call me in to settle an argument because I could see things from both sides. And it kind of stuck with me, you know? It doesn't mean I don't care, or can't love anybody. It just means I have this, I dunno.

This detachment, Daniel says.

Whatever, Hannah says, standing up in the water. She looks at Daniel sitting in the tub, legs bent, hands resting on the facecloth in his lap. A posture of defencelessness. He looks up at her and there is confusion in his face, and anger. It breaks her heart. She feels cruel. Too hard in her heart to love him well. She wants to repent. Wants to reassure him. She can't bear the thought of hurting him, but she's so dissatisfied right now.

I'm sorry, Hannah says, picking the towel off the radiator and wrapping it around her body. I'm just a bit hungover. I mean, I'm really fucken hungover. I'm so hungover I'm seeing mice. I shouldn't have drunk so much. I never used to. I mean, I didn't even know what a hangover was until I came to this fucken country.

Blame England, why don't you.

Oh, don't be so fucken patriotic.

But you had a good time last night, didn't you?

Hannah looks at Daniel, pushes her jaw sideways and nods, as if agreeing were such a sacrifice. Am I so proud?

So why berate yourself? he asks.

Because I have to, she says, squeezing toothpaste onto her toothbrush and jamming it into her mouth. It's in me nature, she says in a mockney accent.

It's because you're North American, that's why.

Oh, now look who's blaming countries.

You just don't know how to have a good time, Daniel says, without punishing yourself. Thing is, it doesn't change anything. You're going to do it all over again next weekend.

Maybe I won't, Hannah says, spitting into the sink.

Of course you will.

Maybe I'm never gonna get drunk again in my whole entire life, Hannah says, bending forward to suck water from the tap.

Famous last words, he says. Problem with you is you confuse ambition with capability. You set yourself goals that you can't achieve and then berate yourself when you don't achieve them. I'll never understand that kind of mentality.

Well, I'm sorry I'm not as sanguine and complacent about my weaknesses as you are.

Oh, that's a nice thing to say about your husband.

Hannah's toothbrush makes a pinging noise at the bottom of the metal cup.

You sure know how to make a man feel loving towards you, Daniel says, cupping water into the facecloth and rubbing his face. Really loving, d'you know what I mean?

Hannah feels a wrenching like drawstrings pulled tight across her chest. She's begun to do it again. Begun to force the love away from her and she wants to run after it, shouting and screaming for it to come back, like she never meant to drive it away. But instead, all she can say is, Just forget I ever said anything, okay? Just leave me alone.

Hannah walks out of the bathroom, gets into bed and pulls the duvet over her head.

A little while later, Daniel comes in and joins her under the covers. Hannah has such a need to feel his skin against hers, so reassuring in its warmth, but she's too sullen to make a move and so grateful when he takes her in his arms.

Hannah wakes and makes herself a cup of tea. She stands at the kitchen window, looking out at the building next door, the hues of pink and yellow in the old brown brick. Against the white sky, squat chimney pots poke up from the flat roofs like elephants' toes. A magpie swoops down and perches on a satellite dish. It's got something red in its beak and its unscrupulous appetite makes Hannah's throat constrict. She recalls the thrill of promiscuity and longs for the whole wide world out there. To relive a night like the one she had last summer when she was working as a waitress at a hotel in Toronto. Her parents had recently moved there and she was staying with them before leaving for England. She was working her final shift and her boss invited her up to the penthouse suite for a bottle of champagne. He was married but said it was a practical arrangement, for the sake of his daughter. His wife was Portuguese and came from an old-fashioned family. He had agreed to marry her, but he wasn't in love with her. His wife had no idea that he cheated on her and that's the way he wanted it to stay. Hannah fooled around with him on the king-size bed, in front of the wide-screen TV, to a soundtrack of music videos. He wanted to go all the way but she wasn't attracted to him enough and so she left.

But she didn't go home. Instead, she dared herself to go to the fifth floor where a customer had told her to come looking for him. Any time of the night, he'd said. A bodybuilder from Alabama, up for a sales conference. He was introducing a new line of power shakes into the market. She got into the elevator and on the way down, checked herself in the tinted mirror. Her hair was tangled and her lipstick was smudged. She felt a little crazy then, standing there like some wild succubus. And when he let her in, they wrestled on the floor, and she didn't fuck him but went down on him instead, because she'd recently made a pact with God not to fuck anyone she didn't love.

And she hadn't fucked anyone from that point on. Until she met Daniel. Whom she loved.

But as she had walked home from that hotel, in the pink haze of a summer morning, Hannah felt giddy in her naughtiness, powerful in her defiance not to care. Because you're free from all reproach when you give up trying to meet the conventional standards of decency. And there was something comforting in the secret knowledge of her sluttishness, the warm knowledge of her badness that she carried like glowing coals, a primitive fire held close to the belly.

A few weeks later, when she had been about to leave Toronto, Hannah took a walk by the old hotel. It had been sold and was under renovation. The entire outer wall of the north wing above her old bar had been torn down. The building looked like a doll's house, each room identical to the next, each with a lighter square on the wall where a picture had been taken down, strips of wallpaper flapping in the breeze, like bunting on a ship, an ocean liner ready to set sail with the memory of a thousand late-night trysts.

Hannah stood on the opposite corner of the intersection and mentally traced her journey from the top floor to the fifth until an eighteen-wheeler came to a hissing hydraulic stop at the red light in front of her, blocking her view. On the door to the cab of the truck was a sticker, a silhouette of a woman with flowing hair, a tiny waist and enormous breasts, leaning on her elbows and kicking her legs provocatively in the air. A Playboy pose. Under the bunny was written BAD GIRLS WANTED. And Hannah smiled because she'd been there too. She knew what it was like to be wanted. Because she'd gone where the bad girls go. Done what the bad girls do. And she had no regrets.

Or few.

12

Party triptych

1. Hannah and Daniel and the usual suspects. Hannah is reeling through the room with a drunken bugbear in her brain, volume cranked. She'll knock a bookshelf over if she's not careful, or break another glass. Lyle is playing his guitar and singing. His voice is like molasses poured over burning coals. He's playing all those songs from the sixties that Hannah is reacquainting herself with because of Daniel. She hums the harmonies and feels this contraction of longing, like a gag reflex, a stretched elastic. It snaps and the feeling drops, like a pebble down a well, echoing its own impossibility. Because there will never be enough, she thinks, to fill me, will there. And Lyle begins to play *Heart of Gold*.

Oh, do that harmony thing, Ursula implores Hannah. I love it when she does that, she says to Daniel, and Hannah is so grateful of her praise.

You see, this painful longing is not unpleasant either. It's like the pleasant sensation of being pulled apart. Of being stretched just shy of breaking point.

2. Ingmar is leaning against the doorjamb, smoking a cigarette and eyeing Ursula. Ursula is dancing with Lyle. She is talking into his ear and Lyle is smiling on her shoulder. Hannah is eyeing Lyle, while Eddie is eyeing Ingmar. Daniel isn't eyeing anybody, although he's talking to Eddie. They're discussing the morality of the imminent invasion of Kosovo by Nato troops. Daniel is eyeing a political event, the only translucent member of the group. He's got nothing to hide. Briefly he looks at Hannah but his expression doesn't change. It's as if he hasn't seen her at all.

3. Just before the sun rises, Daniel is in bed with Eddie. Ingmar is sprawled on the single bed, and Lyle is on the spare futon, flanked by Ursula and Hannah. They are sleeping in their t-shirts and underwear. Lyle is curled towards Ursula, but the mere fact of her hip touching his back is enough to keep Hannah awake. It creates a hot patch like glue. She lies awake and listens to the deep drunken breathing of her friends, like hibernating bears in a pale-blue cave. It almost feels like home.

I could lie here with you for the next five months.

While the dawn creeps in like a red hunter.

13

Norway

Hannah is haunted by thoughts of Lyle. Every time she sees him, her infatuation grows. Is he giving her encouragement? Did he hold her gaze when she caught him looking at her? Is he laughing more than is warranted at the jokes she tells, and lingering at length to talk in kitchens at parties? Problem is, Hannah finds it difficult to have a casual conversation. On the tip of her tongue is the desire to confess her feelings, and this urge is like an obstacle in her mind. Her conversation becomes distracted, fawning. She watches herself dwindle until she is nothing more than the desire to confess her attraction. She becomes a book with only one story. A story with one character. A character with one thing on her mind.

Hannah slow-dances with Lyle in front of everyone. She caresses the back of his neck. Gently circling right there in his living room, Hannah lays her head on his shoulder, one ear like the travelling beam of a lighthouse catching snippets of conversation rising from the furniture, the other listening to Lyle's breath in his throat.

Daniel is sitting quietly on his own, staring at his hands. Hannah's heart aches at the sight, but her body feels too good this close to Lyle. Do I have the strength, she thinks, to step away to comfort my husband? She is relieved the next time she comes around to find Daniel deep in conversation with Ursula. Then in creeps jealousy.

Hannah sits in the flat one night, one night Daniel has to work, and thinks, I am manifesting all the symptoms of being in love. My heart's caught up in a fast drum loop. Butterflies have set up a permanent colony in my stomach. They've pitched little butterfly tents, and they're sipping little butterfly drinks on fold-out butterfly chairs. You're losing weight, she tells herself. You drink too much. You're chain-smoking before breakfast. You're playing the daredevil and courting every chance you get at bravado. There is nothing subtle about this.

When they go as a group to Ingmar's hometown in Norway, Hannah is the first person to take off all her clothes and go skinny-dipping in the freezing fjord. She treads water for ten minutes just to be close to Lyle, to get his attention, to prove how healthy is her heart, how robust and bursting from the seams she is with love.

After the swim, Lyle and Hannah huddle by the campfire sipping brandy. They are the ones who stayed in longest. Your lips are still blue, Lyle says.

I'm okay. And she flicks something off the back of her hand. Hannah says, I can't believe I just got bit by a fly. I didn't swat it because it wasn't a mosquito.

Maybe it was a mosquito, Lyle says, in disguise.

A mosquito, Hannah says, wearing a fly carapace.

She is surprised at how hard Lyle laughs. How could he not love me, Hannah thinks, when I am so witty?

Back in England, Hannah becomes very, very dreamy. She wakes up with plum-coloured bruises after a night on the town. Two on her thigh and one on her arm. She can't remember how she got them. There is a business card in her pocket. A number circled in red pen. When the phone rings, she jumps. Twice she misses the bus stop for Camberwell and rides all the way to Brockwell Park. She can't concentrate enough to read a book and stares out of windows. Just stares and stares, watching the clouds and cars go by, behind the transparent reflection of her face.

She conjures long drawn-out conversations with Lyle during which she confesses her feelings and he reciprocates. She tells Daniel but he refuses to let her go. So, after a dramatic three-way fight and a glorious runaway vacation (usually somewhere in the Mediterranean), and a tearful reckoning (she may be pregnant with Daniel's child), Hannah moves into a fantastic loft in Borough (hardwood floors and exposed brick walls, a rooftop terrace overlooking the Thames). She becomes lover to them both (let's alternate weekends), while driving them out during the day because she's so unbelievably productive with her fabulous novel. But even then, sometimes, when Daniel is asleep in her bed, Hannah is awoken in the middle of the night with a sense of urgency (Lyle needs me!). She sneaks out onto the fire escape in her cerulean kimono and down the ladder into the alley below, to find Lyle waiting for her there with his big hands.

14

Sex, money, food

November rolls around, bored with itself, scratching at doors, irascible and tetchy, eager to spread its wings. Daniel and Hannah are in the flat. Hannah is sitting on the sofa with a novel and Daniel is at his computer, planning next month's movie programme at the Everyman. Hannah isn't reading. She is distracted by his presence. She wants something from him. Wants it simply by virtue of his being there. She wants some attention. Wants to know that he cares that she is sitting on the sofa unable to read. But Daniel is preoccupied, too busy to notice her. He is oblivious of her presence. So self-contained, Hannah thinks, he is perfectly capable of acting as if I'm not here. But it's not an act. Daniel simply knows how to be alone, even when she's in the room.

Hannah, on the other hand, isn't capable of doing this. She is too affected by her environment. She can't engineer a sense of privacy without physically being alone and there is this division within herself: the way she is with people versus the way she is on her own. There is a freedom in solitude, Hannah thinks, born in the absence of a threat of judgment, which allows me to relax and explore my own desires. Without the possibility of solitude, I feel hindered. Hannah is starting to resent that confident, imperturbable calm that so attracted her in the beginning, but which now allows Daniel to continue as before, as if he hadn't even married her, as if he were still single (there is a part of him that he won't share, a part he keeps to himself).

Do you want to go out for a walk? Hannah asks, trying to expel her feelings, going over and standing behind Daniel with her hands on his shoulders.

I'm kind of busy, Daniel says.

How busy? she says, bending forward and putting her head on his shoulder. She puts her hands on his crotch.

I'm working, Daniel says, flicking her hands away.

Fine, Hannah says, backing off.

Sorry, he says. I didn't mean to do that.

Never mind, she says. I'll just sit here and read my book and try to stay out of your fucken way.

Daniel sighs and gets up and puts on his shoes. He puts on his coat. Hannah is determined to ignore him.

Come on, he says, dropping shoes at her feet. He throws a coat over her head.

They go out for a walk. To the park at Myatts Fields. On the path, there's an elaborate Victorian gazebo enclosed in rusty iron latticework. It's cordoned off for repairs. Three boys are kicking a football in a fenced-off playing field. The pitch is covered in gravel and smokes when it's disturbed. The grass is shiny and the air is earthy. The change of perspective welcome.

This was a good idea, Daniel says, squeezing Hannah's hand.

You always like it once you're out, she says, and they perambulate in a happy silence.

That evening they are relaxed. They nestle into quiet, domestic peace. They eat pasta and watch a video, snuggled up on the couch. Hannah feels so close to Daniel it's as if they aren't two people. When they get into bed, Daniel reaches across and starts caressing her breasts. It literally takes Hannah's breath away. Her whole body stiffens. It feels so invasive, her sexuality having retreated to some deep internal place where it lies dormant.

What's wrong? Daniel says.

It's a little weird, Hannah says, letting out a nervous giggle. I wasn't expecting. I just feel like I've been sealed for so long, it's kind of hard to open up. It feels private. Like you're reaching down my throat or something.

It's been a while, I guess.

It's a little painful to admit. I mean, Hannah says, it makes me nervous and yet it's so intense what you're doing. It reminds me of how much I've been longing to be touched and it's paradoxical. I want to go there and yet there's this gulf.

So are we going to lie here and analyse it? Daniel says, and Hannah looks at him.

She laughs. I guess you were just going a bit fast, that's all.

Too fast? Daniel asks in disbelief. All I did was touch your breasts. He rolls back onto his side of the bed.

I'm sorry, Hannah says, remorseful now.

Look at us, Daniel says, and then he laughs too. We haven't had sex in weeks and you keep nagging me about it and so I try it on and –

It was just a bit of a shock, she says. That's all.

Well, I wanted it to be a surprise, he says. I don't fuck on demand.

Tell me about it.

Look, I'm trying, aren't I?

Yeah, you get A for effort.

I can't tell whether you're being serious or sarcastic.

Well, what the hell? Hannah says. You make it sound like you were going for the grade.

It's just that you're always pestering me about our sex life.

Is it such a chore, then, having to fuck me?

It is tonight.

Remind me to buy a dildo, Hannah says, and they look at each other, faces drawn taut with recrimination. Suddenly the absurdity of their situation unfolds as crisp as starched linen, and they both crack up again. They hug and roll around a bit. Then they fall asleep. Warm and cosy between soft dry sheets.

Daniel's father, Albert Steel, spends a week in the flat, installing new kitchen cupboards. A fridge and stove. It is an early Christmas gift.

Hannah helps out, handing him spirit level, square, three-inch screws. She feels like a nurse attending surgery. Out of respect, she restricts her opinions but can't help, at one point, correcting him on a small point of measurement.

So, Albert says, you're not just a pretty face after all.

He is crouched under a U-bend and it makes her seethe.

When the job is done, Hannah feels repentant. It was an act of generosity. I am grateful, she thinks, to have a working kitchen. She puts the hotplate in a cupboard. She keeps opening the fridge and staring at its plastic whiteness. She is taken aback by the racket it makes.

There are two desks in the flat now, side to side. When Hannah and Daniel are seated, they are at most four feet apart.

Let's measure it, he says.

Okay.

And she is impressed with Daniel's pursuit of the joke. He uses string, then measures the string off on a flat ruler: forty-three inches.

Let us, he says, get down to work. And they are concentrated in their efforts. Daniel scans an article about Lars von Triers and the Dogma manifesto. Hannah emails the literary editors of London's major newspapers. She is sensitive to the logging-on sound her computer makes, like the suction tube at a dentist's.

After forty-five minutes of industry, Hannah rises to make a cup of tea. She looks at Daniel and pulls his sleeve. She walks past him and slaps the back of his head. He lurches to grab her and she jumps in surprise. Don't run behind the sofa.

Look, I'm feinting, she says. Just like a basketball player.

That's it, he says, and chases her and tackles her to the floor. He throws her on the sofa. He carries her to the bed. I will, he says, tickle you painfully. I will dig my fingers between your ribs.

They wrestle each other with serious abandon, frisky and vicious as tiger cubs. They punch each other hard while giggling into pillows, armpits, okay okay okay!

111

Stop it, I love it! Hannah yells, wincing from the pain but wanting more.

They have bruises on their biceps like prizefighters.

They are in training.

They invent a phrase that sums it all up: from silence to violence. And it makes them laugh. They hug a lot. Pant heavily into each other's faces, red from the exertion, sweat dampening the backs of their shirts. Hearts pumping into each other's arms.

It is the best that they can do.

Daniel says he won't be back too late. He's going to meet an old university friend he hasn't seen for months. He kisses Hannah and leaves the flat. She doesn't know what to do with herself. Feels, almost immediately, alone. Abandoned, though she knows she has no right. She makes herself dinner. Watches TV. She expects Daniel home around midnight. At 12:30 she goes to bed and reads thirteen pages of an André Dubus novella. By 1:00 her eyes are tired and she turns out the light. By 2:00 she starts to worry. She sees Daniel walking home, weaving drunk. She imagines a mugging. He is hit on the head. A gash. He is bleeding and has fallen into the gutter. Nobody's helping him. Oh, why doesn't somebody stop and help him? Hannah hears the front door open. A flood of relief. Footsteps in the hall. They pass the flat and continue on upstairs. Hannah puts her hands in her hair, turns over and moans into the pillow. She moans herself to sleep. It is a fitful sleep. At 4:30, she is woken again, this time by the sound of loud, uneven breathing outside the door. Daniel fumbles with his keys. He tip-toes in. He thinks he's being quiet. He comes into the bedroom. When he realizes Hannah's awake, he starts to laugh. He stumbles towards the bed and collapses.

Am I in trouble? he asks. Are you mad at me?

No, she says in a grateful voice, drawing him towards her and kissing his hair, privately thanking the gods for bringing him home safely. Because I love this man, she thinks. I really do.

You know, Hannah says to Daniel one day. If you're gonna give me that son at twenty-eight, you've got about a year and half to get me pregnant.

What if you can't get pregnant? Daniel asks.

What if you can't get me pregnant? Hannah answers.

Well, how are your ovaries?

How are your gonads?

When was the last time you had a smear?

That's a good question, Hannah says, and considers it. I should probably make an appointment.

And so it is that Hannah finds herself sitting at a small desk in a dingy surgery on the road to Brixton, across from a young GP fresh out of training who doesn't seem to appreciate that vigorous gum chewing might not lend itself to creating an air of competent professionalism.

Perv, Hannah thinks as the doctor says, Now just relax your legs, running his hands down the inside of her thighs.

Hannah's legs are up in stirrups, so she drops her head back down on the pillow and lets out a sigh. What else can she do? She's in a helpless position. The doctor lubricates the fingers of his right hand and pushes them into her body while pressing down on her belly with the other. Great, he says, and then, sitting down between her feet and spreading her labia, he slips the chilly speculum in.

There's a twinge in her cervix, a little cramp, and she knows the scraping's over. Hannah sits up and notices a piece of bloody gauze at the bottom of a wastebin on the floor beside the examining table. There's a piece of bloody gauze in there, Hannah says.

Oh, yeah, the young GP says, leaning over to have a look, snapping his gloves off and cracking his gum. My last patient was on her period, he says, as if all Hannah needed was the reassurance of an explanation.

113

It reminds her of when she went to get her teeth cleaned by the Vietnamese dentist near the Green. When it came to spitting in the rinsing bowl (which resembled a small urinal), Hannah noticed that on the drain lay an extracted tooth. There's a tooth in there! she exclaimed, and the dentist and her assistant both peered over her head like Parisian waiters and agreed that, Yes, indeed, there was. And that was the end of it.

Hannah couldn't understand this general laxity. Didn't anybody care about anything any more? The quality of services rendered? Were people so unhappy that the idea of taking pride in their work could be met with such apathy and ridicule?

I need to bolster my spirits, Hannah thinks, and she wanders into the market on her way home. Nothing as fortifying as spending money these days, but she only has twenty-five pounds to last her through the week. There is a soft brown turtleneck hanging at one of the stalls. It's going for fifteen pounds. Hannah hesitates before paying the money, then as soon as she does, she starts to feel regret. I've already got a turtleneck, albeit black, but I should probably have saved the money. Daniel never begrudges her this kind of impulse buy (he always tells her that she's worth it), but to appease her guilt of self-indulgence, Hannah decides to buy a nice piece of fish and make her husband something special for dinner. She heads into the local fishmonger's to see what's available. She likes the look of a small red one and asks how much it is.

That one's got too many bones, the fishmonger says.

But how much would it be for two? Hannah asks.

About six quid, luv, he says. But what I recommend is this here lovely grouper. Fresh today and more value for your money.

He picks up a piece that's larger than Hannah would have liked, but he's so persuasive, and he's already wrapping it up.

That'll be eight pounds ten, he says and Hannah's heart sinks. That leaves her just under two pounds for the rest of the week.

Oh, boy, she thinks once she's back on Coldharbour Lane. Super-dooper grouper.

Hannah feels defeated now. Her only consolation is thinking about how she's going to prepare it. With butter and a bay leaf and a touch of nutmeg. When she gets home, she tells Daniel he's got a meal coming.

Babe, I just ate something.

Oh, Hannah says and puts the grouper in the fridge.

She cuts open an avocado and sits down at the table, scooping out the creamy flesh. Daniel comes into the kitchen. What are you doing? he asks, incredulous.

I'm eating an avocado, she says and he tuts for some inexplicable reason and walks back into the living room.

What? Hannah yells.

Aren't we going to eat together? Daniel asks, coming back again.

But you said you just ate.

I had a snack.

I didn't know that, Hannah says. She just wants to be conciliatory. Just tell me when you're ready, and I'll be happy to make something, okay?

Don't knock yourself out, he says.

Daniel works three shifts a week at the Everyman cinema in Hampstead, every Wednesday, Thursday and Sunday. Today is a Sunday. The worst day of the week. A dead kind of day. Everything's closed. Hannah is alone. She is stretched out on the sofa like a golf club, watching TV. She's hungover. The only movement in the flat is the exertion of her thumb on the up key of the remote, and as the channels change, different sounds leap out from the set like the screams of children on a fairground carousel. Children at the mercy of a carousel operator who hates his work, half-crazed with the injustice of a failed love affair, a coat-hanger abortion gone wrong, a crippled bastard son hidden away in a derelict railway car. Who drives the carousel so fast the children lose their balance, fall off their wooden horses and get dragged along the ground.

Hannah practically sprains her neck when Daniel walks in.

Hi, babe, he says.

Thank God you're home, she says, easing her body into a sitting position. Take this thing away from me before it grafts itself to my hand.

What did you do today? he asks.

Fuck all.

Want to go out for dinner? he asks. I scammed thirty pounds today.

That's great, honey. I'd love to.

Hannah takes off Daniel's sweatpants and puts on her army pants, her new brown turtleneck and her old brown coat. They go to the local Indian restaurant and both order the chicken jalfrezi. When it comes, the meat is so tender it reminds Hannah of a chicken she once cooked for Daniel but didn't leave in long enough and how, when she set it down on the plate and pulled the fork out of its tender breast, the blood had seeped slowly onto the plate. She picks at her food and Daniel says, Aren't you hungry?

I had a big bowl of pasta for lunch, she says.

You should've told me. We could have shared.

I forgot.

Aren't you going to eat that?

I'm not that hungry, Hannah says.

That cost money, you know.

I know.

That's seven pounds on your plate.

I know.

Seven pounds we could've put towards the electricity.

I know!

Well, we can take it home, he says, glancing at her plate and taking another mouthful.

I've been thinking about getting another temping job, Hannah says, after a while.

What about the novel? Daniel asks.

Ha, she says.

And your freelance work?

It's not like it's pouring in.

But you've got an interview with the editor of the *Financial Times* next week.

Yeah, Hannah says. To write a book review.

So?

Nobody's ever made a living off book reviewing.

So what are you saying? Daniel says.

All I'm saying is that I think I'm a little depressed.

And what do you want me to do about it? Daniel says, with a look that suggests he's anticipating an accusation.

Nothing, Hannah says. It's not your fault. I'm just saying, that's all.

Well, I find it very difficult, you know? You seem so unhappy these days. I don't know what to do about it.

I don't know what to do about it either, Hannah says, pushing her plate away. I spend so much time in my head and I'm paralysed by indecision. We go to one of Lyle's gigs and I want to be a musician. We go see a film and I want to be a film director. We go to an art show and I want to be a painter. It's like I identify with too much stuff outside myself, I forget what's on the inside. Forget what I want.

You could do any of those things if you set your mind to it, Daniel says, more frustrated than sympathetic. You're such a natural.

Thing is, Hannah says, I dunno what I want any more. I feel like I was brought up to please other people, but I've never been very good at that. I feel like I'm living a double life. Between the polite me that I project and the private me that lives inside, that doesn't want to be cooperative, that isn't housebroken. I want to be selfish, but then I get upset when people think I'm selfish. I don't want to care about what other people think of me, but I can't help it. And it makes me feel constricted. Like I'm not free to be myself, whatever that may be. And it's nobody's fault but my own.

Daniel wipes his mouth with one of the restaurant's big cloth napkins and sighs. His impatience crushes her, but she persists nevertheless.

It's just that sometimes, she goes on, I don't feel smart enough or talented enough or brave enough to do what it is I want to do.

Now that she's revealed herself, Hannah needs some reassurance. She wants Daniel to protest, to tell her all the reasons why she shouldn't feel that way, why he loves her, needs her.

I can't give you the confidence you're looking for, is all he says.

I'm not asking you to give me confidence, she says, hurting too much to want to be reasonable any longer.

Look, Hannah, Daniel says. Life is a series of decisions, and at some point you're going to have to make a choice. Maybe you should concentrate less on being jealous of other people and more on being grateful for what you've got. Maybe you could start by lowering your standards.

What, like you? she says. Scamming the theatre and collecting the dole? Well, I think you're doing an admirable job of lowering your standards. I don't think they could get any lower if you tried.

At least I don't wallow in self-pity every time things don't go my way, he says.

I'm not wallowing, Hannah says, gathering all her strength to crash through her pride and admit, I'm frightened, Daniel.

Frightened of what?

Of not being good at anything. Of failing to make something of my life. Of waking up one morning to discover that I'm not the person I wanted to be and that it's too late to become that person.

All I know is that you can't get good at anything if you don't try.

Since when did you become such an authority on self-help? Hannah says, tears now drowning out whatever impulse she had left to be conciliatory. I mean, how long have you been working at the Everyman? Six years? As a bloody projectionist? My God, Daniel. I mean, it's not like you're getting any younger.

I think you should shut up now before you say something you regret.

I can think of worse things to regret.

I'm going to leave, Daniel says, placing his napkin carefully on the table.

Oh, no you don't, Hannah says. You're not gonna deprive me of the satisfaction. If anybody ever leaves, you better believe it's gonna be me. And one more thing, she says, standing up and leaning forward, I'm not gonna carry you, Daniel. Don't ever expect me to carry you, she says, yanking her coat off the back of her chair and knocking a white vase with a pink carnation to the floor. What the fuck do I get out of this, eh? she hisses. You don't even fuck me any more.

Everybody in the restaurant is listening. Hannah can see Daniel wince under the scrutiny. He runs his hands through his hair and takes another sip of beer. She should apologize, she knows. She should tell him what she needs, how lonely she is. The ways in which he's failing her. They should both discuss the ways in which they're failing each other.

As soon as she's outside, Hannah doesn't feel so brave. The street is full of menace and she wants to get home as quickly as possible. A siren rises out of the city and there's a screech of tires at the precise moment a man bumps into her. The world crouches and threatens to bound into chaos. Hannah catches her balance and bursts into tears and the man apologizes. She waves him off and catches the glance of a teenage girl laughing raucously into a cell phone. She wraps her coat tightly around her body and turns off the high street, pins of adrenaline pricking the surface of her skin. When did you become so frightened, Hannah? What is it you're so scared of?

*

When Daniel gets home, Hannah stands up and goes over and hugs him hard. He tries to push her away but she won't let go. I'm sorry, Daniel, she says. I don't want to fight with you.

Just because I'm not as vociferous as you are, doesn't mean I'm not ambitious.

I know, she says. I'm sorry about what I said. I didn't mean it. I'm a word whore.

You really ought to be more careful, Daniel says, taking off his coat. I don't feel any closer to you when you lose your temper like that.

Hannah can smell alcohol on his breath and craves a drink.

You've got to learn to control your anger, Hannah. It makes me afraid of what you might say. Of what I might do one day. I'm not even sure how I feel about you right now.

Don't punish me, Daniel. I said I was sorry.

I'm not punishing you, he says. I just feel like you crossed a line tonight. You raised the stakes.

Compunction makes Hannah look at her feet, lose sight of the big picture, all perspective. She can only think of the next small step she's going to take.

Look, I'm just telling you the effect you have on me. I'm afraid of your anger.

Hannah was about to beg forgiveness, but now her pride bristles like hackles on the back of her neck. I'm so sick of hearing that, she says, looking up and realizing they haven't made eye contact in a long time. It almost dispels her anger, but she goes on.

At some point, Hannah says, slowly, deliberately. She's holding herself back. Everybody I have ever been close to in my life has said the same fucken thing. I'm afraid of your anger, Hannah. As if I were some kind of monster. The only reason you don't lose your temper, Daniel, is that you're not predisposed to it in the first place. It's not some great act of discipline that makes you so reasonable. Sometimes I feel like I'm living with a goddamn rock.

I'd be careful if I were you, he says.

The only reason I lose my temper, Hannah says, is that I get overwhelmed by my emotions.

But you've got to learn to control your emotions, Daniel says.
Why?

Because maybe one day I won't take it any more.

Is that an ultimatum?

I'm just telling you how I feel.

Well, I'm only acting on how I feel, too.

But you get so angry.

And I do all this damage, Hannah says, as if by rote, exhausted all of a sudden and sitting down on the sofa. And then it's all my fault and I have to apologize and what was done to upset me in the first place gets forgotten and no one ever apologizes to me.

Well, maybe that's the most compelling reason for you to control your anger in the first place. Look! Daniel yells suddenly. This is not my fucking problem!

No, it's mine! Hannah screams, bursting into tears again and flinging herself face down on the sofa, aware, even as she's doing it, of the melodramatic nature of the gesture. I will not stop crying until Daniel consoles me. She hears him go into the kitchen. He is making himself a cup of tea. Hannah perseveres with her tears. She fuels them by dwelling on bad memories, feelings of alienation from her family, frustration at her own passivity, the things she regrets (mostly things she hasn't done), all the books she's never read, the things she doesn't know, all the abuse she's heaped on herself, how she used to throw herself at anyone who offered her a scrap of praise, and she keeps on crying, determined that Daniel should know the extent of her pain.

Hell-bent on some vindication now, she hears him approach the sofa.

Come on, Hannah, he says. Stop crying now, okay? Please?

Daniel sits down beside her and lifts her head onto his lap. He brushes the wet hair from her face. You're a piece of work, d'you know that? What am I going to do with you, eh?

121

Hannah flings her arms around his shoulders and pulls herself up and sits on his lap and buries her face in his neck, as he strokes her over and over again, saying, There, there. It's over now. You're going to be okay. I'm right here.

15

Turn me on

That night they're lying on their backs with their heads on their hands, staring up at the ceiling in an atmosphere of calm but alert reflection.

I want you to tie me up, Hannah says.

What, right now? Daniel asks.

No, not right now, she says.

Good, because I'm not in the mood.

It's just something I'd like you to do, you know? One day.
Why?

Because it would turn me on.

But why would it turn you on?

Because it would absolve me of responsibility. It's the classic rape fantasy. If you're tied up and overpowered then you aren't responsible for what happens and can enjoy the sex unburdened by the implications of colluding with your own submission. Because, as a woman, you're always fucked, you know? And I'm not talking semantically. Literally, you're fucked. And all you ever get is fucked. You're always the fuckee, not the fucker. And if you're a strong, independent woman, then there may be something you resent about that necessary surrender. Always being in the position of having to take the man in.

Daniel is silent.

If I'm gonna submit to a man, Hannah goes on, then I want him to be stronger than me. Because why on earth would I submit to a person less powerful than myself? Where's the dignity in that? Besides, she says, rolling over to look at him. Then you get the pleasure that comes with resistance.

So you want me to rape you, Daniel says.

Well, not in that tone of voice.

But you just said you wanted to be raped.

It's a fantasy, right? There's a difference, she says. Oh, never mind. I'm not gonna beg you.

Imagine that, he says. Begging to be raped.

Hannah can see the vague shape of Daniel's face in the dark, deep shadows in the eye sockets. You just shamed me, she says. Do you know that?

Sorry, he says. I just thought couples did that kind of stuff when they got bored with each other. Not this early on in a relationship.

I guess we don't see eye to eye when it comes to our sexual tastes, Hannah says, and turns to face the window. There's a glow to the sky from a moon she can't see. She really could wail. Just howl. Cry enough for the whole world.

16

Work!

Hannah is leafing through *Time Out* when she gets a call from the editor of a woman's magazine. We like your proposal, the woman says. We want to commission you to write about a day in the life of an inmate at Holloway. Hannah calls the women's prison and is granted permission to spend a morning in the psychiatric day ward. She arrives and is issued a visitor's pass. She steps through the first reinforced steel door and waits for it to close on its electric hinges before the next one opens. For a moment, Hannah is locked into an area no larger than two square metres. I know nothing about being trapped, she thinks, as the second steel door slowly pivots and she enters a stark and deserted corridor.

The psychiatric day ward looks like an elementary school classroom, purposefully bright and cheerful. Half a dozen women sit, in varying degrees of composure, around a large square table. They are dressed in casual sweatpants and sweatshirts. The atmosphere is jocular, teasing but supportive. They are tactile with one another. A fat woman in her mid-twenties, in a sleeveless t-shirt and wearing a baseball cap on backwards, is leaning on the table. Her arms are lacerated with bright red scars, which she scratches from time to time. They are making stuffed animals. Hannah helps a tiny blonde woman sew flippers onto a grey furry seal. Unprompted, this woman tells her the story of how, just last week, she had stabbed her boyfriend to death.

I'd had enough of being abused by him and his uncle. I didn't mean to kill him.

She pushes her needle through four layers of fake fur and tugs it out the other side.

Next time you come, she asks, turning to Hannah, could you bring me some clothes?

Hannah shrugs helplessly.

She is intimidated. They call Hannah a rich snob. She wants to tell them that they're wrong, that she doesn't have any money, but it seems out of all proportion to get defensive, to be affronted by their judgment. They think she's privileged and she is. She can walk out of here for one, and at noon, when she finally leaves the prison, Hannah feels the weightlessness of her freedom so overwhelmingly, she has to sit down on the curb and cry.

She writes the story: two thousand words that promise a thousand pounds. We could go to Canada, Hannah suggests to Daniel. Visit my folks. I haven't seen my sister since the wedding.

But it's so cold this time of year.

What about Mexico? she says. It's cheap. We could take a month. Get healthy. Have an adventure.

But Daniel can't afford to go, nor is he that interested in leaving London. I don't feel unhealthy, he says. I'm happy right here where I am.

Hannah looks down at the to-do list she's just, half-consciously, written.

1. quit smoking
2. drink less
3. exercise
4. write!!!

Hannah had always been a compulsive list maker when listless.

17

Lyle, part 2

The night before, it was Brock and Emma around for dinner. Friends of Daniel's from the Everyman. There is talk that the cinema might be closing down. Six bottles of wine and they didn't leave until 3:00 a.m. Hannah still has a headache but she wants to hear Lyle play at the Porcupine, a pub on Charing Cross Road.

Why don't you come with me?

I couldn't bear, Daniel says, another booze up.

I'm not planning on drinking that much.

But you always do.

Well then, Hannah says, you better not wait up for me.

Before she leaves, Daniel hands her a tape.

What's this?

I made a tape for Lyle, he says. Some Beach Boys he wanted.

That's nice of you, Hannah says.

Can you give it to him?

Of course, she says, and gives Daniel a kiss.

Sitting on the number 36 bus, Hannah feels sick with disloyalty, sorry about her private catalogue of criticisms. She takes off her mittens and holds the tape Daniel made like it's a talisman. She reads the orderly list of song titles like a poem.

> Oh, *Cabinessence*
> Hear *Our Prayer*
> *God Only Knows* this *Little Bird*'s
> Been *Busy Doin' Nothin'*
> So now it's time to *Breakaway*
> *Time To Get Alone*
> Because *Our Sweet Love*

Was *Forever*
Meant For You.

A tree branch grates the length of the top of the double-decker bus, making Hannah jump. It begins to rain. The rain spatters the window in waves, individual drops sliding together, joining up and breaking off, swept up in rivulets or standing alone, the world flipped upside down in their refracted globes.

This is a metaphor for life.

So sad.

Beyond her window, the struggle for life is hard and unforgiving. The bus lurches down the Walworth Road at a halting, sluggish pace. There is so much traffic. A squat row of store fronts, betting shops and solicitors' offices (INJURED IN THE WORKPLACE? GET COMPENSATION!), juts forward like the open drawer of a cash register. Behind this, a volatile mass of domestic life. Enormous blocks of council flats loom against the ash grey sky like communist cruise ships, grim and gargantuan and strictly uniform. Outmoded now and derelict. Forever setting sail, the embarrassment of a facile socialism. There are so many people in this neighbourhood, the sidewalks are lined with railings so people don't fall into the road. Once, in broad daylight, Hannah saw a man crawl out of a kitchen window with a bag slung over his shoulder. Then she saw a boy run back to throw a brick at a shopkeeper who had just hit him with a length of metal pipe.

The bus winds past Elephant and Castle and heads towards the river. Finally, the city begins to look festive. Lights reflecting on the Thames. Floodlit buildings with spires and turrets and small curved balconies. The best part of living in the south is that you get to cross the river.

Walking towards the pub in the freezing rain, Hannah can't see inside because the windows are milky. She opens the door and the place is a shock of noise and heat, and greasy drunken faces. Lyle is standing in the corner, guitar plugged into his amp, amp like a squat black dog on a leash. He's got his eyes closed and he's singing to the ceiling the way rock stars do. Hannah gets this punch of joy at seeing him, euphoric rush of breath and oxygen in the blood to the tips of all her fingers, which she tries to suppress. She adopts a false insouciance. Glances around and locates Ursula, Ingmar and Eddie standing at the bar. She goes up to them and they are happy to see her. Hannah leans on the counter, signalling to the bartender for another round, and Ursula says, So where's Daniel?

He didn't feel like coming out, Hannah says, and then feeling the need to provide an excuse. We had Brock and Emma around for dinner last night.

Yeah, I think I've met them before, Ursula says. So how are they?

Oh, they're good.

Still all over each other?

Wanna hear the latest?

Of course.

Hannah lowers her voice. They've started peeing on each other.

Really, Ursula says, astonished.

Hannah raises her eyebrows and nods knowingly. Yep.

Fascinating.

Not only that, Hannah says, leaning closer. Brock got Emma to pee in his, you know, *dans la bouche*.

No! Ursula exclaims. *Pas dans la bouche!*

And suddenly they realize what they sound like, two old gossips over the fence, and they have to laugh. They laugh for so long it tires them out. It brings them closer.

What's so funny? Ingmar asks.

Just having a good old goss, Ursula says.

Talking of which, Eddie says, have you heard that Lyle might be moving to LA?

Really? Hannah asks.

Apparently he's got an audition for a record label. They heard his stuff and want to put a band together.

129

That's great, Hannah says, turning to look at Lyle, but not before catching Eddie give Ursula a meaningful nod as if to say, See?

Hannah wanders off from the group and leans back with her elbows on the pinball machine. Lyle is doing a Simon and Garfunkel cover, and Hannah finds it moving. It moves her all the way back to Canada and the Greek restaurant she used to work at when she was fourteen, with its vinyl booths and pint-sized jukeboxes, all the golden oldies playing on the radio, Carole King and Donovan. How the cute construction men used to come in at 9:30 on the dot for french toast and scrambled eggs. They'd hug her hips while she refilled their coffee cups. And of Mani, the old Greek cook who used to fondle her in the storeroom, his hands all covered in pastry flour. He'd come out of the kitchen when the restaurant was empty and lean across the counter and grab her hands and pull her forward and slide his thumbs back and forth across her nipples. And I let him, Hannah thinks, because it felt so good, despite the whiskers on his chin and his breath, which stank of coffee and Metaxa.

Oh, how she had wanted some affection back then. Some love, at that point. At fourteen, she didn't have a boyfriend. The boys her age seemed too young, their preoccupations trivial. And their inexperience made her nervous. She'd been a good kid, self-contained and happy, but now she needed somebody's attention. Her parents were busy. They were always busy, attending to the parish, caring for other people's emotions while their own family withered from neglect. The hypocrisy of the situation confounded Hannah. She would sit in a pew on Sunday mornings, listening to her father's genuine and heartfelt sermonizing, and think, but who is looking out for me?

Her dad had missed her big performance in the school play. Then he couldn't make her violin recital. When she broke her nose playing soccer, there was nobody to pick her up after school. If her earthly father didn't care, then how could she believe her heavenly father did? And if he didn't, then why should she? It was a crock. She let her grades slip. She started smoking pot. She dropped acid, then dropped out. There were two arrests. A late-night phone call from a hospital. The summer she was fifteen, Hannah moved into an apartment with a girl from her school who was in a higher grade. Her mother came over once and said, I'm getting you a bed. They bought her a mattress. In August, Hannah moved back home. In time to go back to school. When her parents came to collect her things, her mother said, Where's the mattress?

I gave it to a friend who didn't have one.

But her parents didn't believe her. You sold the mattress for drug money.

Am I not, Hannah had screamed, before slamming the door and walking away from the car, capable of a single act of Christian charity? She couldn't convince them. It was then that Hannah started to feel really abandoned. Her parents had written her off. The vicar and his wife had lost their faith. What was left, but to run away?

And so she did, to California. She was trusting and open and good-natured and the world reciprocated in kind. The world shone the same bright benevolence back at her and California, the entire state, became her home. She took possession of it and found her feet while moving across its rough surfaces, at ease as the observer. And she was lucky. The luckiest traveller she ever knew. Just passing through.

With her back to the pinball machine, propped up on her elbows, Hannah has the long straight highways of America in her mind, velvet and green, golden fields of wheat and corn, stretched as far as the eye could see, under the wide blue brim of an open sky. Lyle is going to LA, she thinks. He's going to California. Soon he'll be eating with the tattooed truckers, at cafés with peroxide waitresses. And Hannah wonders if Lyle is in love with the myth of America as much as she is. He's playing all those elegiac songs of the sixties, mixed in with a few of his own. They liked his songs.

They're putting a band together. But right now, Lyle is putting her in mind of someone else. She can't quite put her finger on it, someone from a long time ago, when she got all her stuff stolen, north of San Francisco. She didn't care. She was so young and fearless then. She'd hitchhiked down Highway 1. Yes, that's who it is. That guy who picked me up. He was driving a Dodge Omni. A beautiful boy. All fucked up and angry with the world. John Wade, that was his name. We spent three days together.

But Hannah knows the pitfalls of this kind of infatuation, illusions born of an imaginative projection. She sinks even lower on her elbows, practically reclining on the pinball machine now. Her stomach sticking out, her chin touching her chest. Hannah thinks of her gypsy vision of the world and Daniel's European intellectualism, grounded in a history dating back to the Phoenicians. Sometimes she thinks they are as different from each other as the famed polarities of mind and body. His rooted intellectualism versus her raw pioneering spirit. They would complete each other nicely if only they could get it together. But it isn't working.

Oh, Daniel, what is going to become of us?

Lyle finishes off his song and there's a riffle of applause. Someone hollers a Ziggy Stardust request and Lyle says, I'll be back after the break.

You're looking glamorous this evening, he says as he passes Hannah, catching her off guard.

She lifts herself up, pulls her t-shirt down, and notices Eddie and Ingmar laughing at her from across the room. Hannah smiles and shakes her head.

I read your review in the *Financial Times*, Lyle says. Must be satisfying to knock down a literary giant like A.S.Byatt.

I didn't do it for kicks, she says. Fact is, I wasn't convinced by the book. I didn't buy it.

That's pretty funny, he says.

It's his hair and his demeanour and the elegant hint of bones beneath the skin.

Well, congratulations anyway, Lyle says. It was a good review.

Thank you. But instead of feeling pleased, Hannah just feels crushed. It costs him nothing to pay her a compliment and yet it means everything to her. He can be perfectly charming because he is perfectly disinterested, politely disengaged. And the more he charms her, the more dejected she becomes.

Lyle can afford to be generous, Hannah tells Eddie at the bar, because he has no attachments, no a priori emotional commitments. He isn't expected to do anything for anybody else at any particular time, so he can be generous when it suits him.

Which means, Eddie says, his generosity is spontaneous, genuine. They both turn to look at Lyle. He's at the microphone again.

Yes, Hannah says. He leaves a strong impression of his generosity on other people, and yet I've never really known him to go out of his way for anyone. I find the general praise of his character unwarranted, undeserved. And yet I do it too. I praise him.

We all do, Eddie says. He's charmed. Always has been.

But then I guess one praises what one admires in an attempt to win it over, Hannah says, putting her hands down on the bar.

So you remain a hypocrite while envying him too, the luxury of his irreproachable selfishness. So what?

Hannah looks at Eddie. You've thought about this before.

Maybe just a little, Eddie says and nods at her nearly empty pint glass.

Hannah finishes off her beer. Where's Ursula?

I haven't seen her for a while, Eddie says.

Hannah goes to look for her in the ladies'. Ursula? she says. Is that you?

Sniff.

You okay?

133

Yeah, I'm fine.

What's up? Hannah says.

Don't mind me, she says, coming out of a stall and wiping her eyes. I'm just having a blubber-fest. It's this thing with George.

Hannah rolls a cigarette and hands it to her, then rolls one for herself. Ursula leans against the wall too close to the automatic hand dryer and the thing goes off. She lays a hand on her chest to settle her heart, laughs a little, then starts to cry again.

Oh, Ursula, Hannah says, stroking her arm, glad to be of use, to be needed.

I think he's started seeing somebody else.

Really? Hannah asks.

Somebody at work.

Are you sure about that?

He used to pad around the house in his slippers, Ursula says. And now he's going out clubbing and doing e. He even got his nipple pierced. I mean, the George I know would never have considered doing a thing like that.

Maybe he's just experimenting.

Now that he's shot of me.

I didn't mean it that way.

I just wish he'd talk to me, she says, reaching into the stall to get more toilet paper. I always thought I'd have his children, she says, dabbing where her mascara has run.

Hannah looks down at her feet. The idea of children is sobering. The prophecy of a son at twenty-eight. It presupposes a level of commitment she doesn't believe she has with Daniel. A level of stability she's never achieved.

But now I'm just being pathetic, Ursula says.

No, you're not, Hannah says. As long as you can still feel pain, it means your heart is open. It hasn't shut down.

I wish it would, she says.

The more you let yourself grieve, the sooner you'll get over it.

But I don't want to get over it because when I do, that's exactly what it'll be. Over. And then where will I be?

Hannah looks down at the tiled floor and chews her cheek. Bereft of boyfriend, she says quietly.

Too bloody right, Ursula says, running a hand through her fine blonde hair and inspecting her face in the mirror. But for now all I am is bereft of drink.

Well, thank fucken Christ that's an easy one to fix, eh? Hannah says. Come on, let's go downstairs and get you a refill.

On the stairs, Ursula says, I just hope Lyle doesn't finish off with *Leaving on a Jet Plane*.

He always does, Hannah says.

That one chokes me up.

You're not the only one. Gets Eddie every time, too. And what with Lyle about to leave for real.

And what about you? Ursula asks, stopping to turn around. She puts a hand on Hannah's arm, makes her feel cared for, for the first time in ages, and the feeling is so tender and her need so fierce that it snags and burns. She loves Ursula, the friendship she's extending.

I'll be okay, Hannah says, and knows this to be true. And anyways, she goes on, it's just a fucken song. And a sentimental one at that.

Nice try, Ursula says. We Europeans can live without nostalgia, but you North Americans are gluttons for it.

And why's that? Hannah asks.

Because you have no history, Ursula says and continues down the stairs.

Meanwhile, in a corner of the pub, his soft brown shirt unbuttoned at the cuff and hanging down at the elbow, his smooth white forearm curved delicately at the wrist, guitar pick held between his thumb and forefinger like a huge thorn snapped from some giant rose bush, Lyle sings.

What I wouldn't give, Hannah thinks, to catch his eye right now. For him to know exactly how I feel.

*

Hannah and Lyle live in the same part of London. They're sitting on the number 36 bus headed back towards Elephant and Castle, back up the Walworth Road. In the narrow seat, Hannah feels nothing but Lyle's thigh pressed against her own.

I'm sick to death of playing bloody covers, Lyle says. I've played those songs a million times and it's always the same fucking thing.

But people love it, Hannah says.

They always do.

You had them all going.

Sure, he says. With other people's music. It's so predictable. People are like sheep.

Well, you won't have to do it for much longer, she says.

I can't wait to start recording my own songs.

Your stuff is amazing.

You think so?

I love it, Hannah says, and Lyle nods rhythmically, not looking at her. In fact, he hasn't looked at her much at all and this upsets her. She really means it about his music. Wishes she could separate the compliment from any hint of ingratiating herself or wanting to acquire an advantage. She wants him to know that his music moves her. That there is a yearning in it she feels too.

So when do you think you might be in LA? Hannah asks.

Sometime after Christmas, he says. Before the spring, I hope.

Maybe we'll bump into each other.

What do you mean?

I'm going to Mexico, she says.

You and Daniel?

Just me, Hannah says. I'll probably have a stopover in LA.

Lyle seems to think about this.

Are you gonna miss London? Hannah asks.

No, he says. I'm fucked off with it now.

And I'm just getting used to it, Hannah says. It's like a dare, an open invitation. It excites me. Like now, I've got this buzz. I don't really want to go home right now.

Hannah is surprised to hear herself say this, it's such an obvious come-on. But even more surprising is Lyle's response.

Well, you're welcome to come back to mine, he says. I just took some ecstasy so I won't be sleeping for a while.

Really? Hannah says, meaning the e. She didn't know he was the type, and it both intrigues and disappoints her, although she's hardly in a position to disapprove.

Have you got anything to drink?

I think so, Lyle says, appearing then to fall asleep.

Hannah turns to the window and wipes the condensation off the glass. The city lights, red and white, fracture on the wet surface.

The consequences, she thinks, of satisfying desire. Now that it's upon her. You're a married woman, Hannah. Does that mean anything to you? Would Daniel even care? He pays you so little attention.

Oh, but something bad would happen. I just know it. Because adultery in women is always punished horribly in the end.

But then nothing's happened yet. All we're gonna do is talk. And maybe we will cuddle up at the end of the night. All I want is a little understanding and affection and I know Lyle is bound to understand me, isn't he? Which isn't to say I haven't dreamt about fucking his brains out, but that's not really what I'm after.

No.

But even if it were? What's so wrong with that? Sometimes a woman gets neglected, you know? Just look at Madame Bovary. Okay, so maybe she was frivolous and naïve, but did she really deserve to puke black bile all over her white wedding dress?

They're sprawled on the kitchen floor. Lyle's roommates are asleep and it's just the two of them. Hannah is lying on her side, holding her head up with her hand, which has fallen asleep, her wrist beginning to ache, wrapped in his roommate's sheepskin coat. She's lying against the wall underneath a window, drawing patterns on a chipped white saucer in the ash from her extinguished cigarettes. Three empty beer cans at her elbow and a bottle of Black Bush. Lyle is sitting across from her, leaning against a row of kitchen cupboards. There are bits of dried food along the skirting board and a brown desiccated teabag, still with its stapled string, wadged under a rusty chrome leg of the kitchen table.

Hannah's got half her mind on the conversation and the other half on her confession. Snagged on some pointy fear of rejection. She looks up when she hears Lyle say, Said I was too selfish.

Who did? Hannah says, her tongue slow and clumsy in her mouth, like it's gone to sleep, a fat slug.

My ex-girlfriend, Lyle says. She wanted me to concentrate less on the music and more on her. When I was this close to making a breakthrough.

I know what you mean, Hannah says. What you do is more important than who you're with.

And she knows more than anybody else in the world, how important this is to me.

Hannah finds herself marvelling at the banality of her conversations with Lyle. She wants to shake things up. Talk about something really important. If he were anybody else, Hannah would be dying of boredom, thinking this guy is so full of himself. Instead, her infatuation picks up the slack, and she can't help but placate him. It's so important to make good use of your talents, she says.

If you work in an office, Lyle says, have a job, not a vocation. Well, then maybe you can give more to a relationship. But an artist is married to his work. That's why I've never wanted to get married. I don't think I'd make a very good husband.

Ah, no?

I think marriage is overrated, he says.

How would you know? Hannah says, sitting up and crossing her legs. She looks down at her hands in her lap.

Her fingernails are dirty. She scrapes the dirt out from one and realizes it's dried blood. Blood under her nails from her period. From playing with herself.

Every married person I know has the same complaints, Lyle says. They all whinge about their sex life.

Hannah laughs out loud. But it's true, she says. Marriage is like a fire blanket. Smothers the life out of passion.

Thing is, Lyle says. You married people make out as if you're all deprived. While everybody else who's single envies what you've got. It's bollocks. I'm sick of the whole fucking thing, he says, sliding sideways and stretching out on the floor. Everyone just seems so dissatisfied these days. It's like, as a society, we're not getting what we need.

I totally agree, Hannah says. But what is it we're missing?

Well, that's the sixty-four-thousand-dollar question, innit?

I always thought I could be satisfied with anything, Hannah says, so long as it was intense. Passion is all I've ever wanted in my life.

Passion can be its own burden too, Lyle says wistfully, like he's looking out over the landscape of his memory.

Well, I'd rather be smothered by passion than a fire blanket any day.

The key to a happy life, he says, is to love moderately and work hard. That's why you have to nurture your friendships. A man's greatest consolation is in his friends.

You sound like a Chinese fortune cookie, Hannah says.

But it's true. Friendship brings out the best in people. It's altruistic. It endures.

You also spend a lot less time with your friends. Demand a lot less.

And you end up doing a lot less damage, Lyle says. Friendship is a great advertisement for restraint.

I hate restraint, Hannah says. I don't want to deny myself anything. I don't see the point.

Well, that's a bit indulgent.

Isn't everybody nowadays?

I don't know, Lyle says. But you go right ahead.

As if you're any different.

I'm as indulgent as the next guy, he says. But I'm getting older.

You're thirty-one, for chrissake.

That's right and I don't have the energy for that kind of all-consuming sexual passion any more. Besides, I have my work to think about. That's what I'm passionate about now.

I just wish I found my work, Hannah says, as diverting as my life.

Modigliani once said that if he had to save a cat or a Matisse from a burning house, he'd save the cat.

So life, at the end of the day, is more precious than art.

Exactly, Lyle says. Though now I wish I'd played around less and worked more.

But don't you see how that's a misguided regret?

Why? he says. Because you admire the refusal to sacrifice pleasure?

No, she says. Your refusal to spend all your time working, despite having talent.

Maybe something is preventing you, Lyle says. Maybe you would have liked to achieve more too.

To please other people? Hannah asks. Or myself? And then she shivers, violently, from tiredness and the booze and the cold linoleum floor beneath her body.

Cold? he asks.

The floor is freezing, Hannah says.

Do you want to go to bed? he asks, and Hannah looks at him, her whole soul pinned by what has just been laid at her feet like a slab of cold white marble. There's a part of her that doesn't want it, that fears it, shuns it, now that it's been offered.

Lyle stands up and Hannah follows him out of the kitchen, solemnly. They walk towards the stairs. To consummate or not to consummate.

Lyle stops at the doorway of an empty bedroom at the end

of the hall and, pointing with his thumb, says, You can sleep in Dan's room. It's empty. He doesn't get back till tomorrow night.

Alright, Hannah says, smothering all trace of disappointment, of humiliation, the offer she had imagined. Without even so much as a hug, she walks into Dan's room and sits down on the bed.

Dan's room. Daniel's room. She didn't even know Lyle had a roommate by that name.

Goodnight, Hannah, he says from the doorway.

Goodnight, Lyle, and she bends to pull her shoes off.

When he's gone, Hannah lies down and tosses for half an hour, then gets up and slips out of the house, walking home through the black and blue deserted streets of a south London morning, the memory of her mistake insistent as a dog's bark. A whole pack of hounds, for that matter, jubilant in tutus and high heels, marching behind her on their hind legs, playing the trumpet and twirling batons in the air.

It's four in the morning when Hannah gets home. The fog has turned to freezing rain. Icy pellets hit the window while she's brushing her teeth. She turns the tap on and the whole world seems composed of water, burbling through pipes, swirling in the basin, tapping the plastic tops of garbage bags sitting on the curb. Hannah puts her toothbrush in the metal cup barnacled with limescale and, leaning on the sink, bends forward and spits into the drain. Bullseye. She straightens up and looks at her face. After twenty-six years, it's still strange to her. Age hasn't altered it though she's not the same person she was six years ago, and yet she is. She lifts her hands and looks at them. She sees nothing but lines and creases, no fortune of a baby at twenty-eight. She looks at her face again and squints. Crow's feet appear around her eyes. Hannah Crowe's feet. More prophetic creases.

You will grow old. Of that, I can assure you. Everything else remains a mystery.

Suddenly cold in her underwear, Hannah runs on her toes into the bedroom and jumps into bed.

Your feet are like ice blocks, Daniel says.

I know, I know, she says. You say that every night.

He turns over and they settle into their most familiar position. Daniel facing away from her and Hannah spooning from behind. She puts her arm around his waist and pulls herself forward, pressing the warm steaks of his buttocks into her lap.

After a while, Hannah asks with genuine sincerity, Do you want me, Daniel?

He groans. Go to sleep, he says. I don't want to have this conversation right now.

I don't mean right now, Hannah says and there is an injury of misunderstanding in her voice. Not sexually, she says. In general.

Why do you always have to bring this up? he says, sighing across his pillow. I'm tired and I want to go to sleep.

A simple yes would have sufficed, Hannah says, rolling onto her back. Is it so hard to say?

It's four in the morning and I've been worried about you all night and now that you're back I want to get some sleep. A simple phone call wouldn't have gone amiss, you know. Where have you been all night?

I was at Lyle's.

Daniel says nothing.

I'm sorry, she says. I should have called.

Yes, you should have, Daniel says, looking over his shoulder. Did you give him the tape?

Oh, fuck, Hannah says, I forgot.

And Daniel turns away again.

After a while, listening to his breathing, shallow and not sleeping, Hannah says. I just wanted you to hold me. Her voice sounds tiny.

Oh, babe, he sighs, as if reaching out to her across a sad, regretful distance.

Daniel turns over and snuggles in behind and puts his arms around Hannah and they lie like that for a while, holding onto each other's arms like banisters on a steep flight of stairs, their thumbs sweeping back and forth in lazy, hypnotic strokes across the skin.

Our thumbs are like windshield wipers, Hannah whispers and Daniel squeezes her then and holds her tighter.

18

Christmas

It is a silver Christmas Eve morning, the sky an immaculate virgin blue. Hannah is walking down Camberwell High Street, squinting in the sun's glare off cars and plate glass windows. On the sidewalk outside Pesh, the local flower shop, there is a display of poinsettias, puffed up with sunshine, waxy and red. Where it remains in the shade, the sidewalk is still white with frost and the plants are decorated with styrofoam balls covered in gold glitter, curls of orange peel and red tartan ribbon. They remind Hannah of every Christmas decoration she's ever seen, and there's a heft of optimism behind the simple act to celebrate that impresses her. The impulse to adorn. She remembers coming around the house one day and seeing the pots of flowers her mother had bought to plant in the spring. How the young, blunt shoots and delicate green buds had seemed to contain her mother's soul, everything that was beautiful about it, full of vulnerable hope and a faith in renewal. How Hannah had felt a crushing pity for her mother then, like a fist tightening around the thick red muscle of her heart at the sight of them. And guilt, too, for judging her so harshly when all she was trying to do was make the best of things.

Hannah goes inside and buys one to adorn the table at the Christmas dinner she and Daniel are hosting tonight. Then she goes to the local Turkish café and, placing her poinsettia on the table in front of her, sips at a mint tea. In light of the compassion of Christmas and in an effort to do the right thing, Hannah decides that a festive exorcism is in order. She must confess her feelings for Lyle, thereby purging herself of those feelings, and concentrate on her life with Daniel.

When she gets home, Daniel is making a trip-hop tape: Howie B, DJFood, Funki Porcini, Kruder&Dorfmeister. He labels it in lower case, *chip shop, christmas, 99*. Hannah stands behind him, looking over his shoulder.

Looks great, babe, she says and he turns to her and smiles. They kiss and it's a sweet and tender feeling.

The phone rings and it's Louise calling from Montreal.

Lou! Hannah shouts. We're having our Christmas dinner tonight and I wish you could be here for it.

Me too, Louise says. I just wanted to call and wish you a Merry Christmas.

How's everything your end? Hannah asks, her voice going soft, full of sympathy.

Well, I just got a pretty good Christmas present, Louise says. Martin's finally come around. He's flying out next week and we're gonna give this whole marriage thing another go.

Oh, Lou, Hannah says. That's wonderful news. Everything's gonna be okay for you two, I just know it.

After she hangs up, Hannah goes into the kitchen and starts preparing the meal. She cleans and stuffs the turkey with bread, onion, celery and chestnuts, fresh sage and cranberries. She peels carrots and yams and parsnips and potatoes. She cuts a cross into the bottom of every single Brussels sprout. Daniel looks at her from the living room and she feels his stare.

You're at your happiest when you're cooking, he says. Did you know that? And Hannah smiles, wiping her hands on a dishcloth, awaiting the party with pride and trepidation.

9:30 p.m. Hannah serves the turkey to the sound of Christmas crackers popping, cheers, laughter and the rustling of paper crowns.

9:45 p.m. Hannah goes into the bathroom, takes two paracetamols for a headache, and washes them down with gin.

11:30 p.m. The water boils dry and the Christmas pudding burns in its plastic container. A cloud of toxic fumes fills the kitchen. Everyone crowds around the open living-room windows and there's a spontaneous rendition of *Good King*

Wenceslas. While they're singing, Lyle appears down on the sidewalk, tired after a late-night gig.

Here comes the rock god! Eddie shouts and suddenly they're all shouting, All hail the rock god! Long live the rock god! Get your arse up here, ya pillock!

Hannah runs down to the door in her socks to let him in. They hug and he follows her up the stairs. She takes his coat and he's wearing a royal blue velvet shirt that makes her want to stroke him. I saved you a plate of food, she says.

1:00 a.m. They push the furniture aside and start to dance.

1:15 a.m. Ingmar turns the music down to make a toast.

I want to make a toast, he announces and everybody groans.

Stand up! Eddie shouts.

Ah, shut your cake-hole, Ingmar says and raises his glass.

Great toast, Ursula mutters.

Here's to the first year of the new millennium, he says. I think it's going to be a great year for all of us.

Hey, who turned the music down? Daniel asks, slow on the draw.

Turn the music up! Ursula shouts.

Give him a chance, Eddie says.

I thought he was done.

Seriously, though, Ingmar says. I really feel like it's going to be a successful year for everyone. Record deals and shoes sold and articles published and big promotions in the city.

And failing that, Eddie says. Suicide.

Come on, guys, Ingmar urges. You've got to admit, we have more fun than most.

What makes this so funny is that Ingmar says it with absolute conviction. Without a trace of irony. And the rest of the group pounce like jackals on this scrap of sincerity and tear it to shreds.

I can't believe you just said that, Ursula says, between sobs of laughter.

Here's to having more fun than most, Daniel says.

More fun than most! everyone repeats.

Here's to making more money than most, Eddie says.

More money than most! they all echo in mock-serious tones, raising their glasses into the air. Then Ursula dives behind Ingmar and cranks the music and the dancing resumes.

2:30 a.m. Hannah passes out behind the sofa. Falls right over, stiff as a board. Bam! Just as Debbie Harry hits the chorus of *Atomic*.

When Hannah opens her eyes, Ingmar has his hand under her neck and is trying not to laugh. I thought you fell out the window, he says. From my angle it looked like you fell out the window.

I really went down, eh? Hannah says, rubbing her head and looking around for Daniel.

Like a tree, Daniel says, crouching down beside her with a huge grin on his face. Sent a chair flying too. You okay, sweetheart?

Just a little shaky, that's all.

I think you spilled some gin down the back of the sofa, Eddie says, peering sideways with his hands on his knees.

I see you're still holding your glass, Ursula says, giving Hannah a wink.

Couldn't pry it out of my hands if you tried, Hannah says.

Yep, died with that glass in her hand, so she did, Daniel says.

Looks like we're going to have to bury her with that glass, Eddie says.

That glass was the closest thing she had to a friend.

A fine friendship, so it was.

And Lyle starts whistling the Funeral March.

3:56 a.m. Eddie and Ursula fall asleep in the bedroom.

4:00 a.m. Daniel pulls out the sofa bed and Ingmar collapses on it. Lyle is sitting with his back against the radiator. He sighs deeply, runs a hand through his hair and says, Man.

4:15 a.m. Lyle puts on his coat and gives Daniel a hearty hug, full of the kind of warmth and friendship that passes between men in the early hours of the morning.

Danny, my boy, Lyle says. Can you handle another year of the same old bollocks?

It's enough to drive a man to drink, Daniel says.

Goodnight, Lyle whispers into Hannah's neck while he's hugging her farewell. The food was fantastic. Thanks so much.

Safe home, she says, and closes the door behind him. Then, as if by some silent, sullen agreement, Hannah and Daniel begin to clear up.

Daniel carries some glasses into the kitchen and starts running the water for dishes. All of a sudden, bent over the coffee table, empty wineglass in one hand, full ashtray in the other, Hannah is gripped with a brave new determination. She has her back to Daniel and, without turning or even telling him where, she's going.

4:18 a.m. Hannah slips out the flat. Softly shuts the door, hurries down the stairs and out the building. She just slips out into the street with only her socks on her feet and starts to run.

The seeping through of cold wet pavement is like a gradual smack to the soles of her feet, and when it hits it has a sobering effect. Hannah is breathless by the end of the block and slows down when she sees Lyle standing at the bus stop. She can feel her heart surging the barricades, storming the ramparts to capture the citadel. She jaywalks the intersection and braces herself against the surprise on Lyle's face. Hi, she says, dragging her teeth across her bottom lip.

What's up? Lyle asks, pulling his head back slightly, as if she were about to strike him.

Um, Hannah says. She pauses, and then they come. All the words with all the force of their repression. The demented lawless rush of momentum. I just wanted to tell you, she gasps, that I'm really attracted to you and it's not like I want to be your girlfriend or your wife or anything like that, I just wanna fuck you, d'you know what I mean? Not right now, obviously, not in the middle of the street or anything like that, it's just that I wanted to tell you because it's been on my mind for so long and it's been driving me crazy and I know I've been acting like a total idiot and maybe you already know, maybe it's really fucken obvious. I mean, I know it must be. But then I wasn't sure and I think these things really need to be said, you know, brought out into the open and there it is. I've said it. And I feel a lot better now and I'm just gonna head back home, and I hope you don't mind that I told you or anything like that, and I hope you had a good night and I'm sorry if I've put you on the spot but I needed to do this so I could resume my life with Daniel. Or maybe not. I dunno. I dunno anything any more.

Hannah laughs. Then she stops and says, Right then.

She's about to leave when Lyle says, I can't let you go home like this. I mean I think we should talk about this.

I don't know if there's anything to talk about, Hannah says, magnanimous in her liberation, feeling a growing sense of ease after the flood of her confession and a new clarity, unfurling in her mouth like fiddleheads, green and cool and quiet in the shade.

I've been totally obsessed with you for the last three months, she says, but I know as well as anyone how false that can be. I don't even know if it's you I've been infatuated with or some idea of you. Some projection on my part. Because we don't really know each other, do we?

Hannah is feeling aloof, almost superior now that she's owned up to her feelings. You swallow the power of deception when you demystify a secret. The power of that secret becomes your own. You acquire it. It's like eating peyote. Digesting the power of things that thrive in dark concealment.

The irony of it all, Hannah says, is that my feelings have actually prevented us from becoming better friends. Because

I've been so goddamn shy around you and I wish I'd said this ages ago but there you go, I didn't.

She shrugs and lifts one foot and then the other. God, my feet are frozen.

Here, he says, giving her his coat.

Hannah puts it on, luxurious with the warmth of his body. It's like an embrace, and she longs to be touched, deep in the solitary soul of her. I'm sorry, she says. I've just been feeling really lonely. What with being in a new city, a new marriage, trying to get on with my work. I'm just finding things really difficult these days.

And you're not the only one, Lyle says. But you've got to keep at it for the rest of us. You have to keep telling yourself that what you're doing is important. We all need to believe that. Otherwise none of us would ever get out of bed in the morning.

I appreciate that, but this isn't really about my work, though God knows it's a conundrum. The fact is I look at you and I want you. It isn't more complicated than that. And to be honest, I don't really have that feeling for the one person I'm supposed to have that feeling for these days and I don't know why.

I wish I could say I felt the same way, Lyle says, sighing in apology.

Apparently, Hannah says, what doesn't kill you, strengthens you.

For what it's worth, he says, I know what it's like. I had a big thing for Ursula recently. But she didn't fancy me.

Really? Hannah says.

Didn't you know that? Lyle says.

Hannah shakes her head. Fucken Brits, man. Nobody ever talks about anything.

They both stand there for a while, staring at the ground. Hannah's socks are wet and the sidewalk is icy.

Daniel's a good man, he says.

I know he is, she says.

I like him a lot.

He likes you too.

Do you want me to walk you home? he asks, and Hannah shakes her head.

She looks at Lyle then, intently, as if for the last time, a hardness to his features she hadn't noticed before. The eyes a little close together, too deeply set. Here, she says, returning his coat. Guess we won't be seeing each other in LA, she says, laughing a little. And then she says, Just joking.

Look, I'm not considering LA a success yet. It's only a fucking audition.

I'm sure you'll do well, Hannah says, and then feels as if she might start to cry.

We met, okay? Lyle says. At some specific point, on this street, in this country, on the surface of the earth, our paths crossed and we recognized each other. We felt a sympathy. That's got to be worth something, right?

Hannah nods. She moves towards him with the simple wish to be held and lays her head on his chest. She can feel his body stiffen.

Don't, he says, putting his hands on her arms and gently pushing her away.

Hannah sighs. Misunderstood again. She bounces on the balls of her feet with a fatalistic shrug. Ah, well, she says, rubbing her arms. Guess that's it then, eh? Fucken cold out here or what?

You sure you don't want me to walk you home? Lyle asks her again.

No, she says, that's quite all right. I'm fine on my own, and she turns around and begins the short walk home, too numb to feel the cracks in the pavement under her feet.

When she gets back to the flat, Daniel looks at her, then turns his back. Suddenly he swings around and hisses under his breath (restrained even in his anger on behalf of their guests), Where the fuck have you been?

I had to go talk to Lyle, Hannah says. I had something to tell him, and I just walked out. I'm sorry, Daniel, she says, fear squirting into her bloodstream. There's something I need to tell you.

Look, I already know you fancy him.

Do you?

Everybody does.

Oh, Hannah says, sitting down at the kitchen table. Why didn't you tell me?

I was waiting, Daniel says, for you to bring it up.

But nothing's happened, Hannah says.

I'm sure, he says. I didn't think Lyle was the type. I didn't think he'd let it.

And what about me? Hannah says.

And Daniel doesn't answer her.

Christmas Day is survived. *The Sound of Music* and hot mince pies with custard. Hannah gets no word from Lyle to mark the millennium. No acknowledgement, no gesture of levity, nothing. She's convinced he has misunderstood the cathartic nature of her confession. All she seems to have done is over-estimate the friendship. And Lyle's capacity for compassion. Some fanciful idea she culled from his song lyrics, foisted on him like a cumbersome corsage and pinned to his chest.

The next time she sees him is at a farewell gig on a boat moored in the Thames, a going-away party. Lyle makes a point of ignoring her. He won't even look at her. Rumour has it that she threw herself at Lyle. Now everybody skirts around the topic like she's brought shame down on the fami-ly. The quiet murmurings behind her back make Hannah want to cry. She finds it hard to breathe and goes up on deck. She sits down on a picnic table in the cold wind and listens to the noise the city makes. The sky is in mourning. Wearing a purple stole over a thin green slip of horizon.

This wasn't how things were supposed to go.

It wasn't supposed to be like this at all.

When she gets back to the party, Daniel is concerned. Hannah sits quietly at the other end of the table. She's trying so hard to follow the conversation (the effort forcing her eyebrows up in the middle), that Daniel gives her a sympathetic look. She keeps flexing the muscles at the back of her jaw, dropping her eyes and staring at her hands. Just sitting there with her hands in her lap. A little girl of six. Waiting for a yellow school bus to come and take her home.

Ah, home.

Daniel catches her eye again. She gives him a hapless shrug, apologetic and embarrassed. She's putting on a brave face and it's breaking his heart. Her desires baffle him but, he understands, not nearly as much as they baffle her. He gives her a little jerk of the head and pats the bench beside him. She gets up and walks around Eddie and Ingmar and Ursula and sits down next to him, taking his hand under the table and resting her head on his shoulder. Daniel puts his arm around her, his prodigal wife, and reunited under that weathered, somewhat torn and tatty umbrella of their love, they look out at the world with one face.

19

Let's negotiate

Sometimes we do things because we want to, Hannah thinks, looking out the window of her bus at the golden rocky hills, small tufts of cactus almost purple under a gauze of dust. And sometimes, she thinks, we do them in defiance of fear.

This trip was for that reason, to chip away at time, the whole aging process, which sometimes seems no less than the slow accumulation of fear. Hannah used to be so reckless, her life a stunning lesson in bravado. And now? Well, she watches too much TV, refrains from speaking her mind too often. She's grown shy and complacent and a little insecure. So lacking in contentment she's begun to commit desperate acts of rebellion. Like going out on drunken binges that bring her home at dawn. Or traipsing off for two months on her own, leaving her husband in that damp flat, surrounded by traffic, under all that cloud cover. To test her own capacity for loyalty and betrayal. Her insatiable need for love and her damned refusal of it.

Hannah came to Mexico to raise her old self back from the dead.

And to analyse her heart, to keep a journal, write a travel piece.

Sometimes we do things in defiance of fear, sometimes for love and sometimes by accident. We panic at the weight of our restrictions and wonder, how did I get here? We do things in defiance of what's prohibited, because it makes us feel free.

It is a sweltering afternoon in the month of March. A woman has just arrived by bus in the small colonial town of San Miguel. Her name is Hannah Crowe. She is twenty-six years old and she is carrying a backpack, a small black case containing her laptop, *Portrait of a Lady* by Henry James, and a thin red book called *Monogamy*.

She gets off the bus and walks around, somewhat apprehensively, until she finds herself being ushered into the front seat of a cab (ostensibly heading into town) with barely enough room for her long legs. She is the third passenger. The driver talks constantly with the two women in the back. Words lift off their tongues like flocks of birds. They laugh as the car climbs slowly through the dusty streets. He drops one of the women off and then, further up a steep incline, in front of a crumbling façade draped in bougainvillaea, the other. Neither of the women pays and as soon as they're alone, the driver turns to Hannah and starts checking her out. She rallies a smile although, in truth, she's annoyed at the unctuous style of flirtation that has suddenly replaced the indifference he showed her while the two women were still in the car. He begins to ask her questions, grinning beneath his bushy moustache.

Perdone, she answers him. *No hablo español.*

Nada?

Poquito, she says. *San Sebastien hotel, por favor.*

Sí, he nods. *Sí.*

After what seems like an unnecessarily circuitous route, they arrive at the hotel. The driver overcharges and short-changes her by thirty pesos. Normally Hannah would chalk that kind of swindle up to first world tourist tax, but this time she insists on waiting at the door of the taxi, palm open, until he has returned the full amount. She hoists on her backpack, picks up her case and walks into the hotel. The San Sebastien is fully booked and Hannah's out on the street again in less than a minute. She checks her guidebook and heads to another budget hotel a few blocks away, but this one is also full. And the next.

It is five o'clock in the evening when Hannah finally gives up, looks up at the sky and wipes the sweat off her forehead with her wrist. Her army pants are heavy and the air so humid it's like walking through steam, damp and dusty at the same time. The soles of her sneakers are soft from the heat rising off the stone sidewalks. She can feel the texture beneath her feet. All Hannah knows is that one more unsuccessful attempt and a sharp little edge of panic will set in. She feels vulnerable with her laptop, foolish in fact, like she's over-dressed for a party, and all she wants to do right now is blend into the background. She doesn't want to draw any attention to herself.

Nobody's been overly friendly so far (she's just another *gringo* tourist) and Hannah doesn't feel confident walking through the streets. That's a privilege reserved for your own hometown, if you happen to have one. Sometimes, Hannah thinks, I don't know where I belong any more. Not that this bothers her. She's still happier to leave a place than stay. But the obvious question is, when does leaving constitute running away? Her guidebook quotes Emerson: *Travel is a fool's paradise*. Is that because you never stick around long enough for anyone to call your bluff? Because Hannah has always tried to avoid the exposure of her inadequacies. But maybe, she thinks, I'm being a coward.

The street opens up onto a square full of pigeons, bordered on one side by an ornate, folklorish cathedral, with a tall and elaborate spire, like a candlestick covered in wax. Hannah stands in the square letting her eyes go out of focus, watching the dust motes on the surface of her eyeballs slide down over her cornea until they disappear. She looks up and finds another one and follows it down across her field of vision, until she feels a slight touch on her bare arm, light as a cob-web. Standing beside her, up to her waist, is a poor gaunt boy. His lips are covered in thick dark scabs and his eyes are two holes drilled into the black cavity of his skull. His fingers crawl down the length of Hannah's arm and softly pat her suitcase. *No, gracias*, she says instinctively, although he isn't offering anything. He doesn't move away, just stands there, quiet and suffering. *Gracias*, she says and turns away and walks quickly down a side street leading away from the square. She is disappointed by her impatience to get away from the boy, anxious as she was not about his poverty but his infectiousness. Don't be so precious about your health, Hannah thinks. Don't be so squeamish. Be sympathetic. In an emergency, would you be the kind of person who shoved your way towards the exit, trampling people? Or heroic, self-sacrificing? A white-haired man hands her a flyer. It's for a poetry reading in English.

Hey! she yells, running after him. Do you know of any hotels around here that might not be full?

Sure do, he says. If you continue straight down this street for about ten minutes you'll come to a covered alley full of artisan shops. Follow that and you'll see some steps. At the bottom, there's a large sign for the Rosa Rosita. You can't miss it.

And they'll have a room?

They won't turn you away, he answers, rather mysteriously.

Hannah wanders up and down the covered alley and comes across half a dozen sets of stairs, but nowhere does she find a sign for the Rosa Rosita. Rosa Rosita, she asks, *donde está*? But no one knows. For an hour she walks up and down a series of stone steps, and then she sits down on the curb. I'm tired of this, she thinks. She's hot and sweaty and her arms ache from carrying her laptop around all afternoon. Her mouth is dry and her face is stinging from the sun. Her head hurts from squinting. She thinks, this is starting to get ridiculous. Then a guy walks down the street. A *gringo*. He's wearing a pair of blue jeans and a shirt and he's carrying a worn brown leather briefcase. Hannah can tell by the way he looks, his red hair, his ruddy complexion, his size and his build, even by the way he walks, that he is American, probably of Scottish or Irish descent, and certainly a drinker. He nods at her as he's going by. He says, Hi there.

Hannah jumps up and blurts out, Do you know of any-where around here I could stay? I mean, I'm supposed to be looking for this hotel, but I can't for the life of me find it and everywhere I've gone so far is fully booked.

I could probably think of a few places, he says, eyeing her from top to bottom.

Yeah?

I've got a directory in my apartment. It's right over there, and a phone. You're welcome to use it, make some calls, see what's available.

Hannah lets her body relax a little. She lets out a sigh and says, Thanks. That would be great.

I'm just waiting for my internet guy to come around with the key, he says. He should be here any minute.

His cell phone rings.

Gary! he booms. I'm standing outside my place right now. I'm waiting for Luís to show up. Did you pick up the phones? Good. Listen, I'm gonna be a few more minutes . . . Just give me ten minutes. I gotta woman here. She needs to make some phone calls . . . Ya, ya. I'm gonna let her use the phone in my place . . . Ten minutes, okay? Listen, where are you? Already? Hey, there's Luís. I can see him now. He's coming down the street. I'll speak to you later.

He stuffs his phone back in his breast pocket and says, So where d'you come from?

Canada originally, Hannah begins to say.

No, I mean today.

Oh, she says, slightly embarrassed. Guadalajara.

By plane?

By bus.

Helluva distance, he says.

It's a long ride, she says.

Well, my name is Shawn McCarthy. And this here is Luís. You got the keys, *señor*?

Sí, señor, Luís says.

Well then, I guess you might as well come on up.

Okay, Hannah says, and turns and lifts her backpack to her knee and does a kind of half-jump to swing it onto her back.

Can I take that for you? he asks.

Thanks, she says and hands him her black case.

Whatchya got in here, he says. Bricks?

They are standing in a dilapidated apartment on a hill over-looking San Miguel. Hannah is looking through a greasy, cracked window at a maze of rooftops, the sun glinting off a tangle of TV aerials and power lines. Shawn McCarthy had told his friend Gary, and Gary had mentioned this place. It belonged to a friend of his who was out of town. Hannah could have it for next to nothing.

So Gary drove them in his rundown jalopy, through steep and narrow streets, to a rusted wrought iron gate leading to the courtyard of a simple square building, so rudimentary it seemed hollow or incomplete. There were bars on all the windows of the ground floor but no glass, just broken shutters pressed against raw cement walls. No sign of life, no movement anywhere, except the soft inhalation and exhalation of dirty grey curtains through the bars. The apartment itself was on the second floor, at the back, and the steps were strewn with garbage, dirty rags and jagged tin cans. The door was crooked, the hinges old and stiff, and Gary had to give it a shove with his shoulder to get it open. Once inside, it looked as if the place had been ransacked and then abandoned, giving off an odour of thieves.

Despite the deserted air, the seediness of her surroundings, Hannah stands at the window and feels an immense peace.

You can go anywhere in the world, but you will always meet good people.

And here I am with two such people. Two big American dudes in a hot country, and I feel a strong sense of affection for them. They seem like reliable guys, the kind you'd want to have around if your house caught fire or your car broke down. I feel safe with them and they are going out of their way to help me, lavishing me with good old American hospitality.

159

Suddenly Hannah feels humbled in the presence of such good fortune.

Then she has a twinge of guilt, which she brushes away like a pesky fly.

A dog walks into the apartment and sniffs at a small pile of its own dried shit.

Isn't the cleaning lady supposed to take care of this? Shawn asks Gary.

The dog doesn't have to stay, Gary says. The landlady can look after it, if you want.

I'm not much of a pet person, Hannah admits.

I think the bedroom's in here, Shawn says, and Hannah follows him through a curtain of red and blue plastic strips into the other room. There is a mattress on the floor covered with a filthy grey wool blanket on which the dog, now seated, has lifted one leg behind its head and begun to lick its balls.

I didn't think this place was gonna be such a dive, Shawn whispers.

Hannah walks over to the window and looks out at the town again. In the distance, across the valley, the hills are red and orange. The sun is starting to sink and the sky around it is heating up, the colour of skin, while the sky overhead cools to a deeper shade of blue.

Hannah thinks of all the places she's been in her life, of all the people she's met, and it never ceases to amaze her.

She glances back at Shawn and catches him taking in the shape of her ass. His friend walks in and says, Well, I got the stove to work. The gas main was shut off. But it's all in running order.

I don't know if she's decided to take the place, Shawn says, and moves towards Hannah, as if insinuating she shouldn't take it.

You know, Hannah says, turning to Gary, finding it hard to turn him down, to deny him his boy scout enthusiasm. I really appreciate the offer, and I don't mean to be ungrateful, but I was hoping to be a bit more central. Closer to the main square. I'll just have to go over my budget and get a hotel room until I find a cheaper place to stay.

Well, whatever suits you is fine by me.

Thanks for going to the trouble, she says.

You know, Shawn says when Gary's left the room. I've got an extra room in my apartment, and I don't want you to take this the wrong way, but you're welcome to stay there tonight. I'm going back to San Francisco tomorrow for a couple of weeks.

Hannah smiles inwardly. Goodbye Gary, goodbye dog shit, hello Shawn.

Now she's in the spare bedroom of Shawn McCarthy's apartment. There's a queen size bed flanked by two night tables with lamps made out of ceramic jugs, a wicker chair and a small desk by the window. Next to the window is a doorway leading out to a narrow balcony with an elaborate wrought iron balustrade. Hannah puts her backpack on the chair and her computer on the desk. She can hear Shawn mixing drinks in the kitchen. She steps onto the balcony and looks down at the street, at all the geometric shapes the buildings create, her eyes fizzing with the effervescence of so many warm colours. The stucco walls appear to solidify and deepen as the light intensifies just before sunset, plump as ripe peaches, heat emanating from their still warm but faded planes of ochre and rose and tangerine. The air is so soft there isn't a muscle in Hannah's body that isn't relaxed.

Oh, Daniel, my love. Where are you now? What are you doing? When will I see you again?

Shawn knocks on the door and Hannah steps back inside. His red hair is slicked back with something sticky and he's changed into a short-sleeved shirt and a clean pair of faded blue jeans. He's wearing soft leather shoes that look flimsy on such a big guy (he's more than six feet tall and must weigh close to three hundred pounds), and it makes her think of Ali Baba.

161

And the house that smelt of thieves.

Men shouldn't wear such dainty shoes. They're too effeminate, she thinks, and so is he. Some kind of gentle giant trapped in the body of a wrestler, looking for a little tenderness. And Hannah's verdict is at once compassionate and dismissive. For herself, she prefers her men lean and wiry. Tough as beef jerky. Hard as nails. Rodeo boys.

Do you like tequila? Shawn asks.

I'm not crazy about it, she confesses.

He hands her a drink. Have you ever had good tequila?

Sounds like a contradiction.

White tequila?

Don't think so.

Taste it, he says. See what you think.

It's not bad, Hannah says.

Now later, Shawn says. You leave later to me. I've gotta go get a few things. In the meantime, make yourself at home. Feel free to use the shower if you want to freshen up a bit. There are clean towels in the closet. And then I thought maybe we could go catch a bite to eat.

Anywhere that's cheap, Hannah says.

No, no, it's my treat. I know a really good place in town. Run by a couple of Americans. Food's delicious there. I'd be happy to take you, if you'll let me.

Are you sure?

It would be my pleasure, Shawn says.

Well, as long as you're sure, Hannah says. She is annoyed now by the prospect of having to fend this guy off. She doesn't relish the outcome of the sequence of events she's just set in motion, and bemoans the likelihood that Shawn McCarthy will settle for companionship. By accepting his offer of dinner, Hannah knows she's crossed a line, agreed to the terms of the bargain, and all her hitherto sassiness is transformed by a hesitation as to the debt she is about to incur.

And all because she thinks she deserves the comforts that money can buy. Feels that a certain privilege is her due.

162

And yet, Hannah wonders why she hasn't learned how to avoid these semantic snares, why she hasn't yet developed a technique. After twenty-six years, she still doesn't know how to make it clear what her limits are, that she isn't available for sex. Is it that she doesn't know what her limits are? Is she afraid to lose this man's interest? Even this man she feels no attraction towards? Or is it simply, on her part, a linguistic laziness? I am willing, she realizes, to end up with the compromise of unwanted sex, rather than work up the word power to avoid these pitfalls, these misunderstandings. An odd reaction for someone who is so sensitive to the nuance of words. A paradox. That I can't muster words to my own life's advantage.

Hannah stands in front of the mirror and runs her hands through her hair, dry and dusty from the bus trip. She leans in close and checks her skin. Satisfied, she opens her backpack and rummages through her clothes. She's got a clean pair of khakis that fit nice and tight around her hips, and a backless embroidered top that fastens with a grey ribbon around the neck. It's a gamble she's willing to take. She hasn't had a proper sit-down meal in a fancy restaurant since she left London and wants to look good, despite the signals this will give him.

Hannah walks down the hall to the shower. She lets the hot water run its hands all over her body. She stands there for a long time. There is a window in the shower stall, which she pushes open. Steam billows out and the cool air blows in. She can see the street behind Shawn's apartment, the dark recesses of open doorways along the narrow sidewalk. A storefront festooned with handmade wooden crosses and mystical beasts, angels and scorpions. A little bone skeleton tinkles like a wind chime as a tourist walks out, fanning her face with a straw hat, wearing a floral dress and flat sandals. Someone shouts and a truck comes lumbering down the street, laden with plastic gallon jugs of purified water, and rumbles on slowly towards the centre of town. Hannah can just make out the top half of the moulded cathedral spire, like the sand-castle of an eccentrically meticulous child. Suddenly it lights up like a wedding cake and her heart feels crushed by the beauty of the world.

Hannah hears Shawn return. He walks past the bathroom while she's drying off. She hears the sound of a cork pulled out of a bottle, and as she's walking back towards the bedroom in a fresh white towel, she can see Shawn's reflection in the glass of a framed picture at the end of the hall. He's watching her move and it makes her hold herself differently.

So far nothing's been declared and nothing's been decided. As far as Hannah is concerned, no ulterior motives have yet come to light. She still has the option of feigning innocence.

Giddy from the first few shots of tequila, they walk down uneven streets towards the centre of San Miguel. The air is full of smells. Coffee, fried tortillas and lime. The dry ticklish smell of laundry soap. At one point, they step off the narrow sidewalk and into the road to let an old woman pass. *Gracias*, she says and Hannah looks up to nod and sees into a launderette. Inside, it is dark and empty. The walls are bare. A woman her own age is standing behind a counter wrapping stacks of folded white sheets in brown paper.

They turn the corner and there's a rickety set of brown saloon doors set into a wall of blue stucco. Beside the door is a poster advertising a bullfight in a neighbouring city. Is that a cantina? Hannah asks.

Yep, Shawn says.

And only men are allowed to go in there, right?

A woman can go in, but only with a man.

And the women don't mind?

They don't seem to.

What happens if a woman goes in there by herself?

Shawn shrugs. A few years ago, he says, this woman came down from California. Or maybe it was Florida. At any rate, recently divorced. Kind of fucked up. Went on a binge that lasted a few weeks. Made a total fool of herself. And she kept insisting on going into these cantinas by herself, when she knew all along that she wasn't supposed to. Eventually, one night, a bunch of men took her to the hills outside San Miguel and gang-raped her.

Really?

Yeah, they just left her there in the hills.

Did she die?

No, she made her way back. But nobody saw her do that again. I guess she learned her lesson.

You call that a lesson?

Well, she knew the rules, Shawn says. She knew what she was getting herself into.

What, getting gang –

I'm not saying she deserved it. But she had plenty of warning.

She needed help, Hannah says, not a warning.

I agree, Shawn says, but it's not the fault of the cantinas. That kind of thing happens all over the world. It's no worse here than it is in America. There are places in the States that a woman wouldn't go on her own, so I don't see the difference.

What I don't like is that there's no equivalent for men, Hannah says. No restrictions like that placed on a man's freedom.

Sure there are, Shawn says. There are places a man can't go. Certain neighbourhoods in the States where he knows he'll get shot.

Yeah, but it won't be a woman who shoots him, Hannah says.

Might be. Anyways, there are certain circles among women that a man can't gain access to.

What, like a fucken sewing circle?

I'm being serious.

Sure, and if a man happens to trespass into one of these so-called circles, he gets his name embroidered onto the Quilt of Impudent Males. Big fucken deal.

Okay, so the consequences might not be that serious.

165

Or violent.

But for a place as seemingly anarchic as Mexico, Shawn says, there is an invisible order at work. Customs, you know? That are still adhered to. For every written law that gets broken, there are two unspoken ones that are upheld. You have to respect a country's practices, and in the whole time I've lived here, that's the only case of violence against a woman I've heard about. In general, I think it's a lot safer here than it is back home.

That's because the women are contained, Hannah says.

It's because family is sacred. Things may be a bit old-fashioned here, he says, but Mexican women are treated with a lot of respect.

You mean, mothers and wives are treated with a lot of respect.

You may have a point there.

As long as they don't get drunk and wander into a cantina.

I wouldn't recommend it, Shawn says. But I'll take you to one if you're curious, how about that?

Exclusion is so provocative, Hannah says. I almost feel like declining.

Just to be unpredictable? Shawn asks.

To pretend I'm not affected by it.

Well, let's eat first, he says.

Hannah's bending over the table, the 8 ball her last. I'm going for a bank in the corner pocket.

I thought you told me you weren't very good, Shawn says.

I'm so inconsistent it's ridiculous, Hannah says, raising her eyes for a moment and then re-focussing. Booze helps, she says, her chin near the green felt. Eradicates hesitation, she whispers and hits the cue. The 8 ball rolls off the cushion, pauses, then drops into the corner pocket. Phew, Hannah says, straightening up and reaching for her drink.

The hostess comes upstairs and tells them that their table is ready. They follow her down to a small round wooden table by an open window with a view of the street. A candle in the saddle of a ceramic donkey flickers between them. Shawn orders a bottle of Napa Valley red and his steak blue.

So I take the ruins, he continues, of one of these fantastic old colonial homes that's been abandoned for years and I dismantle it, stone by stone, and ship it back to California to be reassembled for some film star in Santa Barbara.

A little third world exploitation, Hannah says, cutting into her meat.

I wouldn't say that. They just go to waste here. Nobody wants them.

And it's profitable work? she asks.

All I have to do is pay for the labour and the shipping which, to be honest, is dirt cheap. I hire these massive containers and ship all sorts of things back to the States. Wood carvings, ceramics, old doors, ironwork. You name it, I sell it. And yes, as a matter of fact, I happen to make a pretty good living off it. I've just rented a new house in San Miguel. My assistant is going to move my stuff while I'm away.

How long are you gone for?

Couple of weeks, maybe longer. It all depends. I have a daughter in San Francisco.

When was the last time you saw her?

About a month ago, Shawn says, leaning forward to take another bite.

So you're married.

I'm divorced, he says, but I try to be a good dad.

Do you miss her?

I adore her, he says, making little sucking noises as he chews. Of course I miss her. She turns seven on Wednesday. I just bought her this little outfit. A yellow dress with ruffles at the shoulders.

Sounds cute.

She's a real beauty. And I'm not just saying that. Takes after her mother in that respect. But that's where the comparisons stop. Thank God. And what about you?

167

No kids, she says.

You got a boyfriend back home?

I'm married, Hannah says.

So how come you're not wearing a wedding ring?

I am, she says, raising her right hand. Sometimes I wear it on my right hand.

How come?

Oh, I dunno. She feels a tightening in her lungs. I figure being married is my business. If I want people to know then I'll tell them.

So where's your husband?

He's in London.

And he doesn't mind you being here on your own like this?

He's cool.

Are you separated?

No, we just needed a little breathing space. I hate the idea that married couples have to be joined at the hip. Like if they're not together every fucken minute of their lives, they'll lose each other.

Yeah, but isn't the point of getting married to share your life with that person?

Yes, Hannah says, taking a sip and hiding behind her wine-glass. But things don't always turn out the way you want them to.

At that moment there's a scraping of chairs and two young American women walk past their table. One of them is saying in a loud nasal voice, I told him, I said, if you can walk without that goddamn crutch, then you can sure as hell give Nancy a lift to the airport.

A grateful silence lifts after the women have moved on again, like tall grass trampled by indelicate creatures.

Anyways, Hannah says, raising her glass with a sigh. It was supposed to be the protection of two solitudes. That's a quote.

Well, that's not a bad way of looking at it if you're both independent people, Shawn says. But that's exactly what I liked about being married, the company. I don't like to be alone.

Well, I do, Hannah says, sitting back and folding her arms.

Honestly?

Most of the time, she says. I was in Puerto Vallarta last week and I had dinner on the beach. The stars were out and I was about ten feet from the surf. I had a plate of barbecued shrimp in front of me that were succulent, and I was surrounded by tikki torches, not to mention a couple of hot waiters. Thing is, it was the most romantic setting I have ever been in in my life and I had no one to share it with. Now, that was a moment when I would have preferred not to be alone.

So have you ever thought of leaving him? Shawn asks, tilting his chair back and clasping his hands behind his head.

No, not seriously, Hannah says. She leans forward and rests her arms on the table. Though I do fantasize about a love that isn't possessive.

Ah, it's always your imagination that gets you in the end.

It's true, she says, I'm constantly weighing my fantasies against my options, as if my fantasies carried the same weight as reality. As if the only thing that keeps my fantasies from coming true is choice on my part.

Have you ever had an affair?

No, she says.

What's stopping you?

It would be wrong, Hannah says. Though I'm not blameless. Part of me hates the idea of what I've become. I used to fantasize about the man I was gonna marry. Now all I fantasize about is having five different lovers in five different cities. And isn't that pathetic?

Well, Shawn says, laying his napkin on the table like a piece of punctuation. I think you can get away with just about anything as long as you keep it a secret.

I don't want to lie to him, Hannah says.

Secrets, my dear, are the secret to a happy marriage.

169

But you're divorced, Hannah says, laughing and finishing off her wine.

Exactly, Shawn says. And you wanna know why?

Why?

Because I got caught.

Oh, that's way too cynical, even for me, Hannah says. A good relationship requires full disclosure. I gotta stand by that if I stand by anything.

I think a good relationship requires stability. However that's achieved. And in my opinion, there are some things in life that are sacred, like the family unit, Shawn says and then he laughs, a short breathy *Ha!* Maybe that's why I like Mexico so much. In my opinion, he goes on, everything is secondary to the wife and kids. The family must never be threatened. To me, the most comforting thing in the world is to know that I can go off in some crazy direction, out into the world, be anybody I wanna be, but that I can always come back to the same familiar situation. The fact that it never changes. I would do anything to protect that. That's what I call a marriage that's steadfast.

That's what I call a marriage that's clueless.

If it means protecting the family unit, Shawn says, then I'm willing to go to any lengths to hide what might destroy it.

What about not doing what might destroy it in the first place?

Name me one person in this day and age who can live like that.

The waitress comes over and removes their plates. She asks them if they want anything else. Coffee? Dessert?

Shawn looks at Hannah and she shakes her head.

Cognac? he asks.

Oh, okay, Hannah says.

Dos cognacs, por favor, Shawn says and takes a pack of cigarillos out of his breast pocket. He offers her one.

I think a cigar would make me want to smoke again, Hannah says, and I just quit.

Congratulations, he says.

It wasn't so hard, she says. Thing is, I'd always rather be in the know, not blind when it comes to love.

We're all blind, he says. Most of the time.

I just think honesty is essential for trust and trust requires full disclosure and without full disclosure you don't really know the other person, so why be theirs alone? That is, if you happen to be theirs alone. And if you're not, if your relationship isn't exclusive, then you don't really belong to each other and doesn't that make you feel kinda lonely in the world?

Listen to me, Hannah, we're born alone and we die alone.

I know! Hannah says. But there's a lifetime in between. The quality of which is entirely up for grabs.

I still think there's so much that passes between a couple that is a mystery to the other, Shawn says, rolling his cigar on the flame of a match. I think that's the way it is, always has been, and always will be.

After dinner, they meander through the cobbled streets of San Miguel. They're laughing on the way, joyous with alcohol, warm in the fur stole of a sultry evening. Hannah has her hand on Shawn's arm and is saying, I think it's very important to get drunk sometimes.

I agree, he says.

It's a wonderful release.

Sure is.

Always makes me happy.

That's good.

And it's easier to be good when you're happy, don't you think? Easier to be magnanimous when you take care of your own needs first, wouldn't you agree?

Just then, a man with a cowboy hat comes out of a cantina across the street. The saloon doors swing open and a yellow strip of light flashes across the cobbled stones, revealing the rich texture of the road and the shadow of that cowboy. The saloon doors creak once, twice, and then it's gone.

Oh, my God, Hannah says, tightening her grip on Shawn's arm. Can we go in? Please?

Shawn laughs and, bending forward to make such a grand sweeping gesture he almost loses his balance, says, After you, milady.

Hannah clears her throat and pats herself down. Everything's in place. She wants to enter with all the panache of a gunslinger, Edward Dorn style. So she uses the momentum of her body to part the doors and lunges forward, too drunk to notice the step down as you enter. The ground isn't where her foot expects to find it and she lurches and lands on all fours. The floor is hard packed dirt. Straight ahead a row of boot heels, some worn down and some brand-new. The bar is made from rough timber and all along the length stand half a dozen *vaqueros*, in dark blue jeans and cowboy boots, leaning forward on their elbows. They lift their heads and turn away from their thimble-sized glasses of cheap tequila and bend to look at Hannah as if from a great height, decidedly unimpressed, like the chorus of the swan ballet.

Evening, boys, she says, coughing once and getting up, smacking the dust off her knees and giving the men a quick curtsy.

When they get back to Shawn's place, they pound up the stairs, teeter on the threshold and fall inside. Shawn freezes when he hears his shirt begin to tear. It's caught on the door handle.

I'm stuck, he says.

Aw, let her rip, Hannah says, and they think it's the funniest thing in the world. They double over, slap the walls, wipe the tears from their eyes and then it's time to say goodnight, so they linger in the hallway for a while, swaying like top-heavy tulips.

Well, I guess this is goodnight, he says, serious all of a sudden. He takes a few steps closer and Hannah focuses on his big face swinging towards hers, the pink edges of his watery eyes, his dry cracked, wine-stained lips, the freckled skin pulled tight across flat cheekbones. His face is not a pretty sight, she is not attracted to it, and yet she does not propel herself backwards but forward to meet his mouth. She meets it with a hunger that far exceeds any decision she has yet had time to make.

There is nothing to decide.

Because nothing feels quite as right as succumbing to your worst suspicions about yourself.

Somewhere at the back of her brain, Hannah is sober and coherent. I am not embracing this man, but entropy. I could tell him to stop, but I won't. I am not afraid of him and for this night only will give in to the downward force of my baser nature and revel in depravity.

Hannah pushes Shawn McCarthy away and gives him a look like a hook in the eye. She walks over to the bed. He comes up behind her and she arches her back, pushing into him. She falls forward on the bed and he turns her over. Avoid his face because you don't want to kiss him. Just give me your bulk. Let me bang myself against you.

He lies down on top of her and Hannah brings her legs up. He presses his pelvis into her and she lifts her hips, trying to buck him off.

You're a wild one, he says.

So fight me, she says.

But I want to be tender.

Well, I don't, she says, and pushes and pulls until he's forced to use his knees and arms to pin her down.

He holds Hannah's wrists above her head and slides a hand up under her top. It feels so good to be touched. It's been so long. She lifts her bum and he pulls her pants off and she turns onto her stomach and sticks her ass into the air. She knows how tempting her ass must look, the black line of her thong, pull me apart. She hears his sharp intake of breath and feels the power she has over him. He puts his face to her cunt and she presses back into him. She lowers herself to one side and pushes him off with her foot. Fuck you. He grabs her ankle to keep from falling off the bed and jerks her towards him. She twists away from him again and now their hands are slapping each other. Their bodies colliding. You asked for it, he says. You're gonna get it now. He undoes his jeans and pulls his underwear down. I don't want to see his cock. He gets on top and wraps a fist around her underwear.

Don't, she says. I can't do this. I'm married. For chrissake. Please stop.

He stops and looks down at her, breathless with disbelief. He drops onto an elbow and slides over. Christ, he says. They are both on their backs, looking up at the ceiling, panting for breath.

Goddamnit, he says. You're so fucken beautiful and such a fucken tease.

Hannah's heart is racing, every muscle in her body alert. But she is soaring in her mind, like a bat, quick and invisible in the dark, a rush of air at her ears, at once euphoric and remorseful, giddy with power and sick with it too, her body tingling and bruised from their exertions. I got something out of that, she thinks, but I didn't give myself away. The only way he can have me is to rape me. And he's not the raping kind.

She is triumphant and appalled, drunk and tired and so, so heavy, dropping like a stone into the deep well of her unconscious.

In the morning, she opens her eyes and sees his dry, papery face. He's awake and looking at her. He's caressing her hip.

Morning, gorgeous.

Hannah clears her throat and swallows. A mouthful of regret. She covers her face with her hands.

Oh, Daniel, can you ever forgive me. Where are you now? Do you still love me? How could anybody love me?

Shawn leans in for a kiss and Hannah rolls away, quickly sits up although her head is hammering.

Last night was a lot of fun, he says.

She doesn't answer him.

174

You're some kind of animal, he says.

Hannah leans forward with her elbows on her knees and rubs her face with her hands. She still hasn't said anything. She wants to be alone, but she doesn't want to be rude either. She was never very good at that, though it's done her more harm than good, made her swallow what she should never have accepted in the first place. Hannah almost laughs out loud thinking of a story Louise once told her. Louise had gone back to this guy's house when she was a teenager, because he had tickets to a concert she wanted to go to. But he got strange on her and wanted to tie her up and slap her with strips of cucumber peel. Lou saw him get the cucumber out. Had she said okay? She was scared, but she was more afraid of offending his feelings, so she submitted herself. When Louise told Hannah this story years later, they had laughed about their inability to say no. How well brought up they'd been and what good it did them to be polite in such risky circumstances.

Even so, thinking about last night, Hannah figures she's been callous enough already. Shawn's been nothing but decent to her. She looks at him with the intention of giving him a friendly smile, but seeing his head on the pillow, so intimate, with little white flecks of spit at the corners of his mouth, she can't do it. She wants to run away, lash out at him. She wants to get dressed too, but she doesn't want the intimacy of dressing in front of him. She can't stay in bed any longer though, so she gets up and dresses with a kind of seething ferocity.

He lies in bed watching her with smug propriety.

So I thought you might like to come to Juanajuato with me today, he says, cleaning a fingernail with a wooden match off the bedside table. There are some galleries I want to check out and then I thought we could have a late lunch somewhere, get back in time for my flight to Guadalajara. I've got to be at the airport by six.

I dunno, Hannah says, licking her lips and looking at her face in the mirror. She opens the door and steps out onto the balcony. The sunlight is God's conscience, the jealous Hebrew God of the Old Testament, and it is unforgiving. The street is busy with people who are going about their business, unhampered by guilt or the painful reminder of a hangover. There is a dog beneath the balcony, nipping at its own heels, bent back on itself. It's not one dog, Hannah realizes, but two. Or is it? It is hideously deformed, like some mythical two-headed beast, and seems to carry its deformity resentfully, constantly turning to bite its hindquarters. It is such a miserable creature, cursed and pathetic, that Hannah pities it, this Siamese dog, joined at the tail. And it doesn't seem to be able to coordinate its eight legs long enough to actually go anywhere, darting in one direction, then tripping over itself. It yelps constantly, like a tortured soul, and Hannah stares in wonder at this aberration, this freak of nature.

Shawn gets out of bed and strolls over and hugs her from behind. She twists out of his arms and he asks, What are you looking at?

Hannah points at the dog.

Someone should throw a bucket of cold water on those poor fuckers, he says and realizes from her expression that she has no idea what he's talking about. You've never seen that before?

Seen what?

Two dogs fucking?

Hannah looks at the dogs again and says, No, I haven't.

Sometimes they get stuck in hot weather. They can get stuck like that for hours. Or until someone throws a bucket of water on them. Used to happen on the farm all the time.

You lived on a farm? Hannah asks.

Yeah, I used to run a hog farm.

Pigs?

Belonged to my father.

Hannah nods, then laughs a little and shakes her head.

What? he asks.

Nothing, she says, but what she's thinking is this: here I

am, on this momentous journey, trying to find myself, and what do I end up doing? Throwing my pearls before swine-herds. Sometimes life has such a wonderful way of sneaking up and biting you in the ass.

What's the matter, babe? Shawn asks. Are you feeling guilty about last night? I know how you feel. It's always hard the first time, but you get used to it. I remember the first time I cheated on my ex-wife, I felt pretty bad about it. But it goes away. Just think of it as your initiation.

I haven't cheated on my husband, Hannah says flatly.

Well, technically, I guess not. Not yet, at any rate. We'll have lots more time for that later on.

What do you mean?

Well, what was all that talk about five different men in five different cities?

I wasn't being serious, Hannah says. I told you, it was a fantasy, she says, and suddenly feels nauseous. It rises like a bubble of toxic gas and she needs to get out of there, but she wants to play her cards right too. Shawn offered her the keys to his place the night before. Ten whole nights of free accommodation. All on her own. I did give him my ass, she thinks. I let him press his face into my cunt. That should be worth something. She wants to take it. It would be the easiest thing. But it makes her feel unclean.

And she desperately needs to talk to Daniel.

I've got to go out, she says to Shawn, and he looks crestfallen.

You know, last night meant something to me, he says and so genuinely that, although it meant nothing to her and she can't bear the mere recollection of it now, Hannah perceives his loneliness too, his need for love. She wants to tell him that everything's going to be okay. She wants to reassure the whole world. Tell the whole world that she understands. The nature of its unremitting suffering.

But then Shawn says (changing tack, pulling back, conde-scending again), You're just a little upset.

And Hannah's sympathy drains away.

You'll come around to the idea eventually, he says. Trust me.

I'll see you later, she says, grabbing her bag and pushing past him, running down the stairs and into the street, nearly tripping over those two dogs still joined at the rear.

Hannah sits down at a sidewalk café and orders a cup of coffee. Briefly she wishes she still smoked, though the thought passes and she's back to the regret of last night, her feelings of guilt, and then she wonders whether or not her guilt is sincere.

Nothing would have happened if Shawn hadn't made a move. Hannah was content to go to bed on her own. They had had a nice time. She felt warmly towards him, a friendly intimacy, but he had interpreted that as sexual. The intimacy had turned him on. It was so predictable. Once again, her friendliness was construed as seductive when she hadn't intended it to be.

But then, they didn't go all the way. So at least she feels as if she maintained some degree of fidelity. Because if she's honest, it's not Daniel she's thinking about right now.

So what's upsetting her so much? Wasn't last night just a case of drunken exuberance? Another attempt to find intimacy in unlikely places? Solace in the cold wilderness of her existential solitude? Yes yes yes. But it's not that.

What's making her feel so bad is this nagging and all-consuming sense of self-dismay. In a flash of lucidity, Hannah understands that her remorse is for her wounded vanity. It is her vanity she has offended. Not her morals.

If you had woken up beside a beautiful young man, would you feel any differently than you do now? Less depraved if you had chosen, as the object of your indiscretion, a man who was unquestionably attractive? Not this oaf, this pig farmer. Would you feel so guilty, Hannah, if he had mirrored back to you on the pillow this morning, a flattering image of yourself? Would it have made the experience morally more palatable, if he himself had been?

Is my vanity the only measure of my moral outrage?

Hannah leaves some money on the table and, without drinking her coffee, gets up and goes into the Catholic church across the road. As soon as she slips under its cool slabs of stone, she begins to cry.

This always happens.

She wants to prostrate herself and beg forgiveness. She is sinful and needs absolution. I am selfish, she says, and cruel and pathetic and heartless and nobody will ever love me until I learn to love myself, isn't that right?

But how can I love myself when I am so unworthy? *Not worthy so much as to gather up the crumbs under thy Table,* oh, dear Lord. The words of the Anglican prayer book come rolling back like bolts of purple cloth, enticing and treacherous.

Hannah rests her forehead on the pew in front and feels the tears drop off the end of her nose and chin, leaving a coolness behind, and it feels like a peeling away. She realizes that her heart is inured to something essential. She is afraid of Daniel's rejection but she doesn't feel sorry for causing him pain. She can't empathize with that.

When Hannah looks up, she sees the statue of the Virgin Mary posing in an eternal gesture of supplication by the nave. Mother of God. Her face is chipped and pocked and something like blood has dried on her right temple. Most of her fingertips are broken off and her lace veil, hanging from a rusty halo on her head, is dusty and threadbare, like a cobweb. One hand is delicately held aloft, towards heaven. The other held out towards whoever is beseeching her. It's like she's gesturing to Hannah. Come, she seems to be saying, and rest. Stop running away.

Hannah is sitting at the kitchen table while Shawn McCarthy gives her some last minute instructions. Just a few more minutes and then he'll be gone. She can't wait for him to leave. She's never wanted anyone to be out of her sight more. His presence is like the flu, it makes her sweat and shiver. Shawn gives her a kiss at the door, a wet kiss, and she lets him squeeze her for a while. She feels his body bend forward to envelop her and for a moment she feels sorry for him, pities his need of her. It is a universal need, she could almost take refuge in it for a while. But then he says, Cheer up and stop feeling so guilty. You didn't do anything wrong.

And Hannah can't believe the gulf of miscomprehension that can exist between two people.

If you change your mind, he says, as the taxi pulls up to the door, I can still book you onto that flight to San Francisco. I've got a great pad there. You'd love it.

Poor desperate fucker. What does he know about me?

As soon as she closes the door, Hannah screws up her face and wipes her hands on her thighs as if she could rub off the memory of him. She's in such a state of nervousness she can barely remember her own telephone number in England. Daniel answers after two rings and Hannah's heart is beating so fast it hurts. The line is so clear he could be in the room next door.

Daniel, she says, and something that feels like rain travels across her skin.

Hannah! he exclaims. How are you? And his surprise is so genuine and his delight so pure that it cuts to the core of her and makes her feel faint. Nobody at this point loves me more than Daniel does, so why am I so bad to him?

Oh, Daniel, she says, her voice thick with longing. I miss you so much.

Where are you calling from?

I'm in San Miguel.

Oh, good, so you got there okay?

Ah-uh.

And are you meeting English speakers?

A lot of Americans, she says. I met this guy. He's been very generous. I'm staying at his place. For free. While he's away.

That's lucky.

Yeah, Hannah says.

He says, So how are you?

I'm not so good, Daniel. Not so good. And she starts to weep.

Hannah is sitting on the floor with the phone pressed up against her ear.

I'm so sorry, Daniel, she says, her voice weak, her breathing still jagged from crying.

I know that, babe. You don't need to say that any more.

But I want you to know.

I do know, darlin, and I'm glad you told me, and it is upsetting, but you already feel so guilty on your own, what would I achieve by getting angry at you? I can hardly get mad at you, he says, when you're already this upset. I know you didn't mean to hurt me and it was just a drunken thing and you didn't have sex, so I guess it wasn't such a bad thing after all. It's not like we aren't having our own problems, is it?

Oh, Daniel, why are you so good to me?

You're my little feisty one, remember?

And you don't mind?

I kind of like the fact that you're a little crazy. What am I going to do with you, eh?

I dunno, Hannah says, looking around at Shawn's empty apartment. Daniel's voice is in her head, but he's thousands of miles away.

I love you, sweetheart, Daniel says.

I love you too, Hannah says, silently bursting into tears again. Daniel?

Yes?

Do you think I'm bad?

No, Hannah, you're not bad. You're just trying to live, just like everybody else, the best way you know how.

When Hannah gets off the phone, she feels exhausted, empty, almost indifferent. Absolved, but drained. Scorched and drenched like a forest after a fire, the flames abated, firefighters sitting down at last to rest and catch their breath, the drip and hiss of drops of water still trickling from the gaping mouths of limp hoses that only moments ago were stiff with power. Then gradually, rising from the wreckage, there are stirrings of an ability to tackle the world all over again. Confession has made her weightless.

Hannah walks to the main square. She eats three tacos at a stand where she sees the locals eating. Some fried meat served up on flour tortillas the size of china plates. There are three bowls of sauces, red, white and green. The salsa has fresh tomatoes and chillies and coriander and lime. Hannah drinks a glass of freshly squeezed orange juice, then buys a coconut popsicle from an old man with a handlebar moustache and a ruby velvet vest. He winks and his eyes are the colour of sage. The food is so pure and natural. It is renewing her spirit. The sun makes everything obvious. Her feet heat up. She begins to sweat. Hannah is getting back in touch with her goodness. Her buoyant optimism. A state of calm. It isn't personal, it is an absence of ego. A detachment in her being that is immune to the severity of consequence. That makes her free and independent. That makes her generous, careless even.

Hannah is repentant and determined to behave well, at least until she is overcome by the next temptation. She is deeply grateful to have a husband as forgiving and understanding of her exuberance and sensuality, but his absolution does less over time to reform her thoughts, than it does to allow her to consider doing it again. After a few days, she starts to imagine a certain perverse permissiveness creeping into their marriage space, a grey area where it's okay to do certain things, but not quite all of them.

Like Saint Augustine, she prays, *Give me continence, but just not yet.*

Seven days later and Hannah is sitting in front of her laptop set up at a desk in Shawn's apartment. It is quiet. She is feeling weak, unsure of herself again. She gets up and walks over to a flipchart propped up in the corner of the room. She takes a big blue marker and writes, *I am a good person* across the top. Then she takes a red marker and writes, *I am worthy of love.* Then she takes a green marker and writes, *I am capable of loving.* It is a silly counselling trick, but it makes her feel better all the same, partly because it makes her feel safe, the thoughts being so utterly private, it reminds her that she is all alone, there being safety in solitude.

When Shawn's assistant, Luís, comes the following day to move his things, the phrases are still written on the flipchart. Hannah is standing in the kitchen when she realizes by the smirk on his face that he's read them and drawn his own conclusions.

One thing I have learned, a certain amount of humiliation is good for the soul.

Hannah goes with Luís in his car to Shawn McCarthy's new house on the hill. It is an ostentatious Spanish villa next to another almost identical one, owned by a Texan millionaire. The Texan drives a Range Rover and has a handsome son. What's your name? he asks her. Would you like to go for a spin? Have you been to the hot springs?

All Hannah wants to do is lie low. She walks down to the market in the afternoon and back as the sun is setting. As the candy floss walls of the villa subside to cinnamon, she sits on the balcony overlooking the town of San Miguel and watches the lights come on, all the Mexican families sitting down to eat. She drinks cold beer and watches the workmen fixing the roof of a villa fifty feet below and suddenly she feels like a fraud.

Like I'm some kind of goddamn, rich American bastard.

It is then that Hannah decides. It's time to pack up and head for home.

20

For ever and ever all men

Desire, at the end, was a malady, or a madness, or both. I grew careless of the lives of others. I took pleasure where it pleased me, and passed on. I forgot that every little action of the common day makes or unmakes character, and that therefore what one has done in the secret chamber one has some day to cry aloud on the housetop. I ceased to be lord over myself. I was no longer the captain of my soul, and did not know it. I allowed pleasure to dominate me. I ended in horrible disgrace. There is only one thing for me now, absolute humility.

Oscar Wilde – *De Profundis*

Two months is a long time to be away from your husband and Hannah feels hesitant and impatient as she wheels her bags through Heathrow Customs. The right front wheel of her trolley is spinning and she has to lever the handle hard to keep the trolley on course.

The sliding glass doors part with a whisper and Hannah is confronted by a crowd of people, of all races and manners of dress, some holding signs with unpronounceable names, others holding flowers, all with the same strained, expectant look on their faces, searching and searching. There's a cry and a woman comes rushing from behind, runs right past Hannah to the edge of the crowd. Hannah is so nervous that she jumps, thinking the worst. A crime of violence! A man with a gun! But it is only a mother reunited with her children. The woman crouches and scoops up two young girls with such urgency and passion that it brings tears to Hannah's eyes.

At first she can't find Daniel.

And then she sees him. She hardly recognizes him. She's actually forgotten what he looks like. She looks at him from the outside, like a stranger. And with a pang in her stomach like a punch that takes her breath away, she realizes she isn't attracted to him. And this unforgiving realization fills her with a violent rush of pity.

Oh, Daniel. You are not well loved. And that is all my fault. I will try harder from now on. I promise.

But it is a promise made for the sake of making a promise and it won't hold water, though she doesn't know this yet.

Daniel holds her face and kisses her softly on the mouth.

Darlin, he says.

And the fact that he is her husband, that she has every right to be with him, that there is nothing illicit or forbidden about this union, collapses something inside her that has been held tight for the last two months and she nearly melts. She lets out a sigh and leaning into him, whispers into his chest, Oh, Daniel. I missed you so much.

And in this she is being entirely honest.

Thing is, friendship just isn't enough and Hannah and Daniel were friends. Great, great friends. They could go out on the town and have a rip-roaring time, and loved each other with a love steadfast and true. They talked about companionship, communication, loyalty. They talked about being honest. Only, when it came to the union of souls in the context of erotic love, something was lacking and as a result, they grew further and further apart. A hunger lust grew stronger in them, but imperceptibly, like boils beneath the skin. Erupting at inopportune moments and in ways that were more painful and sinister than either of them wanted to admit.

The grave state of their marriage is beginning to dawn on them.

It begins one sorry night in Peckham.

Daniel and Hannah are tipsy in a pub in Dulwich when they meet two men. One is older than the other by thirty years and they are celebrating the younger man's birthday. The younger man seems in awe of the older man and the older man tolerant, if condescending. The younger man seems to have no one with whom to celebrate the occasion, and the older man is there to remedy this situation in the spirit of a tacit understanding that no man should have to suffer the fate of being friendless. He wants to create a festive spirit for the young man. So, after sitting beside them for a while and sensing their restlessness, and wanting to draw more people into his party, he offers to buy Daniel and Hannah a drink.

They accept with the enthusiasm of two people open to the world and excited by it but on the fringes too, waiting for an invitation, to come into some money, whatever would afford their inclusion.

They were gagging for distraction.

The older man introduces himself as Whitney, a builder. And this, he says, is me partner, Lee. He pats the young man on the shoulder with the soft, almost sexual affection some men show their dogs. And then he asks Daniel what he does for a living.

I'm a projectionist, Daniel says. At a cinema in Hampstead.

So, Whitney says, you must see a lot of films.

I see a lot of them twice, Daniel says.

Ever fall asleep and forget to change the reel?

No, but I've got the order mixed up before. Funny thing is, Daniel says, people don't seem to notice. A Bergman film, for instance. Or Tarkovsky. You skip a reel and put it at the end? It can even be an improvement.

And what about the missus? Whitney asks, turning to look at Hannah.

Freelance, she says, and Whitney nods. But mostly I'm what you call between jobs.

Done a bit of that meself, he says and winks.

When they finish their pints, Whitney invites Daniel and Hannah to join them at the Victory pub in Peckham, a neighbourhood not far from their own, which Hannah knows only as being one notorious for its poverty and crime.

186

They accept the invitation and follow Whitney and Lee to an old Mercedes-Benz, parked down a side street. As they're walking to the car, Whitney flips open a cell phone and makes a call. We're on our way, he says and pauses. Four of us, he says, then closes it up.

He drives fast and loose and at one point, veers off the main road and onto a residential street. He stops in front of a row of houses and turns to Daniel in the back seat. Just going to pop inside for a minute.

Okay, Daniel says.

It is only ten-thirty when Whitney runs into the house. He darts out again in less than five minutes holding a brown paper bag, which he passes to Lee. A tall thin woman with short curly hair, wearing a patterned apron and wiping her hands, waves briefly from the entrance before closing the door.

Whitney starts the ignition and takes the bag from Lee. He opens it and the car fills up with the smell of boiled eggs.

Egg sarnie? he asks. There's plenty here. I told Peggy we were four tonight.

They all take a sandwich and as Whitney guns the car back into the street, Hannah smiles and raises her eyebrows at Daniel to show him that she has understood how strange a life can be, and yet how high she is on the adventure of it all, speeding through dark streets towards an unknown destination. And as she takes a bite, Hannah believes it's the best egg sandwich she's ever had.

There are no more than a dozen people in the Victory and Whitney knows them all by name. A drink on me, he announces. It's Lee's birthday. And everybody cheers. Whitney introduces Daniel and Hannah as university graduates and people seem genuinely impressed.

You see Declan over there? says an old man with a pale green and motionless glass eye. Now his daughter, she's been to college.

187

I might've gone meself, a thin reed of an old woman pipes in, a string of beads under the neck of her prim blue cardigan. If I hadn't been up the duff and kids hanging off me apron strings for half me life.

Her laugh is loud and hoarse.

Not that I'm complaining, mind. Got meself five strapping lads. All settled down nicely, too. Me youngest worked on that millennium dome. Calls it Tony's Money Toilet, which I say is fair enough, given wot he spent on it.

It is refreshing to be around people who appreciate the value of an accomplishment, and they welcome Daniel and Hannah as only people who've known hard times can welcome strangers into their midst. They are people for whom the world is an inhospitable place, whose only protection is to choose a cavalier fatalism over bitterness. And their generosity is such that neither Daniel nor Hannah will pay for a drink the entire evening. At one point, Hannah notices she's got three full pints lined up on the table in front of her.

She's talking to an Irish World War II veteran by the name of Paddy Marsh. You have to promise, he says, to make my eighty-sixth birthday next Tuesday. His hands shake so badly, the froth on his Guinness peaks like meringue as he lifts his glass to take a sip. Hannah feels the moral imperative of honouring this old gentleman. I'll be there, she says. She gives him her word. And in her heart, she really believes she's going to make it.

But she won't.

The day will come and she'll remember the old man, and apathy and a desire to forget this night will overtake her sense of duty. But her failure to fulfil that promise will continue to haunt her for a very long time. Suggesting, as it does, an unreliability she is reluctant to own.

Across the room, Daniel is playing pool with Lee and the lads, over by the jukebox, smoking fags. Daniel takes a shot and misses. Can't get away from the missus, he says to no one in particular, then steps back and leans a little too heavily, landing with a thud against the bar. Holding his pool cue with one hand, Daniel reaches for his pint glass with the other and takes a drink. It's Lee's turn but he scuppers his shot. So Daniel pushes himself off the bar and, keeping his eyes on the pool table, reaches behind to put his glass down. He misses the counter and his pint goes crashing to the floor. He's too drunk to connect the noise of the crash to the glass that's just vacated his hand, and it's only when the barmaid comes over with a broom that he notices a commotion.

What happened? he asks.

You dropped yer pint, she says.

Who did?

You did.

Fucking 'ell, he says.

Not to worry, luv. We'll just clear this away and get you another one. What yer having?

It is two hours past closing and the blinds have been drawn and the closed sign hung from a hook on the door. There is a collective lull as sometimes happens and the barmaid, putting one hand on her polished taps like the wheel of a ship, takes advantage of the hush to sing an Irish ballad about a love affair gone sour and the lovers slain. People gather around the bar. The song goes on for a full fifteen minutes and when she's done, and after the applause, Hannah breaks into a rousing rendition of *Farewell to Nova Scotia* (the only remotely Celtic song she knows). Her performance is so unanticipated, and so enthusiastic, that it erases whatever class distinction there may have been left in the barmaid's mind between the two of them. So she pulls another pint and slides it in Hannah's direction.

At quarter to three in the morning, Lee whispers into Hannah's ear, I think you should go now.

What? Hannah says.

I think you and Daniel should leave.

189

Really?

That's right.

Hannah feels a pang of fear. She leans back and crosses her arms. Looks over at the pool table where Daniel is surrounded by men. Now the place has a sudden edge of hostility, like a bright light has been flicked on to reveal goblins lurking in the shadows. Why? she asks him.

Whitney's turning ugly, Lee says, and I think you should just avoid any trouble by leaving right away.

Oh, okay, Hannah says. Thanks, Lee, and she walks over to Daniel and tells him they should think about going now and in such an imploring, serious manner that he intuits an urgency and pulls on his coat.

Before they reach the door, Declan comes over and offers to put them up at his daughter's place for the night. It's right across the street and she's a policewoman, he says. And I'd feel safer knowing you two weren't out on the streets at this late hour of the night.

Daniel says, We're just a twenty minute walk away. I think we'll be okay.

Suit yourself, Declan says, and walks off, suddenly disinterested now that his hospitality has been rebuked.

Hannah takes hold of Daniel's arm and braces herself. Not knowing the area, she can only think the worst.

Whitney reels across the room. You going?

Yeah, we are.

Fuck off, then, yer posh bastards!

It's the drink, Lee says.

The barmaid unlocks the door and almost pushes them out, shuts the door quickly and locks it.

They find themselves on a dark, rainy street in Peckham, in the middle of the night, vulnerably drunk, and Hannah whispers, Oh, my God.

I have to pee.

Daniel, we're gonna get killed.

But I have to pee, he says, and chooses a spot by a low brick wall bordering a front yard covered in gravel. He stands there in the drizzle, swaying in the hot steam from his own piss. Hannah guards him, hoping nobody will see them. She fears the sight of him might arouse unwanted curiosity. If someone came now, she thinks, they could beat the shit out of us. Out of Daniel. They'd just take me. They wouldn't lay a finger on me. Not yet.

Come on, she urges, and Daniel says, Don't rush me.

Please, she mouths the word, looking up and down the street.

Daniel raises himself on the balls of his feet, shakes his cock and zips up. Okay, he says, rubbing the heels of his hands together. Home, James?

Hannah takes his arm and they make their way towards Peckham High Street, bouncing off each other. A white, souped-up Cabriolet with black tinted windows glides past, pulsing with bass, making the cement vibrate beneath their feet. Everywhere she looks, Hannah can see the black shards of darkened corners, the threat of unlit alleyways, looming estates, misty funnels of light over rows of caged-in, barred-up doorways. Daniel is blathering on about something that has amused him, but Hannah isn't listening.

She is being vigilant.

And concentrating on holding him up.

Near the high street intersection, Daniel starts to laugh. He laughs so hard that he totters to the right and bangs into the metal shield pulled down over a storefront to protect it from vandals. The metal clangs like disrupted garbage cans and Hannah resents the attention he is drawing to himself. Daniel slaps his thigh and doubles forward, then straightens up and falls backwards into a doorway, all the while laughing to himself. Hannah bends over him and begs him to get up.

Please, she says with all the sincerity of her fear. Hannah looks down the street and sees six young men in puffer jackets and baggy jeans walking towards them. This terrifies her.

That's it, she thinks. We're done for.

Grabbing Daniel by the shoulders, she shakes him hard. For fuck's sake, Daniel. Pull yourself together.

Out of the corner of her eye, she sees the men approach and hates Daniel at this moment for abandoning her. She imagines a murky canal, cold mud and prickly bushes, torn clothing, a broken bottle, laughter but you can't see them because you're blindfolded with your own stockings. When the men are nearly upon her, she panics and slaps Daniel hard across the face. She hears someone laugh. Taunts of bravado. But they pass her by. Hannah covers her mouth and lets out a sigh, more like a whimper. She straightens up and starts walking away.

Meanwhile, Daniel is holding his cheek and feeling enraged.

What the fuck did you do that for? he yells at her back.

Hannah ignores him and keeps on walking. Daniel catches up and swings her around.

What the fuck was that for? he demands again.

Fuck you, she says, pulling away from him.

Don't walk away from me! he yells and runs after her, grabbing her and pushing her up against a parked car.

In a drunken, bumbling, ineffectual way he pins her against the car. She resists him, but Daniel leans his weight forward until she is bent back over the hood. He relaxes his body then, sort of lying on top of her, and becomes belligerent.

Don't you ever, ever do that to me again. You have no right to hit me, you hear?

Hannah can see more people coming down the street. She thinks they might figure Daniel is beating her up and take it upon themselves to come to her rescue. Now she is worried about his safety.

Get off of me, she says, first angry, then imploring. Seriously, she says, this isn't a good idea.

I'll tell you what isn't a good idea, Daniel says, their noses an inch apart. Hitting me in the face isn't a good idea.

Just get off of me! Hannah yells and using all her force, pushes him sideways and jumps up. Then she runs. Down the high street. Daniel in pursuit.

He catches up to her and reaching for her shoulder, trips on her heel and goes crashing to the ground, pulling Hannah down with him. She sits up and looks at him. He is lifting his face out of a puddle. He puts his hand to his mouth and then looks at his fingers. There is blood on his fingers.

You did this to me, he says, holding out the red evidence. She says, You're an asshole.

Hannah stands up and is startled by a tall black man standing a few feet away, in the open doorway of a chip shop, placidly eating his chips with a plastic fork, looking down at her and shaking his head.

Hannah looks back at Daniel, still kneeling on the greasy sidewalk. She closes her eyes in mortification, then walks away. Two blocks later, Daniel catches up to her.

I can't believe you fucking hit me in the mouth, he keeps saying.

Listen! she yells, stopping abruptly and turning towards him, her temper snapping like an elastic. I didn't hit you in the fucken mouth, okay!

Like a child having a temper tantrum, Daniel pushes Hannah in the chest. She trips backwards and falls heavily. When she hits the ground, she becomes incensed. She jumps up and, reaching with the full extent of her arm, grabs Daniel by the neck and pushes him up against the brick wall outside Camberwell Art College. Hannah pins him. Fuck, she is strong. Daniel's arms are flailing helplessly, and he's making pathetic, exaggerated choking noises.

Even as she has him pinned there, Hannah notices the heightened melodrama of the situation and wonders, who is this person with their fist around Daniel's neck like this?

She drops her arm and Daniel's hands shoot up to protect his neck. Are you crazy? Hannah whips around and runs across the street, the sound of a car horn trailing after her. She runs towards Camberwell Grove, taking the path that runs behind the Gothic church near where they were married. It is badly lit at night and lined with tombstones. A woman was raped here at knife point, then stabbed. She slows down, regretting her decision now but unable to turn back. Hannah reaches her own lighted street and, fumbling with the keys for a minute, lets herself in and flings her body down on the sofa in the dark. Shadows of the branches outside the window like long thin fingers wagging admonition on the empty walls of the unlit living room, the only animated presence in the flat apart from her.

Apart. From her.

When Daniel gets home, he leaves the lights off. She hears his knees crack. He kneels by the sofa. What was that all about, hey?

I dunno, Hannah says. She accepts his embrace, presses her face into his neck.

Pretty shameful behaviour.

Oh, Daniel, it was awful.

This, he says, has got to be the nadir.

I can't bear to think about it.

Let's just forget about it, okay?

Hannah nods. How's your lip? she asks.

It's a bit sore, he says. You really must've hit me hard.

Babe, you busted your lip when you fell in that puddle.

You hit me in the face.

I hit you, but I didn't bust your lip.

At any rate, it doesn't matter.

It does matter, actually.

No, actually, it doesn't.

Your refusal, she says, is wilful. It's gratuitous.

Daniel gets up and goes into the bathroom.

Oh, God, Hannah thinks, turning to bury her face in the sofa. I can't stand living like this.

When Daniel comes out again, he lies down beside her. His

194

arm draws her in. They lie there in the quiet of the night, listening to the wind through the bare branches of the trees, the occasional sound of a car braking for the speed bump on the street, then accelerating. Braking again for the next one.

They want us, Daniel says, to go visit. It's just three days. It's just my parents.

It makes Hannah feel like she's drifting.

Adrift.

Of course we'll go, Daniel. I'm happy to.

Hannah has no ties, no family in this country. No job. No schedule or responsibilities. She can get up and go for three days and there's no disruption. Nothing to disrupt. And all their plans for the next six months are things Daniel wants to do. Whereas Hannah seems to contribute nothing. Control nothing. Initiate nothing.

When you're crying in bed, she thinks, and the person beside you doesn't react, even if it's because you're so good at hiding the fact, it makes you feel invisible.

But why should you be so good at hiding the fact? So well practised?

Finally, the long dull winter cracks. It is the first warm sunny day in May. The pub doors are open. Hannah is having a drink with Ursula Bishop at the end of a crowded picnic table on a brick terrace with empty flower pots. They are tipsy and animated. The sunshine, Ursula says, is making me feel euphoric. They get talking to some handsome young men, Oxbridge types who buy them a round, and then Ursula has to go.

Oh, don't go, Hannah says.

But I have to, she says. My parents are coming and the place is a tip.

Hannah sighs.

Why don't you stay? asks one of the nice, young Oxbridge men. Have another drink with us? He has pale skin, dark curls and plump red bee-stung lips.

How can I be faithful to just one man, Hannah thinks, when there are so many beautiful men I'd just love to taste, to try, just the once, for one extremely passionate night.

Yeah, Ursula says, giving Hannah a look as if to say, do you dare? Why don't you stay? She lifts her handbag to her shoulder, bends to give Hannah a kiss and says, Call me later.

Hannah huffs incredulously as she watches Ursula walk away, but sure enough, three hours later, Hannah finds herself going home with Alan Cummings, a nice young Oxbridge man who claims to be, at the green age of twenty-two, a qualified chef with his own TV show. He lives in Old Holborn, in a palatial top-floor flat owned by his parents, with an original Miró over the fireplace and eclectic but expensive designer furniture.

I demand, she says, to see your knives, Alan Cummings.

Pardon?

I wrote a piece on kitchens, she says. The restaurant manager told me that any chef worth his salt owns his own knives.

Like a good country doctor Alan unrolled them from a canvas pouch and laid them on the couch, sharp as scalpels.

Very good, she says. I can vouch for your authenticity, Mr Cummings.

They sit down to play a game of strip chess. After swallowing two flaming sambucas and staring for five interminable minutes at the pawns on the board (he actually set his chess clock), Hannah becomes disenchanted with the game. So Alan Cummings suggests they play strip checkers instead which, compared to chess, is like flying Concorde. It's over in a flash and Hannah finds herself naked in this young TV chef's kitchen, insisting that she's married and really must be going now that it's, oh, my God, three o'clock in the morning.

Married? he says and Hannah nods. But you're so young.

I'm older than you are, she says.

But it's so cruel, he says, to deprive us men of a woman like yourself.

196

Hannah laughs and says, I'd better get out of here before you sweet-talk me into something I'll regret.

Wait, he says, coming over and putting his hands on her hips. Before you get dressed, I want you to do me a favour.

Hannah looks at a desire in his face she cannot fathom. What?

I want you to shave me.

Shave you?

I think it's sexy when a woman shaves a man, don't you?

Hannah pauses. Where?

I'm thinking right here.

It's a bit cold though, isn't it? she says, rubbing her bare arms.

I'll light the hob, he says, and sparks all four of the gas burners on, cranking them to max. He says, Wait here, and leaves Hannah alone in the kitchen, listening to the blue gas hiss into the silence.

Hannah leans back against the counter and crosses her arms. She thinks, this is crazy. I am naked and alone in this beautiful kitchen. How do I get myself into these situations? But she is feigning scruples. Because hiding behind her disapproval is an undeniable delight, a thrill of superiority born of experience that she gets from these encounters. Do I not partake, she asks herself proudly, in the daring, heady culture of human dissipation? Have I not lived?

When Alan Cummings gets back, he's tucked a towel into the waistband of his trousers and his chin is lathered. He pulls a wooden chair over to the kitchen sink and sits down. He runs the hot water and hands her a straight razor. You can, if you like, sit down. Hannah straddles his lap and pivots his head with her fingertips. Just a little to the side, she says, and while she drags the blade in scratchy strokes over his jaw, Alan Cummings curls his fingers around her ass. She shaves and feels the keen sensation, his fingers now inside her. It makes her tremble. Her lungs are two fish caught in a net. Her breath leaps and tosses. She turns her face to sigh and catches an unexpected glimpse of her reflection in the window. Her hair is up in a loose ponytail and her skin is luminous. Her small breasts are round and firm. Her arms smooth and muscular. But I am beautiful, she thinks. Why doesn't he see that any more?

Watch, Alan Cummings says, what you're cutting.

When she gets home the sky is light. Hannah runs a bath. Daniel comes in wearing a bathrobe and sits down on the toilet. Hannah is full of something indistinct, of elation and foreboding. Giddy and packed tight with an excess of it. She is nervous about telling him what she's been up to, but not as much as she's embarrassed by it. It's like she's been caught wading in a public fountain, nothing serious, just silly. She bites her lip and fights off the urge to laugh, to giggle. She must try to seem repentant. She tells him about Alan Cummings.

I've seen his show, he says, if you're wondering if he's for real. Daniel is annoyed, but he doesn't appear to be angry.

Aren't you going to rail at me?

I haven't the heart, he says. He shrugs at the news and leaves the bathroom.

I didn't kiss him, Hannah tells him from the living room, still drying herself off.

At least it wasn't somebody we know, Daniel says, his voice flat, defeated. He is pouring hot water into a plastic coffee filter balanced on a mug. He wields the kettle with an economy of movement, as if begrudging the effort, or unable to summon it. His back is turned and Hannah watches him for a moment. He looks so boyish in his bathrobe, so vulnerable. And his shoulders that were once so square seem rounded now, like a stone wheel ground down over time.

It's been months since they made love.

Apathy, whether adopted or genuine, is corrosive, and gradually Hannah becomes cavalier. She allows herself a sexual dalliance. And then another. While she feels remorse at these lapses of integrity, she doesn't have the resolve, or the energy, to change her situation. How can I be faithful, she thinks, when I feel this unwanted? And yet she doesn't have the confidence, nor is she that certain she should leave. She has had such great expectations for love, fantasies of what it means to be devoted. But her marriage isn't even coming close. And still, she finds it hard to give up on that dream.

Daniel, too, finds it easier to forgive Hannah than to delve for a darker explanation. Delving might lead to giving up his autonomy. He knows he should probably make a compromise, but he can't relinquish his habits and his routine, his one-bed flat, the straight, uninterrupted path into his future. The idea of giving Hannah a son at twenty-eight is beginning to feel like a mistake. How unwelcome the disruption of a son would be.

Daniel's forgiveness appears to be generous, but it leaves Hannah feeling forsaken. I would like him to stop me, absolve me of the guilty burden of being the one so obviously in the wrong. She wishes he would put his foot down. He did it once, when she packed her bags and threatened to leave. When she got to the door, Daniel said, You walk out and you never come back. So you care, Hannah said. Yes, I care, he said, and that had made her stay.

But now she has begun to notice a saintly forbearance in Daniel's face. A sanctimonious immunity to the facts. An avoidance of responsibility. Gradually, Hannah's encounters become more risky, her confessions to Daniel less remorseful, less thorough. She may have left a few things out.

She becomes cynical about her own unhappiness. She mocks it. She compartmentalizes. My life with Daniel is here, and my life without him is over there. It is the only way to cope with such emotional disarray. Such hearty lonesome neglect. She doesn't feel loved and yet she cannot, officially, love another. She begins to catalogue her dalliances the way some people catalogue holiday snapshots. And then there was the time when.

Hannah catches herself boasting about a conquest to her friends. They laugh at her story. Ursula Bishop says, You're crazy, Hannah, and shakes her head. Then Ursula starts talking about her own unfulfilling sex life. Then Eddie does. And no one seems to disapprove. They seem to envy Hannah. They admire her spunk. In their minds, her life is one big unfettered adventure. She meets with no resistance. I want, she says to Ursula, to meet a powerful force. Something to stop me. I am heavy, Hannah thinks, with the weight of my sexual betrayals. They are drying me up. But she can't stop. She is hungry for love.

And yet she loves the look on Eddie Webb's face too. They are at the back of a noisy tapas bar. They are drunk on red wine, eating chorizo and black olives. In Hannah's words: We kissed in the bathroom of a crowded bar in Soho. She kept whispering how I tasted of cinnamon.

Did you know, Eddie tells her, that you and Lyle are vying for first place on my list of the top five most fucked-up people I know?

Really? Hannah says, and is taken aback. Her life has been observed and yet she feels unknowable to herself. She hasn't thought about Lyle in months. How is the old rock god anyways?

Last week he was taken to hospital on a drug overdose, Eddie says. He could see out of his eyes, but he couldn't move a muscle.

Oh, my God, Hannah says. That's terrible.

Just wait till I tell him about the cinnamon.

Oh, please don't, Hannah says. It's not the same thing. Honestly, Eddie, I feel like I'm trying to be good in my life.

You call this being good?

Well, I'm not a drug addict for one, Hannah says. And I don't get into fights. And I'm not a thief or a liar or intentionally malicious.

But you were barely married when you fell in love with Lyle.

That was my heart, she says. You can't blame me for that.

You and Daniel should have been a gay couple, Eddie says, taking a gulp of wine, little red horns staining his upper lip. I didn't think heteros had arrangements like yours.

We don't have an arrangement.

It's only a matter of time.

But my dalliances, she says, are always the product of drunken exuberance. Not a single one has ever been sober. And they're never premeditated. I feel, actually, like I'm holding myself back.

Well, thank God for that, Eddie says. Here's to restraint. Greater London need not be put on alert.

I will have you know, Hannah says haughtily, waving her wineglass in the air, I have never, not once, gone the whole way.

That you know of.

That I can remember.

Well, congratulations are in order, Eddie says, for the amount of integrity you rescue from compromise.

It is the death knell of innocence. Hannah and Daniel are clinical in their approach. They agree to draw an arbitrary line between faithfulness and full penetrative sex.

You say snogging, but it's really a euphemism for everything else, Daniel says.

I mean hugging, kissing, petting, Hannah says. That's all I ever do.

Dry humping, Daniel says, oral sex, blow jobs? What's next?

Do I get the go ahead for mutual masturbation? Hannah asks sarcastically, while in her mind she sees a tree full of white blossoms wither on the branch and fall from their stems to cover the floor in confetti.

As long as there is no penetrative sex, Daniel says, the rest is a tonic for the relief of unbearable urges.

I feel, Hannah says, after envying them for all these years, their sanctioned indulgences, their cycle of sin, confession and absolution, I have finally become a Catholic.

Alas, he says, your Protestant days are over. Your idealism rotten to the core. It is finished.

Daniel and Hannah comfort themselves with words like bohemian, liberal, open-minded, appetite, curiosity, adventure. And it is some small consolation. But lurking in the wings of their big wide open hearts is a growing panic that the embittered hag of resignation may be squatting there, spraying her territory with the poison of paralysis, wearing the damaged rags of apathy.

But not every compromise has to be a resignation and maybe this is just maturity and maybe this is experience and maybe this is understanding and maybe this is love and maybe just maybe.

At the height of summer, drunk on white wine and an empty stomach, Hannah snogs a prominent movie critic at a party Daniel takes her to, in front of everyone, even the press. Daniel had left on account of a hangover, but Hannah was on a roll. When Daniel asked her if she wanted to leave, she had said no, kissed him briefly on the cheek, then disappeared into the crowd. And the movie critic, who was older and shorter than Hannah, had to stand on a champagne crate to kiss her and the whole debacle got written up in a gossip column of the *Daily Telegraph*.

This is how Daniel finds out about it. He is reading the paper at the kitchen table on a Tuesday morning. Your name's right here in print, he says, slapping the column with the back of his hand. They call you an essayist. I was wondering what you are.

Hannah admits, I ended up at the Groucho that night, snorting coke off the back of a toilet in the men's washroom. But in truth she had woken up with a cement dread in her stomach and a fear of the telephone ringing. She had blacked out again and couldn't remember what she had done.

And I bet you thought you'd hit the big time, Daniel says.

It's a bit of a blur, to be honest.

Jesus Christ, Hannah. What are you like?

I'm sorry, she says.

Why didn't you tell me?

I dunno.

But we promised to be honest with each other! Daniel shouts.

Why? Hannah says. So that you could lord your moral rectitude over me?

So that I could decide.

And feel smug about being the one to bestow forgiveness.

I'm getting tired of forgiving you.

Then stop forgiving me! Hannah cries. Tell me not to do it!

It's not up to me, Daniel says. I won't be your policeman.

But why don't you try and stop me, she begs him, kneeling on the floor and wrapping her arms around his legs. I just want to know that you love me.

But how can I love you? Daniel asks, pushing her away. When you behave this unlovingly towards me?

They stop and look at each other then. Their faces ugly with anguish.

Perhaps, she thinks, I am like a child, testing the limits of Daniel's tolerance. They are at a small soirée at Ingmar's, and Hannah has thrown herself at his best friend, Peter Straun. Peter is back from Berlin for the weekend. It is the end of a wild night, a debauch that will cause such chagrin the next day that a mildly embarrassed composure will descend upon the group. Even Eddie Webb will settle down a little after this, and surprise everyone by getting serious about his work at the bank.

Still, it is Daniel who sets the tone. Hannah is talking to Peter Straun and drinking a glass of champagne. Suddenly she sees, across the room, that Daniel is naked. Stark bollock naked. Although he is laughing, like he always does, with his hands smacked together and his head thrown back, Hannah has a rush of pity for him. A rare loyal impulse to protect.

I will get undressed as well.

In front of Peter Straun she slips out of her dress. Eddie has beaten her to it, leaning back, he flings his boxers onto a lampshade. Ursula strips off, then Ingmar, and lastly, Peter Straun. In a few minutes everyone is naked and Hannah senses a higher pitch. People continue to stand around and talk, only now they lunge at the champagne and laugh a little louder at the jokes, cruder jokes.

Later on, there is hugging. It was on a dare, Daniel explains, from Ursula. Ingmar has a hold of Peter's cock, he is weighing it. Eddie can't bear this. He is drinking heavily on the futon. Now Ingmar goes into the bathroom and doesn't come out. Daniel and Ursula continue their heart-to-heart. He is comforting her. You should put her to bed, Hannah says to him. And through her tears, Daniel leads Ursula to bed (Hannah will find him in the morning asleep on the floor under a lumpy nylon sleeping bag). The party deflates into silence. The flat seems to shrink in size. All the lights are on and Hannah and Peter Straun are the last ones standing.

If it wasn't for Daniel, Peter begins to say, a hand on the small of her back, and Hannah bends over the kitchen sink.

Just fuck me, she implores. Fuck me.

But Peter Straun restrains himself. Though he presses up against her for a moment. And sighs.

In the morning there is confession (serious shame this time causing her palms to sweat, her heart to rattle in its cage). His refusal becomes a matter over which Daniel seems to bond with Peter Straun.

I admire his restraint, he says. I take it as proof of his loyalty. This, Daniel seems to be implying, will deepen their friendship.

And I don't feature in the repercussions much at all, Hannah thinks. So who is it, exactly, who is having the relationship here?

It isn't until Peter has left for Berlin that Daniel cracks up. They are sitting at the kitchen table having breakfast when, all of a sudden, Daniel stands up and swipes everything to the floor. Newspaper, food, cutlery, plates, glasses. They all go smashing to the floor.

I can't stand this any more! he yells. You are my wife, Hannah! I want you to behave like one!

Hannah jumps up. She backs around her chair and stands against the wall. Daniel comes over and holds his body an inch from hers. He is trembling with anger, his flesh possessing a dangerous potential. Hannah is frightened and exhilarated. Finally, a reaction. Even if it is to banish me, at last you are looking at me.

She wants him to kiss her, to take her to bed, but he takes her wrist and squeezes it. He raises his other hand and Hannah turns her face and closes her eyes.

I need, Daniel says, and his voice is uncompromising, to be on my own for a while. I need, he says, a break from all of this.

Are you going?

I'm not going, you're going.

I'm going?

Daniel lets go of her wrist and walks out of the kitchen. Hannah hears the front door close and slides down the wall. She wishes he had hit her. Anything to collide with his body. But he doesn't even want that kind of contact.

Hannah knows what he is asking her to do. She must go, like a wayward child to a boarding school, to her parents' place in Toronto. They have already talked about it. The only real option. The only one they can afford.

He's not being violent with you, is he? Hannah's mother asks.

No, Hannah says, sobbing down the phone.

Well, you know you're always welcome to come and stay with us for as long as you need to.

Thank you, Hannah says, and so they make arrangements. They cobble together the air miles.

*

At the airport, Hannah feels the helplessness of an imminent loss she can't prevent. I don't want to go, she says. I don't know anybody in Toronto. I'll be lonely without you.

I'll give you Matt Riley's number, Daniel says, kissing and stroking her head. I went to university with him. He lives in Toronto. You'll like him.

Oh, Daniel.

It's time to go, Hannah.

I can't do this any more.

Call me when you get there.

21

Essential differences

As soon as Hannah walks into her parents' home in Toronto, it feels like a giant step backwards. A failure to progress. She misses her London life. The familiarity of Daniel's presence. Even their cramped one-bedroom flat. She calls him every day and cries with missing him.

I find this so confusing, he says.

I know you do, she says, leaning her forehead against the sliding glass doors in her mother's kitchen. It is the end of summer and there is a blue jay on the lawn and a fat black squirrel running along the fence. I'm sorry, Hannah says. I don't know what's wrong with me. I just feel so heavy.

I read an essay today by Susan Sontag, Daniel says, about the films of Bresson. She talks about the difference between grace and gravitas. That too much seriousness stamps out the possibility for grace. You used to have so much grace, Hannah, when I first met you. You've got to work out how to invite a playful levity back into your life.

But how? Hannah asks.

Work, Daniel says. Be productive. Why don't you get back to your novel?

I'm so much happier when I write, Hannah says. It puts everything into perspective.

So do it then, he says emphatically.

But I can't, she says.

Why not?

I dunno.

Write one paragraph, he says. Just one.

Hannah's mother appears in the doorway of the spare bedroom. She's doing her best to ignore a fear of her daughter's rejection, but she's tentative, a little nervous. She can sense that something's wrong. Her daughter isn't happy. She wants to help but her most trusted palliative is faith in God. She's already tried that one with Hannah and it didn't work, but it's been a while. Years since she tried to foist Jesus.

What are you doing? she asks.

Nothing, Hannah says, sitting up in bed. She puts her notebook down. What?

I know you don't go to church any more, her mother says, leaning in the doorway. But your dad is giving the sermon tomorrow morning, and as the assistant pastor, he doesn't often get the chance, and he's such a wonderful speaker.

Why can't she, Hannah thinks, just tell me the reason she wants me to come is that she hates going to church alone. Hates the scrutiny of sitting by herself in a pew, in all that cavernous space. The surprising dearth of intimacy beyond the initial warm greeting at the door. I could sympathize with that.

I just thought that maybe you'd like to join me.

I'll think about it, Hannah says.

Her father comes to the door. Hello there, ladies.

Hi, Dad.

Does my married daughter want to accompany her old man on a jog?

What's that supposed to mean?

What's what supposed to mean? her father asks.

Your married daughter, Hannah repeats.

I just think it's a little funny having a married daughter back at home, he says.

Do you mind?

No, he says. I don't think so.

Well, let me know if it bothers you, Hannah says. She feels a sting behind her eyes. Her parents can make her cry so easily.

I didn't mean anything by it, he says, tying the waistband of his running shorts. Just thought you might like to come for a jog, that's all.

I'm working, Hannah says.

Okay, well, her dad says. See you later then.

I'm making a cup of tea, her mom says, and Hannah says, I'm fine, in such a way that it shuts down the conversation. So her mother smiles and nods and leaves gingerly, like she's pulling away from something explosive, and as soon as she's gone, Hannah regrets her defensiveness, yearns for something intimate.

Hannah picks up the phone and calls Daniel's friend, Matt Riley. I'm Daniel's wife, she says into the receiver.

No way! Matt yells. I'm so glad you called. How is the old sonovabitch, anyways?

They meet up for a drink and Matt Riley tells her how he and Daniel used to get drunk every day in the student pub when they were at university. How much he loves the English, but can't handle the booze.

I know what you mean, Hannah says. They never socialize without it.

Neither do I. I just socialize a lot less.

Matt is teaching at a high school, doing guidance counselling part-time. First week back on the job, he says, and today I listen to a gay kid tell me how he wants to commit suicide. I had to call a counsellor in another high school for guidance. I mean, I'm just doing this part-time because there's a shortage. I'm not even qualified. This other counsellor, now he's a real pro. He asked me if I had the list. What list? Apparently there's this list of things to look out for, so you can judge how serious the suicide threat actually is. This kid said he wanted to kill himself, but he hadn't planned how he was going to do it, or where. That put him at about a sixty-five percent rate of success. A hundred percent and you're lucky to be alive.

I feel lucky to be alive, Hannah says. And I guess about sixty-five percent married.

Daniel was saying you guys have your rough patches. He told me to watch it. He said it in a nice way.

The thing is, she says, and this is the most absurd irony of all, but marriage has given me the best excuse to say no. It's given me a licence to date, so to speak.

We're not dating.

I know. You're Daniel's friend. Don't worry, I've learned. I mean, I never used to kiss a guy without going all the way because I never had a good enough excuse or compelling reason not to.

You mean you couldn't think of one.

I mean, I really couldn't see the difference, and maybe it was a lack of self-worth, but I simply thought, why not? And more often than not, enjoyed the sex a lot less than the chase, but that's beside the point. Now when I want, I can kiss a man, grope him and be groped, and I don't even have to investigate my conscience.

Lucky for you.

All I have to say, repeatedly and in the heat of the moment is, no, no, no, we can't do this, I'm married, please stop, and so on. Until eventually we both roll over and look up at the ceiling, or separate in the back of a cab, him with his hard-on and me feeling smug.

Man, you're a piece of work.

It's just this sensation of having been desired and desiring someone else, and managing at the same time to feel completely unviolated and pure, much more pure than I ever felt when I was single, because I've been able to keep things on an innocent level.

Except nobody else would see it that way.

I know, I'm sure it's perversely inappropriate to feel so irreproachable at the moment of such moral impropriety, but that is the effect.

Hannah likes Matt Riley a lot. They get along well. She senses a flirtation, but decides she needs friendship now more than she needs a fling. And this act of decisive negation gives her a whole new thrill. It liberates her conscience and puts her at ease. They play pool, then take a cab back to Matt's place. He lives in the basement of his grandfather's house, with a tank full of tropical fish and a big fat, moth-grey cat.

I've got beer in the fridge, he says, and a bottle of Glenfiddich.

They go outside to smoke a joint and Matt pukes off his grandfather's porch. He offers to share his double bed and Hannah declines. She crashes on the sofa with her hands under her head. I've just declined the offer of a bed, she thinks.

Matt calls to tell Hannah about a reading she might enjoy. His friend Stan Carver is reading with Norman Peach. Stan's a laugh, he says.

I think I'll pass, she says.

Look, Daniel said you haven't been out of the house at all. At all, he said. Come on, it's Toronto nightlife.

Okay, okay. Hannah gets ready and as she's pulling on her black tights, she feels that familiar buzz of anticipation fluttering at the periphery of her thoughts.

Walking along Queen Street with Matt Riley, Hannah thinks Toronto looks like a built-up gold-rush town. There are second-hand stores selling old suede jackets, cowboy taverns and faux English pubs and weeds growing out of the sidewalk. It's as if, she says, the city's only recently been laid down.

It's a thin veneer of civilization, Matt Riley agrees. It's so relatively young, untamed nature can still be seen pushing up through its foundation. Beside a solid, red brick Victorian house, a lopsided timber shack. The eclectic style, the anarchic distribution of Toronto's buildings, suggests there was no grand design. Just random development.

It's so different, Hannah says, from London.

Yeah, well, London's got architecture. It's got authority. London's a city that sits thick on the earth.

The reading is well attended. The back room at the Rivoli is crowded and dark. But it is not what Hannah had expected. I

used to go, she says, to these sixties-style coffeehouse read-
ings in Montreal.

Matt looks around. There are a few women here tonight, he
says, whose fashion sense could rival the best of them in
London.

You're right. There's a whole new level of urban sophisti-
cation.

Rather, he says, taking a swig of beer and lighting up a
cigarette.

A woman in a green dress and fishnet stockings taps at a
microphone on stage. Can you hear me? she says and people
begin to sit down, or turn their chairs to face the front.
Norman Peach is first to read and he reads from a book of
short stories set in his hometown of St John's. His writing is
intelligent and insightful. Rare in its quality. Confessional
without being cloying. And it is full of humour. He's good,
Hannah says. I'm surprised.

Didn't you know we had writers of this calibre in the
colonies?

She laughs. I used to think I came from a glorified truck
stop culture. But now –

We've come a long way, baby.

Then Stan Carver gets up to read. He is part Mohawk and
pure cowboy, he has sharp angles to his face and sideburns.
He is reading from his novel about an ex-con busking his way
across the Yukon with a banjo inlaid with mother-of-pearl
and a stray mutt called Jango. Hannah laughs out loud three
times and when Matt introduces him later, Hannah thinks, I
like how cocky he is, because she knows how often this is the
belligerent side of a reluctant sensitivity.

Stan is ranting against the cult of Margaret Atwood and
this amuses Hannah. She keeps trying to interrupt him, but
he's holding court. At one point she finds herself leaning
across a crowded table, pounding her fist and screaming,
You're just a wind-up mouse!

This makes him stop for a moment and give her a look and

212

then she knows his whole tough-guy act is just a front, that he probably takes off his sideburns every night before getting into bed, and puts them in a little box on top of his dresser, after taking off his cowboy boots and blue jeans.

I don't think we've been introduced, Norman says, squeezing in beside Matt and leaning towards Hannah. I'm Norm Peach.

And I'm Hannah Crowe, she says, and gives him her hand. There is something about how close he dares to hold himself that makes Hannah feel weak. It's so invasive.

Don't mind him, Norm says of Stan. He's just trying to impress you. But it makes it hard for the rest of us to get a word in edgewise.

I miss this breed of Canadian men, Hannah tells Matt. The beautiful struggle between their sensitivity and their machismo.

The beautiful struggle, Matt says, to choose between their wives and the rest of Toronto's women.

The next time Hannah talks to Daniel she wants to tell him what a good time she's having. I didn't realize how much I missed Canada. I wish you could be here with me. Matt is great, she says. You were right about him. I wish you could see what it is I love about this country. The leaves are changing colour and the air is so crisp.

Great, Daniel says. But he sounds distracted and aloof.

What's wrong, babe?

I have something to tell you, he says, and Hannah is gripped with panic, claws digging into her stomach.

I don't know how to put this, he says.

What is it?

I sort of, Daniel says. Last night. I spent the night with someone.

Oh, my God, Hannah says, gasping for breath. She doesn't know what to say. Do I know her?

No, you don't.

213

And then she starts to laugh, her laughter spilling over with relief, the gratitude of a misery that finds company, of guilt upon discovering that it is not alone. And then Daniel laughs too. And they laugh for a very long time. At what they cannot understand. At what they are unable to control.

At dinner the following evening, Hannah's parents announce that they are moving again.

Jesus, Hannah thinks.

To Victoria, her father says. And hopefully, this'll be the last move.

We want to be closer to Connie and the kids, her mother says.

We want the opportunity to enjoy being grandparents, her father says.

Maybe one day, her mother says, you and Daniel might.

Might what?

Think of moving out there too.

Hannah nods. Maybe, she says. And though the thought of living near her family stifles her, she feels a little deserted too.

After dinner, she gives Louise a call in Montreal. It's been such a long time and it's so good to hear her voice.

And how are you? Louise asks.

Lonely, Hannah says. Nothing's changed. And I just met these two guys the other night. If either one of them had asked, I would've gone home with him.

Why didn't they?

Oh, a girlfriend. The other one's married. But I'm glad nothing happened. Who needs another drunken one-night stand?

And being ignored and feeling used.

Yeah, trying to pretend that you aren't emotionally attached. Listen to me, I'm already in mourning and nothing even happened.

You like men, Hannah.

I like the warmth of an evening.

That's the thing that men don't understand, Louise says.

Women are propelled by their hearts. They don't fuck around without entertaining the possibility of at least falling a little bit in love.

Is it cynicism? Do you think there are essential differences?

Absolutely, Louise says. Look, men are interesting because they do interesting things. A woman is interesting simply by virtue of being interesting. Do you know what I mean?

Not really.

Women draw from an internal source, whereas men draw from things outside themselves. You gotta read your John Berger.

I feel oppressed by my internal source.

What does Daniel think about this?

I don't know, Lou. I'm so sick of talking about it. We've analysed our feelings to death and it isn't any clearer.

Sometimes I think, when you get to the over-analysing phase, it's already too late.

What do you mean?

I mean, the constant evaluation is a sign of too much dissatisfaction.

But everybody feels dissatisfied.

Not as much as you. Not in the last couple of years.

Really?

You're always complaining to me.

Am I?

The problem is, Louise says, her voice soothing, nobody wants to be alone. You make a compromise to be with someone because you don't know any better. It might not be perfect, but it's better than anything you've had, and you do it because there's no guarantee that something better's gonna come along. So you enter into this thing and maybe it doesn't make you happy. You want to get out, but it's hard to extricate yourself. It's hard when you've got integrity. You, for instance, are much more caring than you give yourself credit for. You don't want to hurt Daniel so you disregard the pain you're causing yourself. The thing is this. Love is rare. Much rarer than we think. I don't think you've ever really had it. You'd be sure if you had. I mean, you'll be so sure when you do. Wait for it, Hannah. I wish somebody had told me that.

Wait for it.

When Martin and I split up and I came back here, I realized I couldn't live without him. I didn't have the strength. And maybe I'm weak because of it. But you've always been more independent than me. Whenever you spend time away from Daniel, it doesn't seem to confirm anything, it just confuses you more. I don't think you should keep ignoring the signs.

But I don't think I have the ability to leave him, Hannah says.

Are you in love with him?

I don't know, she whispers. I just can't give up like that.

But he's not enjoying this any more than you are.

But we were gonna have a baby, Hannah says.

Children have never improved a bad relationship. You have to be a hundred percent sure about that one, no fucking around. Trust me, I know.

What are you saying?

Oh, nothing.

You're not pregnant are you?

I dunno if this is something you want to hear right now.

Fuck that.

It's only been two months.

Oh, my God, Hannah says. I've got goosebumps on my arms. Oh, Lou, she says. I love you.

22

The opposite of love

When Hannah returns to London, she has a new decisive-ness. She flies back to London tired of the hypocrisy of her situation and determined to split up with Daniel. It is her twenty-eighth birthday and Daniel takes her to their favourite restaurant the day after she gets back. Hannah thinks it might be a good time to broach the subject of a sepa-ration, but when they get to the restaurant, the first person she sees is Peter Straun, sitting at the end of a long table, read-ing a menu. He looks up and smiles. Hannah thinks, he must be in from Berlin. But why didn't he call? He must be here on the sly. Some illicit affair with a woman in Camberwell. What a lying bastard. But then Hannah sees Eddie Webb and Ursula Bishop and Ingmar and George Tuff even, with his new girlfriend, Beth. And they're all looking at her with these irrepressible grins, and then slowly it dawns on her.

Is this for me? she asks, turning to Daniel with all the pure delight of a child, tears loosening in her eyes. This is, she says, the nicest thing that anyone has ever done for me. And for the first time since she can remember, Hannah really feels as if she belongs somewhere.

And just when I am about to leave.

That night she gets drunk as an act of gratitude. Things get rowdy. Hannah flashes her tits at the waiter and Ingmar stands up and puts his testicles on a plate. The restaurant is agog with noise. Ursula is sitting across from Hannah. At one point she slaps Hannah on the back of the hand and says, Did you hear the latest?

No, what?

Ursula nods in George's direction. George and Beth are getting married.

George is getting married? Hannah shouts.

You didn't know?

I've been away.

Yeah, yeah, they're going to tie the knot.

Hannah turns to look at George and his fiancée at the other end of the table. Wow, she says.

Have you ever met his parents? Ursula asks.

Hannah shakes her head.

They're very straight-laced, she says. Very middle class. Last week, George took them to meet Beth's parents. A meeting of the in-laws. Apparently Beth's father is a loose cannon, bit of a liability, if you know what I mean, and he likes his lager.

Ursula is pitched forward, a hand on her chest. Hannah is frozen in anticipation. She's forgotten what a good storyteller Ursula is.

Well! By the end of the evening, he had them all outside in the backyard, with a javelin.

A javelin! Hannah shouts. Who owns a javelin?

Aluminium alloy, Olympic-standard javelin.

You might expect a round of croquet.

He said: before you leave, who can hit the bin bag at the bottom of the garden?

Can you imagine?

And George used to think my parents were hard work, Ursula says, leaning sideways in her chair, weak with amusement.

When the restaurant closes, Daniel leads the party, winding like the body of a snake, down to the Lemon Grove, a Camberwell nightclub. He is unaware at the time that it is lesbian night and as soon as the friends walk in, they all hit the dance floor. Unruly bunch of heteros (bar Eddie, who at this point is too inebriated to dance), brash with a sense of their own entitlement, they are completely insensitive to the atmosphere that may have proceeded them or indeed, the steely resentment over their intrusion. After a few exhilarating dances under the disco lights, Hannah walks off to the loo and strikes up a conversation with a buxom Jamaican woman waiting in line ahead of her. After a while, a thin sallow woman comes out of the stalls and makes straight for Hannah, grabs her face and smashes her head into the wall and walks out.

What'd she do that for? Hannah says, rubbing the back of her skull.

Just ignore her, luv, the woman says, pulling Hannah towards her. I take it you're not one of us?

I've had some experience, Hannah says, her words muffled in the woman's large consoling breasts.

I guess she didn't like what you were saying, the woman says.

But it's my birthday, Hannah says.

Happy birthday, sweetheart, she says, stroking Hannah's hair.

At which point Ursula walks in to find Hannah with her head on this woman's ample bosom.

It's not uncommon to find you in a compromising position, Ursula says, but could you tell me what's going on in here? Hannah launches into a vivid description of her assault and they both storm out, round up the rest of the group and, announcing that Hannah's been attacked, exit the nightclub with all the camaraderie of a chorus line.

In the morning, neither Hannah nor Daniel has the heart to talk things over. She says, When you spent the night. With that woman. Did you spend it here?

Are you crazy, Hannah?

So you went to her place? Who was she, anyways?

It was a woman I met at the Everyman. It was nothing, Daniel says. I mean, it is nothing.

Somehow it's never the right time. A few days go by and they resume their domestic routine. It is autumn and the impulse is to hunker down. A few weeks pass and it's as if Hannah never left. They've been together for nearly three years now. It seems like an immeasurably long time, but when Hannah tries to pin it down it escapes her. She can't conceive of her life with Daniel as a sequence of events, with a beginning, middle and an end. Some things in the past are so vivid in their proximity, while so many things have been forgotten.

All Hannah knows is that she is being borne down a river on a raft. She is never anywhere but on the raft, so she cannot gain perspective. She has only the present moment in which to live, to feel. And nothing seems to accumulate. Things either approach or they retreat, but they do not accrue.

On the sofa one afternoon, Hannah cries after watching *Death in Venice*. Daniel strokes her hair and says sincerely, You are the source of all my joys and all my sorrows.

Hannah is struck by the depth and breadth of this sentiment, the position of central importance it gives her in his life, which she hasn't felt for so long. She feels an overwhelming gratitude that she can't convey. It suggests that Daniel still loves her. But it's a love she wants to shrink from because of the work that it implies, the effort it would take to rekindle it. But how can I have gone so long feeling only his indifference? And where have the last few months gone anyways? What happened to my resolve? My determination to bring this agonizing purgatory to an end?

Instead of coming to a decision, Hannah and Daniel have sunk to the level of somnambulance. They are going through the motions unaware of how precious a commodity is time. They are knee-deep in the warm, thick mud of habit.

But where could she go? Hannah was broke when she got back from Toronto. She could never afford her own place in London and she's been living off her credit card for months. Standing in line at the ticket counter at the Oval tube station, Hannah realizes she must be the only person in London who pays for a single ticket with a Visa card. Then one day, the rumours are confirmed. The Everyman is closing down. In one month, Daniel will be out of a job. It is time now, Hannah thinks, to go out and get a full-time job.

So this is where they're at. Christmas comes and goes. Then New Year. Hannah calls her temping agency and starts work as a receptionist for a law firm in the City. Daniel finds a new job reading film scripts for a Soho production company. They are still hard up. Still have separate bank accounts. Still linger in the flat, with their wish lists pinned to their sleeves like convict numbers, unable to leave.

But when should a person leave? When does the hard work of being together equal too much hard work? Can someone please help me here, because I really don't know what I'm doing.

Stay until you can't stay any longer, Hannah.

Stay until you can't not leave.

Absolved of the responsibility of filling her time, Hannah finds contentment in the mindless days at work. The lawyers are patronizing, her colleagues, mainly women without career ambitions, overly chummy. But once she gets the switchboard down, Hannah likes to answer the phone. She gets a rise of satisfaction from putting a caller through to the proper extension in a clipped, efficient and courteous manner. She keeps a tidy desk. She is poorly paid.

Today, on the way to work, it felt like spring. There was a damp smell of earth in the air. White and purple crocuses sticking their fists out of the black dirt. The green asparagus tips of daffodils a cause for celebration. And so it is that two months into the job, and after some insistence on their part, Hannah accepts an invitation to go to the pub and have a drink with the other receptionists and secretaries of the firm. She feels a scant affinity with most of them, but is pleasantly surprised when one of her colleagues, a quiet, middle-aged man, admits to being an ex-Catholic priest.

Defrocked, he says, is the proper term.

After a brisk first pint, Hannah confesses that she's been stealing cutlery from the kitchen at work, solid silver-plated forks and knives. I almost have a complete set of six, she says.

Better quality than I could ever afford, and I figure it's fair enough. Do you know that after thirty-five hours a week, I only come away with a hundred and eighty pounds after tax?

When you steal from an employer to compensate yourself for what you feel is inadequate pay, the ex-priest says, it's called occult compensation. If you went to a bona fide priest with that confession, he'd have to give you the corresponding penance for that sin.

How do you know what penance to give? Hannah asks.

Oh, there's a list, he says.

A list of sins?

A veritable directory, he says. And it's very long and very detailed and very medieval. Pretty much any sin you could possibly think of is itemized and categorized. It's all very bloodless and cerebral. I couldn't hack it. And besides, he says, lowering his voice, I fell in love with a fellow seminarian.

It is 10:30 when Hannah takes her leave and 11:00 when she's sitting on the bus for Camberwell. After four pints of lager, she is buzzing with energy and the idea of home feels claustrophobic. She decides on a whim to pop into the Hermit's Cave for one last drink before going home. She orders a beer and stands in the crowd for a while. She watches two young men in the corner, heads coming together occasionally to talk, but otherwise just looking around, scoping the joint. One of them has blond curly hair and olive skin. He looks Greek and Hannah feels an attraction for him that is almost maternal. She would like to run her fingers through his hair.

She walks over and shouts above the noise, Are you two alone?

They nod and introduce themselves. They need to get close to talk and the conversation is tactile. At one point, Hannah tosses her head back to laugh, showing off her long white throat, and then she says to the man with the golden curls, You're very beautiful, you know that?

They buy two more rounds before the place closes. Hannah is feeling expansive, unable to shrink back down to size. She

222

is as big as a flying saucer and full of light. She would like to descend and squat on the city, suck all the people into her shiny chromium belly. She doesn't want to go home. She wants to glide through the air, feel it push against her skin. Her cheeks are burning and the air is cold. She wants to hold herself open to it, let it stream around her. She wants the cold air to fuck her hot body. Knock her down and nail her to the ground.

She kisses the two young men – mwah, mwah – and says, You guys are so cute, you really are. Ciao! And then she sways forward into the street, her feet dragging behind, rushing to catch up with her massive floating head.

As she's moving down the street, something catches her eye. The door to the Nigerian nightclub is wide open and she can see the bar inside, an orange glow. There is a rhythm coming from within, a luring calypso beat, so Hannah walks through the door and goes up to the bar. She is the only white woman in the place and a few people turn to look.

You looking for someone? the barmaid asks in a foreign accent.

No, Hannah says. Just wanted a drink.

You sure 'bout that?

Hannah nods, eyelids heavy.

Whatchya want?

Rum and coke, please.

Okay, girl. Have it your way.

Hannah turns around and leans her back against the bar and feels the urge to dance. Shake that spirit free from her body. She closes her eyes and feels the music in her lungs.

You planning on drinking that alone? a man asks her.

Hannah opens her eyes. The man is her height, with a heavy build and a handsome, round face and close-shaved head. He is wearing a brown suit and a crisp white shirt.

Not any more, she says, and they have a drink. Let's dance, he says and while she's thinking how wonderful it is to dance with a man who really knows how to move, she notices that the two young men she met earlier are sitting in the corner. They nod and she can't help but feel they have followed her in to keep an eye on her.

Hannah and the man in the brown suit dance until they're breathless and sweaty and then he takes her up a short flight of stairs to another level. Hey Julian, he says. Hey, Carmela. He introduces Hannah to a handsome couple in matching Hermès outfits. They look like Louis Vitton suitcases sitting side by side, like they're going on a trip.

Pleasure to meet you, Julian says, extending his hand. He's wearing a gold ring and a gold watch, half tucked under the cuff of a light pink shirt. I was just telling Carmela here how I had the rare privilege today of seeing, in a private collection, an early self-portrait by Giacometti. It was beautifully rendered in the style of the Impressionists.

Really? Hannah asks.

Carmela says, He's always talking Giacometti.

His later portraits are less representational, more psychoanalytic. But oh, they're not nearly as pretty as the one I saw today.

Julian looks at Carmela. And I thought what a shame it was that he abandoned the beautiful style he had when he was young.

He'd never have become famous, Carmela says, if he'd continued painting that way, Jules.

You've got to be innovative, Hannah's man says.

Or else the people get bored, Carmela says, looking at Hannah. Wouldn't you agree?

I think that's a very interesting question, Hannah says, leaning forward and knocking her rum and coke into Carmela's upholstered lap.

Oh, my God, Hannah says. I'm so sorry. I can't believe I just did that, she says, going to wipe the woman's skirt and then realizing it might be overly familiar.

It's fine, Carmela says in a tone that suggests it isn't. Get me some soda water, she barks at the waitress.

Hannah sighs and raises her eyebrows and says, I'll get my coat.

But the man in the brown suit says, Come with me.

Hannah follows him through a door in a wall like the entrance to Anne Frank's secret hideaway, and up a flight of stairs connecting this building to the one next door. Walls have been torn down and there are four different stairwells going off in separate directions. Hannah follows the man down a narrow hallway and into an apartment that has a lonely feel to it. Through an open door, Hannah can see a boy asleep in a king-sized bed under a zebra print duvet. Then she's in a room with black leather sofas and girlie posters on the wall. On the far side of the room is a stack of hi-fi equipment, decks and mixers and six-foot tall speakers. There's a hatch through to a kitchen with liquor bottles on the counter. She can smell fried chicken coming from the fast food restaurant below.

You want something to drink?

Hannah shakes her head.

Have a seat, the man says and comes over and sits down beside her. He puts his hand on her thigh and pushes her skirt up a little. Hannah takes a deep breath. The man leans forward and she leans back. He puts a hand behind her head and covers her mouth with his. His tongue darts in, eager to penetrate. She pushes him away.

What's the matter?

Look, Hannah says.

Don't you like me? he asks, nuzzling her neck and putting his hand under her shirt. He slides his hand up to her collarbone, and then the man in the brown suit puts his hand on her breast. His hand is warm and dry and feels so good on her skin that Hannah relents a little. Then he squeezes her nipple. That feels good too. He yanks her by the hips towards him, pulling her down on the sofa and kissing her again. Hannah can feel her pelvis widen, flatten out, the pressure rising and pushing her groin forward, gravitating towards some sexual release.

If she just closes her eyes and imagines it's somebody else. Lyle, for instance. But she loses patience with the thought of him. She can't do it. Look, she says again, this time more forcefully.

Is it money you want? the man asks. You need some money? I know how hard it can be. I could get you a mobile. If you needed to reach me, any time. You need clothes? I could get you some clothes.

And his questions take her back to another time.

When she was young. Just fifteen years old.

She'd been panhandling after school for a dime bag of pot. She was with Louise. They had come up with a story. They needed a certain amount of money to get the bus back to Ottawa. They met a man who said he could give them the full amount, only he had to go back to his place for the money. When they got to his apartment, they could see he had a lot of coke paraphernalia on the table. He asked them if they wanted to smoke.

They said, Sure.

They got high and he asked them if they wanted to go to a salsa club.

Okay, they said again. Why not?

Then he said, It's a formal place, and opened his closet. It was full of designer women's clothing, all brand new, still in their plastic wrapping.

Sometimes my clients pay me in clothes, he said. Choose anything you want to wear.

Hannah chose a black leather skirt and a silver top with sequins. She can't remember what Lou wore. Then they went to the club, one on either side of the dealer. He didn't order individual drinks but bought a whole bottle of whiskey, which they drank neat. There were lots of other men there. They kept coming up and giving Hannah and Louise little white envelopes full of powder to snort in the bathroom. Hannah got so high, she felt delirious. She couldn't remember ever having been paid this much attention to. It all felt so loving.

She just kept spinning around on the dance floor, laughing with all the men and being passed around, until the dealer grabbed her by the arm and said, You're with me tonight. As if he owned her. Stop looking at all the other men, he hissed.

Hannah remembers being frightened by his reaction, but also indignant at having her freedom restricted. She flashed him an angry look that he seemed to find erotic. She realized she liked to feel his power too. It was this power that she expected to find in men. Something she would hunt for all her life. Something to challenge her own strength and fearlessness.

And then, hours later, Hannah found herself alone, back at the dealer's place. He took her into the bathroom and started undressing her. He ran the hot water and they fooled around in their clothes. He bent her over the bathtub and licked her cunt.

She'd never been licked there before.

They got wet in their clothes and she worried about ruining the leather. They did sixty-nine on the floor and, numb from the coke, all she could do was marvel at the flat fillet of skin between his testicles and his anus. She was fifteen years old and she'd never seen that before.

When he fucked her, she didn't feel much. It was probably the coke, but she didn't know for sure because it was only her second time. It hurt a little too. But if she closed her eyes, the pain was satisfying, in a punishing, debasing, comforting sort of way.

This was also something she would seek out in her life.

Look, Hannah says, pushing the man in the brown suit away from her. That's enough.

What's the matter, babydoll? he asks, taking hold of her and exerting force.

I gotta go, she says, sobering a little from the pressure of his hands on her body. Suddenly, the danger of her situation launches itself in her mind like a ship on a slipway. Daniel doesn't know where I am. I'm drunk in a room above a bar, with blacked-out windows and a widescreen TV and I'm all alone. With a man I don't know. Who is stronger than me.

What the fuck are you doing here, Hannah? How the hell do you keep getting yourself into these situations? And it hits her like a hammer. I can't bear to be like this any more. The thrill isn't worth the weight of shame.

I'm serious, she says, as the man pulls her down, fumbling to undo his pants with one hand. Stop it, Hannah says, trying to sound casual, but her voice is falsetto with fear.

What did you think we were going to do? he asks.

I dunno, she says. I wasn't thinking. Look, it's been great, but I gotta get home. My boyfriend's waiting for me, she says, wondering about her reluctance to reveal her married status, even to this guy.

So you have a boyfriend, he says. That's okay by me.

Well, it's not okay by me, Hannah says, and yanks her arm away from him. She falls off the sofa and crawls a few paces along the floor, then gets up and runs down the hall.

The man has the handicap of a hard-on and can't follow her immediately. Hannah goes downstairs and grabs her coat and leaves, noticing that the two young men from the Hermit's Cave are no longer there.

As she's walking down the street, the man in the brown suit comes running after her. You want me to walk you home?

No.

You need anything? he asks, catching up with her.

No, she says, standing still. I'm fine, thank you.

Here's my business card, he says. You call me, any time.

Okay, she says. Goodnight.

Are you going to call me?

Hannah nods with her eyes closed.

Promise?

Sure, she says. I promise.

Hannah walks down the silent corridor of the office building where she's been working as a receptionist. Past the empty meeting rooms to the kitchen at the end of the hall. She takes a bottle of wine from a case in the cupboard reserved for receptions (not receptionists), and puts it in her handbag. She finds two plastic champagne flutes with screw-on stems and puts those in her bag as well. She has handed in her notice.

On the way back to her desk, Hannah goes into a meeting room and listens to the white noise of the ventilation system. She stands at the window overlooking the City and feels the sun on her face. She can smell the warm leather off the high-backed, well-padded swivel chairs. She can see St Paul's copper green dome, grey stone carved in patterns like dirty old-fashioned lace. She will miss this view. The jagged angles of a London skyline. So busy the eye has to flatten them. Like the view along the Thames that she found so disappointing at first, so void of the sweeping vertical gestures of North American skyscrapers, but which she loves now for its clutter. The furious detail behind an apparent uniformity.

Promptly at six o'clock she gets a call from the security guard downstairs. Daniel is waiting for her. She'll be right down.

They kiss a greeting and walk outside. Daniel offers her his arm, in a gentlemanly fashion, and Hannah takes hold of it, curling her fingers around the inside of his elbow. They often walk like this. In the summer months, when his arms are bare, she loves how soft his skin feels.

So where are we going? Daniel asks.

I dunno, Hannah says, but I'd just like to wander until we find a good spot. I've got a bottle of wine and my Swiss army corkscrew.

They have a party to go to at nine. Two hours to kill and it's a sunny evening in early May. The air is cool, but there are patches of warmth if you keep out of the shade.

They stroll for twenty minutes, aimlessly. Hannah is improvising, following her nose. They weave through crowds of men in suits, women in high heels, wearing shiny flesh-coloured nylons.

What about right here? Daniel says, pointing to a bench on a small patch of grass next to a roundabout.

No, Hannah says. We can find a better place than that.

But you have no idea where we're going, he says. We're meandering.

Just trust me for a little while, okay? she says, wishing he would be more patient but not wanting to start an argument. Hannah has faith in the existence of a spot cut out for this excursion, one destined for the moment. If only he would give her time to find it.

Another fifteen minutes and Daniel starts to sigh. He hates the lack of planning and direction. I find, he says, this exploration of the interminable present tedious and misplaced.

He's not thinking about faith. This is not a matter of destiny. It's a question of expediency.

Just give me five more minutes, Hannah says, stubborn in her optimism but strangely sanguine, and then they come upon a pretty little square. Backyard to three council estates, secluded and quiet, with the wide green umbrella of a chestnut tree in the middle, and children playing with a dog in a fenced-off playground, with brightly painted metal shapes to climb all over. Ta-da. She smiles at Daniel and he concedes the victory.

They sit down on a bench and Hannah says, Wouldn't that be a great place to live? pointing to a two-storey coach house converted into studios with tall windows, wooden beams, brick walls.

You always say that, Daniel says, and Hannah shrugs. Whenever we aren't in Camberwell.

I've said it about places in Camberwell too. She hands him the bottle and the corkscrew. When Daniel looks up again, she's beaming at him, holding out the plastic flutes. Bet you weren't expecting a glass.

Daniel pours the wine and they tap glasses and drink. Daniel sighs deeply. They lean back together to take in the pretty picture of their little park. Daniel says, You were right to wait. I didn't think we'd find a spot like this.

It's great, isn't it? she says. London is full of these secret oasises.

Oases, he corrects.

Whatever, she says, and watches the children in the park, playing with their little white dog. That dog sounds like a box of matches, Hannah says as the children chase it between the monkey bars, between the chains the swings hang from. It runs, Daniel says, like a Kleenex box on wheels.

They drink more wine and Daniel talks excitedly about a film script he just read and Hannah thinks how smart he is. So much smarter than she is. He's wearing the black turtleneck sweater that she likes because it strengthens his jawline. And his hair is messy, giving him a boyish, mischievous look. She can see why she fell in love with him. Could still be in love with him for all she knows. If she knew anything at all any more. She feels a deep bond, a true respect, and an intimate knowledge of his habits and his quirks. She wants their marriage to work. At least, she thinks she wants it to work, and yet she feels defeated by the stagnancy of the last few years. The lack of change or any movement away or towards a mere conviction. Even a soft conviction would do. Anything. Just something to say, I'm sure about this. This is what I want.

I'm gonna go away, Hannah says.

I know, he says.

And it's gonna be different this time, she says.

I know.

I'm gonna pack up all my stuff as if I'm leaving for good, and leave it in the hall until we decide what to do.

It's a good idea. We need to make up our minds. We've been living in limbo for too long and it hasn't been good for either of us.

But I don't want to go, Daniel, if it means it's over in your mind. I mean, you're not decided, right?

I don't know how I'm going to feel when you're gone.

Because if you know it's over, then I'm not going. I mean that. I don't want to be six thousand miles away with all my stuff in boxes and be told it's over and have no recourse. I don't want to be in another country when you say it's over.

I don't know what I'm going to say, he says.

But you will in six months' time.

That's what we've agreed to.

And you honestly don't have an inkling what your answer's gonna be?

No, he says. I haven't a clue. Do you?

Hannah shakes her head. Her eyes well up with tears. She looks away. At the children playing in the park. She takes another sip of wine. Holds it in. The whole world inside her ribs.

I just feel so split, Hannah says. Straight down the middle.

Me too, Daniel says.

And I don't know if that's enough.

Me neither.

But I love you, Daniel, I really do.

I love you too, Hannah, and that's not going to change. We're just trying to work out whether we should be married, that's all. And we've tried so many ways to work it out that I don't think we're going to know until we simulate a separation. And not just another temporary one. A real one this time. We need to create the illusion of permanence.

What's permanent? Hannah thinks and at that moment the dog escapes from the playground, someone yells, Dog's a fucking cunt! and the children go running after it in a long line around the tree and stream out the other end of the park like the tail of a kite.

Daniel says, I don't think you ever really believed that I loved you.

Perhaps I doubted it too much.

Daniel puts his hand on Hannah's head and strokes her hair.

Did I hurt you much? she asks, turning to look into his dark blue eyes. I was never sure when you were hurt.

I held stuff back, Daniel says.

Why?

Because you were the one who always seemed to be having such a hard time of it all.

232

Did I hog the hurting? Hannah asks.

You know that night you kissed the movie critic? Daniel says. When I left the party early on account of a hangover?

Hannah nods.

That night, when I got back to Camberwell, I bought a falafel and ate it in the park. I sat on a bench and ate the whole thing by myself and I thought, what am I doing here? Why am I sitting here on my own? Why isn't Hannah here? Why didn't she leave the party and come home with me? I remember going up to you and telling you that I wanted to leave. I asked you if you wanted to go. You hardly looked at me. You were on such a roll. It was like you wanted to be anywhere except with me. It made me very sad. It hurt a lot. I felt very lonely then.

Oh, Daniel! Hannah cries. I didn't know you felt that way. Why didn't you tell me?

You seemed to be having such a wild time on your own.

But I was unhappy too.

It didn't seem important, Daniel says.

But I never knew, Hannah cries, if anything I did had any affect on you!

There was a lot of distance.

I thought we could handle things on our own.

We're very independent people.

But I'm not so sure about that any more, Hannah says. I used to think it was a weakness not to want to be alone. It was like nothing was ever supposed to take precedence over my individual plans. Plans for myself, my ambitions, my individuality.

Maybe we've both been guilty of too much independence. The opposite of love isn't hate, Daniel says, the opposite of love is individuality.

That's nice, Hannah says.

I read that in a letter Walker Percy wrote to Shelby Foote. It's a quote from D. H. Lawrence.

It's kind of devastating, Hannah says and thinks, what a long way we've come from the protection of two solitudes to arrive at this.

The opposite of love is individuality.

Babe? Hannah says.

Yes? Daniel says.

I wanted to cherish you and be so good to you. I wanted to be completely faithful to you and only ever be with you. I wanted my whole body to. I didn't want to belong to anybody else. But then I forgot. I lost track. I didn't care and it was such a desecration.

It wasn't just your fault, Daniel says. Nobody's to blame.

But look at what we risk to lose, Hannah says, the force of grief ripping through her.

And Daniel slumps under the weight of his own helplessness, and a tragic silence solidifies between them in place of what cannot be said, of what will not repair itself.

At Heathrow airport, Hannah is confused, trembling. She looks haggard, strained. Daniel stays with her while she checks her luggage in, and then it's time. Time to go through the metal detector, to say goodbye. She looks at him and is filled with fear, a hopelessness that knows no bounds.

I'm gonna miss you, she says. I don't know what I'm gonna do without you. Maybe we shouldn't split up, you know? If it's this difficult? Her eyes are wet, but she starts to giggle. She is helplessly hysterical.

It's the right thing to do, Daniel says, giggling too now, in the chaos of emotions. We have to do this.

Oh, that's right, Hannah says. I forgot. You're Mr Fucken Granite over here.

Careful, Daniel says, and they laugh at that old familiar phrase. They need the jokes to release the agony. They are both on the verge of weeping.

You know, I don't have to go, Hannah says, after a while. Just say the word and I'll stay.

You give me so much power, Daniel says, shaking his head.

But I don't want any power, Hannah says and starts to cry. She presses her face against Daniel's chest and sobs into his shirt. She breathes in all the warmth and comfort she can avail herself of in the final minute before she pushes herself off, wipes her face, looks into his eyes and says, Goodbye, sweetheart, I love you.

23

The wedding girl, part 2

Hannah stands at the stern of the ferry, crossing over to Vancouver Island, and leans against the railing. Feels the wind on her face. Breathes in the sea. Remembers this smell from when she was a kid. Distance unravels itself as the shoreline recedes, rising then flattening out, as it sinks into the horizon. The sky is a transparent blue, almost colourless. Seagulls caw and linger like gypsies, follow the ferry out into the open channel. Hannah looks down at the water churned out by the engine, mesmerized by the white foam folding in on itself like egg whites. A small killer whale appears, diving in and out of the boat's wake, massaging itself in the forceful stream of bubbles. She turns to an old man standing beside her and asks, Did you see that? What was that? Was that a baby killer whale?

He says, That's what it looked like. Never seen that before in my life. Not in all the time I've been taking this ferry.

Hannah is thrilled by nature, the fact that it hasn't gone away, that it's still here, despite how oblivious she's been to it, that it thrives in its own persistent way beyond the borders of the cities. She had forgotten there existed anything beyond the borders of the cities.

Hannah stares at the ferry's wake. A long white wedding veil trailing in the water.

Victoria is quaint. There are no two ways about it. Houses like gingerbread. Their gardens frothy with rhododendrons, lilac, heather and azaleas. Hannah's parents are away in Europe, so she weeds her mother's garden with the sun on her back. Pulls up dead roots, turns the soil, shakes it through a sieve to get the rocks out and empties three wheelbarrows of compost under a spruce hedge. Occasionally she stands up to stretch her back, looks east across the water at the snowcapped Rockies on the mainland, axe blades left out to rust through the winter, topped with snow.

They are ominous, foreboding, inhuman.

Hannah never did like the mountains. They make her feel hemmed in. Crushed. She can feel how cold they are.

Three weeks go by and except for visits from her sister Connie, Hannah is alone. She likes the solitude, the quiet, but not this limbo. This infernal uncertainty. She's tired of it now. She has no fight left in her. She watches her mother's garden bloom and wishes she had a home.

She goes out to buy Fig Newtons, soya milk, a piece of fish and pasta. On her way back, a crow swoops low over her head, rises and perches on a power line. It fixes her with one beady eye as she walks by twenty feet below.

As soon as she's forgotten, it happens again. Hannah can hear the brush of its wings as the crow glides up from behind and skims her head, stray hairs caught up in the swoosh. It perches on the power line again and fixes her with its black-currant stare. This happens two more times as she is walking home.

Are you my spirit guide? Hannah asks it. Returning to caw at me from the rooftops?

By the time Hannah reaches the driveway, she is frightened and mystified. She has never heard of anyone being stalked by a crow.

As she's digging for her house key, Hannah notices, with a start, that the crow is perched three feet away, on the slanted lintel over the front door. She gets inside, bolts the door and decides it isn't safe to leave the house.

Hannah calls Daniel on the phone. He sighs when he hears her voice and this makes her want to cry. There was a time,

237

she thinks, when Daniel would have been overjoyed to hear from me. But those days have passed. I've lost the sweet eagerness in his voice.

How are you? Hannah asks, a note of false cheer.

I'm great, Daniel says, and she nods into the phone.

I really miss you, she confesses, weak with her need of him.

I miss you too, he says. It's a flat, begrudging voice.

Where have you been? I didn't know where you were.

I went to see Peter.

Did you have a good time?

Yes, I had a great time. I'm really getting to know Berlin.

What did you do?

Oh, went to a few galleries, stayed out, played pool, got drunk.

Did you snog anyone? And as soon as Hannah asks, she knows that she's betrayed herself.

I don't really want to talk about this right now, Daniel says.

You don't want to feel accountable.

I'm not going to talk about it, he says.

Just tell me, okay? Hannah pleads. I won't be mad.

I don't think it's your place to ask me that any more.

What do you mean? We're still married, Daniel.

But we're separated.

Did you sleep with her?

I'm not answering that, Hannah.

You did, Hannah says, and an axe comes swinging down and hits her in the heart.

Look, we both agreed to this separation. You can't go back on your word just because you're finding it difficult.

But we're six thousand miles apart. I have no friends here. I'm a guest.

I'm enjoying having the flat to myself.

I'm sure you are.

I'm just getting on with my life here, he says. Living quietly, doing my own thing.

Every positive assertion feels like an indictment. Hidden

jubilation at her absence. I can't believe you slept with some-body else!

Please, Hannah.

It hasn't even been three weeks! And the shock of Daniel's attempt to make a clean break shudders through her with such brutality. How could you have been so stupid, Hannah? You loved him all along. How could you not have known? Why did you have to go and squander this?

I can't do this any more, he says.

I've never done that, you know? Hannah says, her voice feeble with anguish, but also indignant. Never fucked anyone in the three years that we were married.

Never gone all the way, you mean.

You're breaking my heart, Daniel. I can't breathe.

I hate to hear you like this, Hannah, but I can't handle this either.

Hannah isn't thinking any more. She's just feeling. And it's physical. Like a stroke. I'm gonna hang up now, she says, searching the room for the receiver. I can't hold the phone any more, she says, and everything looks foreign. What does a phone receiver look like? Is that it? No, there it is. The base. I'm gonna hang up now, she says and drags her hand down, guiding it with her other hand away from her ear.

Hannah!

Click.

Hannah lifts the phone and bangs it down again. Click, click, click. And then she contracts. Her whole being. From distant rooms in foreign cities, a double-decker bus, a balcony in Mexico, all her various selves come hurtling back to her in a reverse explosion, sucked back through a pinhole in her gut and in an instant the hole seals over and she's gone. That's it. There's nothing left. Just a question. And a cold tight blankness. An emptiness in which nothing seems to exist. Not even air.

I'm just gonna kneel down here on the kitchen floor where it's cool. Lie down, in fact. That's better. Put my cheek on the lino.

Hannah is lying on her stomach. Her hands are facing backwards, her knuckles are on the floor. Her back feels cold, like her clothes have been peeled back, stripped to the waist, and her back feels weighted, as if with stones. She thinks about how they used to crush a man with stones, and beneath the skin, the soft pink wings of her lungs struggle for breath as her ribs cave in.

I am so heavy. I don't think the floor can hold me up. No, I'm falling through the floor. I have lost everything. I am disappearing. There is nothing left.

So this is what it means to be prostrate with grief. Bereft.

24

Victoria

Two months go by and there is no word from Daniel. He won't answer her calls. He won't reply to her emails. Their friends are apologetic, but helpless. Hannah passes her days in a kind of numb trance. She goes for long walks through Victoria. At the age of twenty-eight, she finally takes driving lessons and aces her test. Her parents come back and she has a fight with her mother. She doesn't tell them what's going on.

Daniel's doing really well, she says. He's working for a production company in London. He sends his love.

She talks to her father about God, about his enduring romance with Christ. The words enduring and romance seem antithetical to her and her dad agrees. It is harder these days, he says, to sustain romance because it requires discipline, and we so often rush into commitment. We want immediate gratification and there is no courtship period to earn a person's love or prove its worth.

Her father is a big fan of the long engagement. Romance dies, he says, when you live in an age without restraint.

Hannah thinks that romance dies when the grass is always greener, in an age without constraint. When all you think about is yourself. When you find yourself at every juncture dogged by freedom and tempted by choice. As if one choice could be any different from the next. As if there existed, out there, a relationship that won't entail work and compromise and some sort of sacrifice. And all you have to do is find it.

As long as people believe that gratifying their own desires is making the best use of their individuality.

Because what you miss when you lose a partner is not so much their love of you, she thinks, but your ability to love them back. Being denied the privilege to love that person is like being taken prisoner. You look out through the bars of your damp cold cell that is always in the shade at a patch of sunlight on a square of green grass surrounded by yellow daffodils and you weep. You simply buckle at the knees and weep.

Hannah decides that if he still wants her, then she will go back to Daniel.

She will accept it as her lot. And all the things that irk her, she will pull like weeds. And all her inappropriate sexual cravings she will smother like unwanted kittens. She will not wield her sexuality as a means of satisfying her need for approval, but will devote herself to Daniel. She will be forgiving. Gentle and maternal and magnanimous. Look at him with only love, uncritical and passionate. She will nurture a monogamous, erotic appetite.

She will commit herself to commitment.

Because she's never really committed herself to anything. Never given up her precious independence for the good of something greater. And it's all she wants.

The self-erasure that comes with total commitment.

And right now, on this day, at this hour, it doesn't feel like a compromise but a relief. It is a relief to have made a decision, regardless of the outcome. Finally Hannah has a conviction and there is consolation in that, though who knows how long it will last.

Hannah gets a job as a cleaning lady. It's the only job she can get in Victoria which starts immediately and requires no qualifications and entails no social interaction. She gets paid in cash and is astounded by the filthy conditions people live in. She finds, in a ball of dust under a bed, a forgotten letter written by a teenage boy to his family. In it, he tells them he knows what a drain he is and that is why he's running away.

She is down on her knees one day, straddling a toilet, wiping the floor behind with a rag. The toilet feels cool, reliable, pressed up hard between her legs. She pulls herself closer to the toilet, her pelvis tensing against the smooth white porcelain. It's a surrender to the physical sensation of something touching her there. Then she laughs, thinking how far she's come.

So lonely I'm humping toilets now.

Six weeks go by like this. Hannah realizes that, according to the conditions of their so-called agreement, Daniel could take another two months to get in touch with her. She needs a plan for the future. And one that doesn't include living with her parents. This isn't doing my confidence any good, she thinks, and I need to get back on my own. A car, she thinks. I have nine hundred dollars in savings and that will buy me a second-hand 1986 Mercury Lynx. The engine's in good condition. No rust on the body. It's never left Victoria. She calls Matt Riley in Toronto. I'm looking for a job, she tells him.

The Toronto school board, he says, is always looking for substitute teachers. Let me talk to the principal at my high school and get back to you.

Hannah checks the internet for an apartment and finds a list of sublets on an artists' co-op website. Norman Peach's name comes up. Hannah remembers the reading a year ago. She'd read his book and loved it. That's a good omen. She emails him and asks if he remembers her.

Of course I do, he replies.

And this surprises her.

What are you doing in Victoria? he writes.

I'm cooking red snapper tacos and drinking a cold Corona. Is there parking with the flat?

There's room enough to swing a cat.

Hannah asks if he'll take a hundred dollars less a month than he's asking for and he says he'll have to think about it. Hannah realizes that she is flirting with him. I am supposed to be avoiding, she thinks, opportunities like this for the sake of commitment.

Norm writes back: You're lucky I have a good deal in St John's. It'll be spotless on the first of the month.

She asks him what he's planning to do in St John's.

Mend a broken heart.

Hannah feels the excitement of a new adventure blooming in her chest and the futility of pretending to be somebody she isn't.

She waits a week then packs her things, says goodbye to her family and heads east into the heart of Canada.

25

On the road again

There are the Rockies which, when you are in them, are not nearly so oppressive. Hannah finds that the good old cowboying ways are still alive and well in the mountains of Canada and there are ranches and Ukrainian hostels and bears by the side of the road almost every day at sundown. Once she spots a silver fox. Every time she comes this close to something wild and alive, the life she lived in London seems less real. The past is clouding over but the view through the windshield of her car is in sharp focus. Her mind is numb, so her eyes take over.

As long as I keep moving, Hannah thinks, I can just about live in the moment. When she is static, standing still in one place for too long, it is time that passes through her. Then the present feels caught between memory and ambition. But when she's on the move, physically pushing through space, she becomes contiguous with time and inhabits the present. She is suspended, without nostalgia and without hope, without expectations of any kind, and this makes her feel unencumbered. She is porous. The country passing through her. This beautiful country of damp redwood forests and high mountain passes clogged with glaciers and lakes so powder blue they look like plastic and a whole host of animals living heedless of the strivings of the cities, and it's like Hannah is rediscovering something sacred. Something peaceful and meaningful in all this uninhabited space. She embraces the indifference the natural world shows her. Takes refuge in its disregard for what she wants, immune as it is to the vagaries of her own mistaken judgment.

She stops the car when she sees a lone bear and watches it. Its bearish imperturbability reminds her of Daniel. The way it ignores her. Continues the meticulous task of collecting berries, one at a time, with its raspy pink tongue. And suddenly it dawns on her. Over the years, I have watched my husband become a bachelor. Like this bear, he has no need of me. This bear has the whole country. And my husband, Hannah thinks, will always be a bachelor.

The prairies are silos and train tracks and gas stations and the creaking of signs in the wind. Hamburgers, all dressed, and well-mannered farm boys in baseball caps and dusty jeans who take their caps off to eat and hang them off their knees. The cows are rust coloured. The fields an electric green. The Mercury Lynx breaks down just off Gasoline Alley and sparks a whole new fear in her. The fear of being in some real danger, and not just an emotional crisis. Hannah sends up a prayer of thanks that she didn't break down a hundred miles in either direction and walks to the Canadian Tire in Red Deer. That'll be a new battery and alternator, miss. She puts it on her credit card and is back on the road in less than three hours.

In the prairies, the sky is the thing. It is the widest film screen, and Hannah can breathe again at last. She would like to be swallowed into outer space. Sent into orbit in her Mercury Lynx.

The rocky outcroppings of the Canadian Shield start rising up on either side of the highway at the border into Ontario. Hannah pulls over at Kenora and goes skinny-dipping on private property. She reads on a tourist sign that there are 14,000 islands in Lake-of-the-Woods and thinks it must be a typo. She rents a motel room and wakes up on her knees, sobbing into the mattress. It smells of hay and car fumes. Her resistance is slowly unravelling. To be proud. It is no longer what she wants. She doesn't have the strength to keep pretending that she's in control. There is nothing to control, certainly not her fate. There are no justifiable grounds for disappointment. She deserves nothing more than to be grateful. The only thing that she can do is love. What is right in front of her. Even if it appears to be nothing at all.

This is the longest time that Hannah has gone without a word from Daniel and already things are changing. She is forgetting. Growing apart. Getting used to. There is a curiosity that keeps her going. An appetite for life. A resilience.

Oh, but how easy it is to remember as well. The laughter. The good times. How quick the human spirit strides in to mythologize.

Listening in the dark to the electric clock on the bedside table, the chuck of the minutes changing like score boards at a baseball game, Hannah understands that time will always be a contributing factor. Time is a wilful agent, she thinks. There will always be three people in any equation. You, the other person, and time.

Hannah leaves Kenora determined to make Toronto in one last push. She drives all day and into the night. Some time after midnight the highway deteriorates into gravel, a few orange construction cones. Occasionally, the flash of an eighteen-wheeler appears like a UFO and runs her into the ground but apart from that, everything is deep black. Hannah can see nothing beyond her headlights and doesn't know if she is driving on the shoulder, in her lane, or on the wrong side of the road.

At the next rest stop, Hannah pulls over and tries to sleep. She starts off in the front seat, then ends up across the back with her feet out the window until she realizes the bugs are too bad. She wakes up in the dark, curled over the handbrake, her head trapped under the wheel, the car pinging with moths and a semi idling noisily seven inches away. It is covered in orange and yellow strip lighting like a travelling casino.

Hannah sits up and witnesses a man screech a pickup truck to a halt and walk drunkenly into the Tim Horton's on the other side of the parking lot. She decides to forego her cup of tea and starts the Lynx. She drives for another hour but has to pull over again. She falls asleep in a dark cul-de-sac beside a gas station closed for the night. When she wakes, the gas station is full of people and she's in plain view, drool on her chin, sweaty and stunned, the car hot as a bread oven.

She calls Matt Riley from a phone booth. I'll be there in three hours. Within forty minutes, she's already making the turn-off from the Trans Canada highway and soon she's knocking on his door.

She feels reborn, a virgin, breakable. Never felt this prudish in all my life, she says.

Well, prudishness is back, Matt says.

Prudishness, Hannah says, is the new black.

It is at Matt's place that Hannah finally hears from Daniel. It's been nearly five months, and at last he calls her. Thanks, he says, for giving me the space and time. Then he says, It's over.

Are you sure? Hannah asks.

Yes, he says. I've made up my mind.

She is both incredulous and already accustomed to the news.

I've changed a little bit, she says.

Yeah.

I could devote myself to you.

This makes Daniel cry. I'm not convinced, he says. I know you too well. Remember how much we bickered?

No, Hannah says, I can't. Her face is wet with tears.

We couldn't get through a meal at Pommedoro without getting into a fight. To the waiters you were that woman who always cried into your pasta.

Thanks, Hannah says, her lungs sucking in large gulps of air between sighs. Her whole body is juddering.

Come on, Hannah, it hasn't worked.

I thought it could, she says. I thought the failing was effort on our part.

248

Our relationship was nothing but mitigation and equivocation.

I don't know what you mean.

I don't think either of us were ever convinced that this was what we really wanted.

It's just the parting that's so hard, she says.

You've always been a risk taker, Hannah, except when it comes to rejection.

Just tell me what went wrong.

It was a lot of things, he says.

So that's it? Hannah says, drained of everything now, even the yearning. Is it over?

She listened hard. Her hand hurt from holding the phone. She knew he was probably nodding.

26

Norman Peach

A strange calm pervades the things she does. Hannah sleeps on Matt's couch and feels safe. His basement apartment is hot, the air thick. She doesn't mind. She likes the stifling heat of Toronto, how it makes her sweat when she goes jogging. How purging it is to be soaked from head to toe in a wetness from within. Reverse baptism.

There is freedom in failure, Hannah thinks, in being powerless. And as she runs she thinks, the sun is my friend. The grass is singing to me. The air is swimming into my lungs and filling me up like a helium balloon. I may just float away. Beyond Toronto and the CN tower, beyond the world into thin mid-air where human souls orbit silent and solitary with only their memories for comfort. And Hannah thinks of Daniel and Ursula and Eddie and Ingmar and that time at the Porcupine when she caught them laughing at her, leaning back with her elbows on the pinball machine, her belly sticking out, and how funny they thought she was and how much fun they'd had together and how much she loved those people who had enriched her life and hoped no harm would come to them and what a joy it is to be in this world though it entails pain and loss unimaginable as a child.

There is so much you can't imagine as a child. So many hopes that have to be crushed. But Hannah is beginning to accept her limitations. Not begrudgingly but with the true compassion a mother has for a daughter who isn't very pretty, who understands that it is her own failure to see beauty and not a lack of it on the child's part.

Hannah gets very drunk with Matt. It's been such a long time. Everything seems funny to her. She laughs a lot. Her face cracks open like a nut. It's been a while since she's laughed with a friend and remembers the importance of being drawn out of herself, vows to make socializing a priority.

I must be generous, she declares, raising her bottle of beer.

Praise people, Matt says.

Not be afraid of them.

In the morning, she calls Norman Peach. To make an appointment to see the apartment. She arrives and walks up the fire escape. She finds him sitting by the back door on a broken chair, using a handful of silver teaspoons to stretch a floppy tire back onto a bicycle rim. She experiences the old ping of a chemical attraction.

Hi, Norm says, with a wicked grin. You must be the subletter.

And you, she says, must be the new landlord. She remembers Ursula's advice. The best cure for a breakup is to jump into bed with the next person you see. But although she's free, Hannah doesn't want to be cynical. She's wearing the thin new skin of her reborn self and doesn't want to thicken it too soon. In order to preserve what innocence she has left, she can't afford to be naïve.

Thing is, Norm moves her. He makes her dinner. They like the same foods. They go for a walk. They end up in a bar. It's late when they get back and he invites her to stay over and the following morning, when they wake up in his bed, she doesn't hold back and for the first time in more than three years, Hannah goes all the way with a man other than Daniel.

She is expecting guilt, turmoil, conflict, but instead she experiences an unapologetic peace and a sensuality that breaks free like a caged panther, sinuous and lethal. Every inch of her body is tingling. Coming back to life after a long sleep. She feels so close to this man and connected and unguarded and he is being so attentive, so gentle with her, and yet there is a dangerous manly power behind his tenderness that takes her breath away. A strength she could never control.

And he has a readiness for humour that suits her. A willingness to be silly. He had stood naked in the doorway to his

251

bedroom the night before, wearing only his electric guitar and singing a Handsome Family song. She knew the tune and harmonized. We sound good together, he said. Her heart exulted. Reacquainting itself with this emotion.

Later in the day, after making love again, Hannah starts to cry.

What's the matter? Norm asks.

It's like you've pulled the plug on me, she says. Everything's falling away.

Is that a good thing?

It's a great thing, she says. I thought I'd have all this baggage with me, but I feel weightless. I feel oddly in synch. There's no resistance. Between my head and my heart and my body.

The sex is so simple. There is no analysis in her head. No interference or conflict of interests. They're lying on their backs and Hannah has her head on his arm, her neck at a sharp angle. She's looking down the length of her body.

Sometimes I think a person's genitals should be closer to their head, she says, at chest level. They seem so far away. If they were closer to the mind, closer to one's thoughts, it might do away with some of the trouble they cause. You know, the whole mind body split that's such a dilemma. It's almost as if there's another couple in bed with us. Us and them. A foursome.

Hey, kids, Norm says, rolling on top of her. What's going on down there?

While they're fucking, Hannah says, This sex is wild. It's as if our bodies already know each other.

They're frisky, he says.

We're like dog owners sitting on a bench, she says, watching our dogs frolicking at the end of their leashes.

Just going at it and getting their leashes tangled.

It feels so natural, she says.

It's muscular, he says, thrusting his cock into her.

252

I feel so comfortable with you, she says.

It's totally relaxing, he says, and Hannah likes hearing him say the word totally. It reminds her that she's in a familiar place, that they have similar backgrounds, growing up in Canada in the seventies. Daniel would never use the word totally.

They spend five days together before Norm leaves for the summer. Back to Newfoundland, where he is from.

Will you email me while you're away? Hannah asks.

Yes, Norm says, though I'm not promising you anything. This has been a crazy five days, but I just split up with my girlfriend of seven years and have a broken heart to fix. And two months is a long time.

Hannah wants to pin him down, wrestle a promise out of him, but she resists the urge, understands the source to be a weak one.

Besides, you're still a married woman, Norm says.

How could I forget?

Hannah drives him to the airport. She has a mixed tape in her car stereo. One that Daniel made for her. Elliot Smith, Thelonius Monk and Jim O'Rourke.

We are married, Norm says, and Hannah's heart lurches. In our musical tastes, he says, and she turns to him and laughs. He kisses her while she's driving, her eyes looking sideways at the road.

Words Norm used while they were in bed: inimitable, anointed, cherish.

When she gets back, Hannah sits in his place, alone again in the thick grey heat, the first of fifty-nine days before Norman Peach returns. There's a tornado warning on the radio and Hannah spots a dragonfly on the wall. It terrorizes the apartment like a small helicopter. She catches it in a clear plastic tub and examines it. Head like a coffee bean. Wings like delicate Japanese screens. Now she yearns for him, wanting to share these small details. But she shrugs at his absence and

253

misses him with a wistful insouciance that is uncommon, not a shred of desperation. She has come unhinged from all that. Has relinquished expectations in the face of a dragonfly's wings.

I've got to be able to take him or leave him, not need him.

She is not even suspicious of the speed with which she may be falling in love. Aware only of how she is like a frail green shoot pushing up through the soil. Towards the light. Utterly blameless.

27

Daniel at the edge of a crowd

Daniel calls to say he's found a cheap ticket to come and visit Hannah in Toronto. He thinks they ought to say goodbye in person and Hannah wonders what it will be like to see him again. She emails Norm to tell him that her husband will be staying in his apartment. Norm says, Well that's a biggie.

She tells him not to worry, that there's no chance of a reconciliation.

He says, You never know.

Hannah supposes there could still be a small window open to the possibility, but all the obvious entrances are shut. Already the past is fading beside the bright urgency of the future.

Hannah drives to the airport to pick Daniel up, thinking about the last time she drove there. She is late and when she arrives, Daniel is standing at the edge of a crowd looking lost and anxious. She notices he is not even holding a bag. Just the leather satchel he sometimes used to carry books in. From a distance, he looks like a boy scout on an outing. Up close, he looks older than she remembers.

Somebody's not planning to stay very long, she says, miffed that he is still insisting, even now, on controlling events. Daniel turns to Hannah and embraces her reluctantly, the way you would embrace a person you know is infatuated and don't want to encourage.

I'm flying back tomorrow evening, he says, and Hannah nods.

The car's parked over there, she says.

Back at Norm's, Hannah cooks a meal. Grilled eggplant and red peppers. Pasta with lemon and parsley and chunks of hot Genoa salami. Daniel sits on the balcony and looks out at the parking lot. It's obvious he is here on business. He is aloof and nervous. He is avoiding making eye contact. Hannah finds this deliberate negation of their history depressing.

That's a great little car you got there, he says.

And Hannah says, Can we get to the point?

Now that she understands Daniel has made up his mind, Hannah wants to get the details sorted. I'm flat broke, she says.

This makes Daniel panic. Is that all you can think of?

This move has cost me a lot of money.

I can't believe how crass you're being.

Crass? Hannah says. Well, I'm not the one who ran off to Berlin and fucked someone while the bed was still warm.

What are you talking about?

When you were in Berlin.

I didn't sleep with anybody there.

So why did you let me think you had?

We were separated. I didn't think it was any of your business what I did.

Well, we obviously had different ideas about what this trial separation meant. You could have saved me a lot of grief if you had wanted to.

I did want to, Hannah, believe me I did. But I had to be strict with you. You weren't capable of letting go on your own. I had to break you down.

And you did, she says. Congratulations.

It was the best thing for both of us. We're happier now, aren't we?

Hannah looks at him and shrugs. She doesn't want to give him the satisfaction.

I should tell you that I'm seeing someone now, Daniel says, at once sorry for and bracing himself against the potential hurt this might cause her.

And you think you're the only one? Hannah says, a slight curve at the corner of her mouth.

The relief that spreads across Daniel's face is so obvious that it makes Hannah melt. They both laugh and this allows them to relax, to pull a few barriers down, their prickly defences.

It's so perverse, Hannah says, but I've never known two people to be so happy with each other's guilt than the two of us.

Even the leaves of the trees out back seem to bristle with relief, shaking themselves out like passengers on an overnight train, roused out of sleep by a clanging noise and then shifting into a new position, reassured of their own safety.

Do you want to go play pool? Daniel asks.

Yes, Hannah says, I'd love to.

They go out and get drunk. They play pool. It's just like old times. Daniel finds Hannah funny and she likes that. They walk home arm in arm. There's an awkward moment before they go to bed. There's only a futon. The sofa isn't long enough. We'll have to sleep together, Hannah says. And so they lie down, straight as two fence posts, frightened to brush against each other.

How about, she says, one last shag?

Last shags are always in the past, Daniel says, not the future.

I was only joking, Hannah says, and eventually they fall asleep, like homophobic men forced to share a motel bed.

In the morning, they walk to Queen Street and go out for breakfast. At one point, as they're walking, they take hold of each other's hands. It's an old habit. But they look at each other and shake their heads. No, they say, that's too intimate. The spell is broken.

Can I drive your car? Daniel asks. Let me drive to the airport.

It's early evening, the traffic pouring home from a day's work. Hannah has rarely seen Daniel drive. I like, he says, that you carry my music in your glove compartment.

When they say goodbye, it is with all the tenderness of two old friends who know they might not see each other again for a long, long time.

When Hannah gets back from the airport, she finds it hard to be indoors. She walks to Little Italy for anchovies and garlic.

257

There's a religious parade down College Street. Brass bands playing mournful minor music, the musicians swaying from one foot to the other, like they're all one body, ambling slowly down the street. There are girls dressed as angels and virgin brides, carrying sponges on sticks and lengths of rope on silver platters and other more obviously symbolic things. A group of men walk by carrying Mary, the one who succours sinners, on their sweaty shoulders. She is sitting in a pile of roses. And then comes Jesus, bleeding as usual, but this time from the knees.

Hannah feels like she's in Sicily. The city feels so exotic. She thinks, there may be something for me after all, something of a mystery here among what's familiar.

28

The handsome policeman

Norm has left her a yellow, old-fashioned Czechoslovakian bike. It has no gears and a braking distance of about ten metres. She cycles to Matt's house for dinner. He has invited some colleagues from the high school faculty where he works. A visiting teacher from Brazil is bringing *feijoadá*. Hannah helps to set up the two trestle tables in the back yard. Her silver rings clink like cutlery. There are fairy lights in the trees and when it comes, the food looks so good people hesitate to touch it, in deference to what they are about to eat. And that, Hannah thinks, is prayer enough.

Please, Matt announces, dig in, and people start to scoop and ladle and pass the food around.

I just got back from Moose Jaw where I was doing some archival research, a woman says, halfway through the meal, waving her wineglass with a flourish. Red wine swells at the lip then drops back again like the viscous blue liquid in a wave box. And the place was overrun with grasshoppers. She says, The grasshoppers were fucking. It was existential.

I hear the bugs are particularly bad in the prairies this year, the Brazilian man says, offering up cigarillos.

Every time I got hit by one, the woman says, I thought, what am I doing here? I need an urban setting. Because this is disgusting. They were fucking everywhere.

Get a room, Hannah says.

And the ones that aren't, you want to say, why aren't you fucking? Can't you get laid?

There is laughter in three different languages and crickets between the blades of grass, serenading the dinner party, playing their hearts out.

As she's cycling home, Hannah falls in love with the world

again. She feels like a queen on her bicycle, the air fluttering the hem of her linen skirt. The night is sultry and the trees look artificial in their stillness, sagging a little bit in the city heat, drooping at the shoulders as if they've finally given up the dream of living in the country. She can't believe Norman Peach left this for St John's. There's a pale blue haze blurring the ends of streets, mysterious aureola around the lampposts. Downtown, the streets are blocked off for a Caribbean parade the next day and people are drifting and mingling. There is a sexual quality to the soundtrack of the evening, a sultry R&B voice overlapping a reggae tune coming from a car stereo as it prowls the back alleys. Catcalls cracking the hush from time to time. A woman with white leather knee-high boots, white shorts and halter-top, struts her stuff like she's been waiting her whole life to do this. Hair piled on top of her head like a wicker basket.

Hannah rides her bike at a relaxed pace through the downtown area. At the edge, where the crowds have thinned but the streets are still blocked, she crosses a quiet intersection. To her left there are the headlights of a cab turning left towards her. She assumes that it will stop, but it doesn't. She brakes and watches as the bumper rolls towards her and smacks her in the leg and then she closes her eyes. She understands that she has hit the hood. Her eyes open for a second and she sees the sky and the pivoting edge of a tall building as she slides off the hood and hits the ground. She is lying in the road. The tarmac is warm, soft even. She can see the undercarriage of the cab and its chrome fender as it looms above her like a shark. Threatless now the engine's off, harmless as a fourteen-foot tiger shark preserved in a glass tank of formaldehyde. But there it is again. *The physical impossibility of death in the mind of someone living.*

Who keeps threatening me with these stuffed animals? Hannah wonders. These reminders of my own mortality? God must be a post-modern taxidermist.

You okay? the driver asks, pulling Hannah by the arm. You

gonna be okay? You look okay to me. I think you gonna be okay.

I'm okay, she says, pulling her arm away and doing a quick mental check of her body.

There are police around for the parade and one comes over and, kneeling beside her, tells her not to get up.

Why are policemen so handsome? Or is it that help appears good-looking in a crisis?

You alright? the officer says in a soft intimate fashion, like it's just between the two of them. Can you stand up now?

I think so, Hannah says. She takes his hand and stands up. She feels as solid as a glacier. The past has cracked off her like an iceberg.

Wow, she says, and then she feels faint.

You look pretty ashen, the cop says, helping her over to the curb.

My name's not Ashen, she says.

I think you should sit down again. Jokes like that call for the paramedics.

Hannah wonders if the cop can smell wine on her breath. She has no light on her bike and she's not wearing a helmet. The bike! she thinks and then she thinks of Norm. She wishes he was here. Or Daniel. Someone to go to the hospital with her if she needed to. She realizes that if she had to stay overnight in a hospital in this city she might not get any visitors. It would take days before anyone noticed she was missing.

Does that hurt? the policeman asks and Hannah looks down. She's bleeding from both knees.

Always takes a little time to recover, he says. Better not to get up just yet. Lucky he wasn't going any faster. Real lucky. I've seen a lot worse.

She looks all the way up his blue uniform. How true this is. How lucky am I. How much worse it could have been. Could always be. She smiles and shakes her head, and then she starts to laugh. Little puffs of breath like steam rising from the spout of a teapot. Her chest contracting painfully. Tears pooling in her eyes.

Oh, Hannah, she says out loud. These rebirthing metaphors have gotta stop. These rebirthing metaphors are gonna kill you.

Daniel is not impressed. It's five in the morning, did you know that?

I'm sorry, Hannah says. She feels cold and shaky from the adrenaline come-down. She grips the phone for reassurance. But all he says is, I'm sure the nausea will go away.

Okay, Daniel, goodnight.

She emails Norm and in the morning there's a phone message from him full of passionate concern.

She calls him back.

What are you wearing? he asks.

That top you like.

Your Saskatoon rose.

I'm only wearing four pieces of clothing, Hannah says. And two of them are on my feet.

Hmm, he says. And then, What are you eating?

I'm eating almonds.

Say almond.

Almond.

Again?

Almond, almond, almond.

So you pronounce the *l*, he says.

Yeah, don't you?

I say awe-mond.

Like the French. *Amande.*

I'm gonna look it up, he says. Hold on.

In the distance Hannah can hear him shout, I'm getting the dictionary!

Okay, he says, back on the phone. See? No *l*.

Well, Hannah says, I've been pronouncing it like that all my life. And I don't think I'm unique in that.

262

You may not be unique, he says, but you're wrong.

Me and all the other people who pronounce it with an *l*. You know if enough people pronounce it with an *l*, it can't be wrong. The English language is dynamic.

You'll be right in fifty years. You're fifty years ahead of your time.

This waiting for you to get back, Hannah says. It feels like such a long time. It's making me irritable. I'm gonna be real pissed off when I see you again.

We'll have a fight, he says.

I'll pout until you fuck me.

It will be, Norm says, a tricky thirty seconds to negotiate.

29

Nice car

Three weeks go by and Hannah gets no invitations. She starts to feel lonely. She calls Matt and they go out to a bar and Hannah confesses her loneliness.

It's hard not to be lonely in a big city, Matt says. You're constantly reminded of all the people who don't know who you are.

Do you know what Stan Carver is up to these days?

How do you know Stan?

I met him at the Rivoli with you.

He's having a kid.

Good for him, Hannah says. He'll make nice kids.

His wife is a knock-out.

Great, Matt. You're making me feel great.

Hannah is drunk when they say goodbye.

You sure you don't want me to walk you home?

No, I'm fine, she says, and wanders off along College Street, singing to herself. At the corner of Ossington, a yellow Corvette pulls up beside her.

Can you tell me where Dundas is? the driver asks, leaning towards the passenger window.

Hannah leans on the roof and points him in the right direction.

You going that way? he asks.

Yep, she says.

You wanna lift?

Okay, and Hannah gets into the car. Nice car, she says. How fast does this baby go?

I can open her up on the highway.

And Hannah says, Why not?

She puts her toes up on the windshield. The road straightens out.

Where are we headed?

Pickering.

Hannah watches the needle dip to 170. The lake to her right. He shifts one last time and she opens her legs. He leaves one hand on the wheel, the other on her cunt. Look at me now, she thinks. Isn't this crazy? It's like a scene from a film. The wind rushing in. It's not the physical sensation, but the scenario that Hannah is enchanted with. The cold idea of herself. From the outside. She's got to get herself back in.

The next morning when she wakes, she is heavy with guilt, vestiges of an old habit she had hoped to set aside. It's a certain kind of callous behaviour, the residue of a failure. The failure to be intimate in a way that she wants to be. Hannah emails Norm to tell him what happened. She waits for his response. She waits an hour, then two, then three. Finally, after four dreadful hours: I can't do it, he writes. I won't give my heart to something I can't trust.

Have I blown my chances? She pleads with him a little, while maintaining the appearance of an aloofness that is a lie.

Not caring. It is this guise she can no longer bear. She is tired of sacrificing her sensitivity to the need to appear indifferent, without weakness, without need. As if she couldn't care less what other people think because she's so fucken happy all on her own. But the fact is she does care. She cares a lot. She used to care so much, she became afraid of the cost of caring.

If I'm not careful, she thinks, if I don't leave this all behind, I'm going to turn into a pillar of salt.

30

10 proverbs

Hannah calls Louise in Montreal. She sighs into the receiver. I need your help, is all that she can say.

In all the years I've known you, Louise says, you've never once asked me for help. Girl, this is music to my ears.

I'm so private when it comes to my feelings, Hannah says.

Tell me about it, Louise says.

But there are things that I'm ashamed of. I fear your judgment.

I haven't judged you.

I don't want you to think that I'm not trustworthy or that I lack integrity.

I don't think that.

But I get scared sometimes, Hannah says.

We all do.

And I try to hide it.

You know, Louise says, you don't have to deal with all of this on your own. Why don't you come to town? Martin will be at work. You can lie on the couch all weekend and I'll feed you chicken soup. Have you got enough for the bus?

Just about, Hannah says.

We'll split the fare, okay?

Thank you, Hannah says, feeling all the gratitude and humility of being rescued.

Hannah loves the anonymity of travelling Greyhound. The dingy last resort of bus stations. She climbs on board and takes a window seat. The air is dry and dusty. A cool current rising from the air vents along the window.

I could sit here on this bus for the next five months, Hannah thinks. Suspended in this moment of the unfurling of a picture outside my window, an endless scroll of scenery.

The sun goes down and Hannah switches on the reading light. Takes out her notebook and starts to write.

Written on the bus to Montreal, sometime around midnight, August 2001.

10 proverbs for riding the Greyhound:

1. Do not get drunk with people you don't know well.
2. Confession can be a way of transferring guilt without learning what that guilt has to impart; in other words, do not seek an easy absolution or forgiveness from the outside but embrace the discomfort and let it change you.
3. Shame inhibits your freedom. Shame is gravitas; a clear conscience is light-hearted.
4. Pretending not to care can have disastrous results.
5. Though you may not be in control of your life, you can still control your ways.
6. A terror of being misunderstood may presuppose a level of understanding that doesn't actually exist.
7. Claim what you are responsible for and then accept your innocence.
8. Flogging a dead horse can ruin the meat.
9. Progress is always two steps forward, one step back.
10. React in haste, lay waste.

Hannah is sitting on the couch, in a pair of Lou's jogging pants and a clean white t-shirt. She's just had a bubble bath and her body is limp from the heat. It's good to be in Lou's house, around the things she's known her to have had for years. A Chinese screen. A lamp with the base of a bronze Shiva. Louise walks out of the kitchen lighting a cigarette. She puts on Stevie Wonder's *Songs in the Key of Life* and turns to Hannah, Feeling better?

Much, Hannah says.

You look better, Louise says, sitting down and pulling Hannah's feet onto her lap. You were in a bit of a panic earlier on.

Hannah nods.

You're too tough on yourself, you know that? You've got to have more faith in your goodness.

It's hard when your goodness isn't that obvious, Hannah says. I know this sounds ridiculous, and I know things appeared crazy on the surface, but I did have a kind of integrity in my marriage.

I know that.

I was honest with Daniel and I never transgressed my own standards. Okay, so they were low, but I stuck to them. I never broke my pact with God.

Your pact with God.

Not to fuck anybody I didn't love. Five years ago, I'd had a string of one-night stands. I got an STD. I was scared. So I made a pact with God. He would protect me from serious harm and in return, I'd stop fucking people I didn't love. It was easy for a while, but when I was married –

You were unhappy, Louise says.

I had to compromise.

You drew an arbitrary line between penetrative sex and everything else.

That's right.

You permitted yourself a couple of blowjobs.

So I've given a few blowjobs in my time.

As long as there was no sperm in your cunt, Louise says, God didn't mind.

He was okay with that, Hannah says.

But you could take it in the mouth.

God turned a blind eye to come in my mouth, Hannah says, running a hand through her hair. This is some conversation.

I just wonder, Louise says, why you had to go through all this in the first place? What drove you to such extremes?

I dunno, Hannah says. When I was a teenager, I felt aban-doned and unloved. But it wasn't my parents' fault. I'd pushed them too far. I did the same with Gerald and Daniel. I may have left them physically, but I pushed them to a place where they couldn't love me any more. How is Gerald, by the way?

He's still with Harriet, Louise says. I think she's pregnant.

Fabulous.

Thing is, you've always been adventurous and indepen-dent.

At the same time as being dependent and in need of love. When I was young –

Your mom was depressed and your dad was absent, I know you told me.

But it made me feel unlovable.

Oh, Hannah, Louise hugs her. So you recreate this situation over and over again.

That's right, Hannah says. Because sometimes knowledge is as comforting as love.

When you're young and you get neglected, Louise says, you think it's your own fault, when it's just circumstance. You think it's because you're bad, when it's just a bad combi-nation. You're carrying around way too much guilt, Hannah. You've got to learn to forgive yourself.

I guess so, Hannah says. But I find it hard to sort out all this stuff in my heart because I'm in the habit of taking refuge in my head. I find it hard to talk about my feelings in a heartfelt way.

You're like a man that way, Louise says.

Maybe that's why I seek their company so often.

Hannah, Lou says. What it is you really, really want?

To be feral, Hannah says. To be absolutely myself.

Can you do it?

I'm gonna try.

31

Lying in the sun

When Hannah gets back to Toronto, she starts looking for another apartment. She finds a basement studio owned by a quiet Portuguese couple. It is small but clean and well lit. When she moves in, Hannah realizes it's a whole new perspective, watching people from the knees down. Pedestrians often stop not far from her window to talk. They don't know that she's there. Hannah can eavesdrop on the soap opera of the street from the comfort of her kitchen table.

Norman Peach gets back from St John's and when they see each other for the first time, he can hear Hannah's heart beat. He tells her this. They make love. It is passionate and physical. That night he moves her around his bed like the hands of a clock. Tick tock, tick tock. When he comes inside her, he tells her that he loves her. She says it too. Then Hannah asks him if she can say it again.

Norm says, You can say it as many times as you want.

Hannah feels herself getting attached, but Norm refuses to make a commitment. He says, If you go out for dinner with some guy, I don't want to hear the agonizing details.

Hannah welcomes this jealous prohibition because it seems to be an indication of a desire to commit. The following evening, she calls him up. I'm having dinner with a friend, is all Norm says. When Hannah puts the phone down, she feels rebuked.

The next time Norm comes around, Hannah says, I can't keep sleeping with you if it's not exclusive. It feels too intimate. I don't want to share this with anybody else.

He says, But I'm not ready to be anybody's boyfriend.

Then you can't fuck me any more, she says.

I'm sorry about that, Norm says.

But you said you loved me, Hannah says.

And I meant it when I said it, Norm says. But I don't think I've ever misled you into thinking this was going to be something exclusive.

Oh, Hannah says.

I'm sorry, Norm says.

You don't know the half of it, and when he's gone, she bursts into tears.

Hannah sits down at her kitchen table. She drinks half a glass of white wine and feels her heart break in the middle of the afternoon. Oh, fuck this whole scourge of falling in love! She gets up and empties the rest of the bottle down the sink. That's it, I've had enough. Looking around her small apartment she thinks, at least I have my own place, my own pictures on the wall.

Hannah has painted her bathroom door bright fuchsia and the walls an Indian white. On her desk, she has a small candleholder, a drinking glass decorated with rectangles of coloured glass that she's had for seventeen years. It's the one thing she's managed, partly by accident, to hold on to all these years and as a result it has acquired symbolic significance. It seems to hold proof of her personality. It seems to be coming back to her these days, this personality. Something closer to what she was when she was young. More sure of herself. Of what she wants. An occasional giddiness in the world. And now it's nearly winter and everything is dying, making her feel alive, reminding her of the worth transience gives a thing. Everything is changing. Everything's in flux. You can never step into the same marriage twice.

The phone rings and it's Norman Peach. He says, Your husband just called me. He's looking for you. He didn't know you'd moved. I gave him your number. Your husband.

That's it? Hannah says.

Yeah, he says. Look, I'm sorry, Hannah. I'm just not ready to settle into something. Anyways, I just called because it occurred

271

to me that maybe your husband didn't have your number for a reason.

It's okay, she says. I don't mind.

As soon as she hangs up, the phone rings again.

Hello, Daniel, Hannah says.

How did you know it was me?

It doesn't matter.

Look, he says. I'm doing the paperwork on our divorce.

God, this is some afternoon I'm having.

It's kind of strange, isn't it? Thing is, I've got to decide which category to serve as grounds.

Can't we just agree to an amicable split?

Not in the eyes of the law, Daniel says. The system is so archaic, to get a fast-track divorce, it has to be this way.

Fine, she says, sitting down at the table and resting her head in her hand.

So I've got three choices here, Daniel says. I can put you down for adultery, unreasonable behaviour, or desertion.

They both laugh out loud at this. The laughter is contagious. It builds momentum until the tension and the sense of failure has passed.

I thought adultery, he says.

But that isn't strictly true, Hannah says. And anyways, I don't want to go down in the books as an adulterer. What about unreasonable behaviour?

As far as I can tell, Daniel says, that category's for domestic violence. And I'm not really comfortable with that going on the record.

Well, what about desertion? Hannah says. That's pretty innocuous.

Yeah, but it takes more time to prove.

So what you're saying is we're left with adultery.

That's right.

Why can't you put yourself down as having committed adultery? Hannah asks.

Because I'm the petitioner. I have to accuse you.

Right.

It's pretty standard, darlin. I think it's what most people cite as the cause.

Fine, she says. Give me adultery for five hundred please, Bob.

Are you sure about this?

Hell, you can put me down for all three, Hannah says and they laugh again, as an antidote to pain, baffled by the way things have turned out, weak with the absurdity of it all, but not resentful. At least not that.

On a more serious note, Daniel says, when the papers come, you might be a bit surprised by the wording of it. The solicitor was dictating and it's a bit brutal, but he assured me it's all pro forma. They have a standard way of putting these things and it's not personal.

Not personal? Hannah repeats.

You know what I mean.

And sure enough, it feels a bit vindictive when three months later, sitting all alone in her kitchen in Toronto, Hannah opens the brown A4 envelope and reads the following in Daniel's handwriting:

(12) the respondent has committed adultery with a man and the petitioner finds it intolerable to live with the respondent. Particulars: The respondent has told the petitioner that she has met a new partner.

Hannah stares at the papers and wants something to happen. Something monumental: a drum roll, thunder, pestilence, strings.

Why haven't the fucken strings kicked in? she says. Where are the goddamn strings when you need them?

But nothing happens. Hannah squeezes a few tears out like she's wringing a rag, in deference to the occasion, but she doesn't feel as much anguish as she thinks the moment deserves. She is a little disappointed by the smallness, the anti-climax of it all. She waits for that film reel of nostalgic moments to start running through her mind, but all that happens is her stomach growls and she feels a little hungry. She gets up and goes over to the fridge. She opens the door and stares and stares into the cold white light. She makes herself a sandwich and can hear Toronto work itself out above her. A sense of grace and heat and clarity comes to her. Although it is the middle of winter and there is snow on the windowsill and the sun has set now and the snow on the ground is blue and the air is icy, there is a warmth and an orange glow to her kitchen. A gentle absent-minded rhythm hums from her appliances. She will call Matt. She will make friends with Norm. Get anchored here. I no longer want to feel, Hannah thinks, like I'm drifting down a river on a raft. She stands up. I want to feel like I'm lying in the sun.

Acknowledgments

The author would like to thank the Canada Council for the Arts and The Ontario Arts Council.

Many people have supported and inspired me in the writing of this book. I wish to thank Lisa Livingstone, Natalie Loveless, Helen Oswald, Elisabeth Unna, Alissa Edney, Katia Opalka, Carle Steel, Alexis Mills, Stephen Finucan, and Ricardo Sternberg.

Thanks in particular go to Joanne Howes, Peter Wood, Einar Holstad, and Richard Skinner.

I am also grateful to Anne McDermid, and to Lee Brackstone and Angus Cargill at Faber, for taking on the book.

And lastly, to Michael Winter, for bringing out the best in both the author and the work.